PARNELL HALL is a part-time actor, a former private detective, and full-time writer of novels and screenplays. An Edgar Allan Poe Award nominee, he is the author of nine previous novels featuring his acclaimed hero, Stanley Hastings: *Detective*, *Murder*, *Favor*, *Strangler*, *Client*, *Juror*, *Shot*, *Actor*, and *Blackmail*. Parnell Hall lives in Manhattan with his wife and sons.

MOVIE

PARNELL HALL

THE MYSTERIOUS PRESS

Published by Warner Books

A Time Warner Company

MYSTERIOUS PRESS EDITION

Cover design by Rachel McClain
Cover illustration by Marc Burckhardt

The Mysterious Press name and logo are registered trademarks of Warner Books, Inc.

 Mysterious Press books are published by
Warner Books, Inc.
1271 Avenue of the Americas
New York, NY 10020

A Time Warner Company

Printed in the United States of America

Originally published in hardcover by The Mysterious Press.
First Printed in Paperback: February, 1996

10 9 8 7 6 5 4 3 2 1

For Jim and Franny

1.

"I love it."

Sidney Garfellow held the manuscript aloft and gazed at it almost reverently. He was a tall, slender man with curly black hair, wire-rimmed glasses, and a thin, sensitive face. He wrapped long, bony fingers around the manuscript, held it out at arm's length, and said again, "I love it."

I watched with more than passing interest. Sidney Garfellow was a hot young movie producer. What he was holding happened to be my screenplay.

Yeah, I wrote a screenplay. Which shouldn't really surprise you. Everybody and his brother wrote a screenplay. I was in a cab the other day, and the driver had not only written a screenplay, but Al Pacino had optioned it and hired him to do a rewrite. If that was true, by the way, it was one hell of an ominous portent—the guy sold a screenplay and was still driving a cab. The old maxim for those in the arts: Don't quit your day job.

I haven't quit mine. I still work five days a week chasing ambulances for the law firm of Rosenberg and Stone. Stanley Hastings, private eye. Sound glamorous? Guess again. It's a job-job, just like driving a cab or waiting tables.

Something we in the arts do when the arts ain't paying. Which is pretty much all of the time.

Except now.

Maybe.

Sidney Garfellow nodded as if in agreement with himself, said, "Love it," one more time, and tossed the screenplay onto the coffee table.

I felt an immediate sense of loss and had a wild impulse to pick it up and hand it back to him. After all, this was my baby, my first, my one and only screenplay. I'd written it over the past year while on the job in stolen moments in hospital corridors, waiting for prospective clients to come out of surgery, or in my office, waiting for job assignments, or sometimes even in my car.

The end result was a hundred-and-ten-page screenplay entitled *Trial by Fire*. It was a murder mystery/courtroom drama featuring a young, unconventional, hippie lawyer. It was pretty damn good, if I did say so myself, and I was sure glad to find someone who agreed.

Particularly Sidney Garfellow. A hotshot young producer with just enough clout to get it made.

I fidgeted in my chair. I was incredibly nervous. After years and years of frustration, with the prize in my grasp, I was terrified it might slip away.

As if sensing this, my agent leaned in and said, "I just knew you'd be pleased."

My theatrical agent, that is. As opposed to Warren, my literary agent, who handled my short stories, magazine articles, and what have you. But Manny Kricklestein was my theatrical agent. Or my Hollywood agent, if you will. He handled my screenplays. Or screenplay. And it was he who jumped in now.

We were sitting in the living room of Sidney Garfellow's East Eighty-fifth Street apartment, the one furnished like a Hollywood home, with the framed movie posters on the walls, and the built-in projector and pull-down movie screen, somewhat of an anachronism in the days of VCRs, still a Hollywood touch.

My god, I'm telling this badly. It's all coming out jumbled. If my screenplay were like this, there wouldn't be a chance of getting it produced. But I was calm when I wrote it. 'Cause then production was pie in the sky. Now it's a reality and I'm scared to death. I'm trying to describe people, places, actions, and how I felt all at once, and I can't get any of them right.

But you gotta understand, Sidney Garfellow was not just some Hollywood studio executive who might make a recommendation. No, he was an independent producer who worked out of New York, who raised his own money and produced his own films and directed them too. He'd done two movies already, both documentaries, both critically acclaimed. One was *Down and Dirty,* an inside look at child pornography. The other was *Straight Shooter,* a brutally frank look at the AIDS epidemic. The latter had been nominated for several major awards, including the Oscar. Which put Sidney Garfellow near the top of the tree.

Sidney Garfellow leaned back in his comfortable chair, cocked his head at me. "I want to tell you how I work," he said. "I want to give you some idea of how it's gonna be."

My heart nearly stopped. It was only gonna be if Sidney Garfellow said so. He hadn't said so yet. But he was talking as if he *had* said so. Which was enough to drive me around the bend.

I gulped. "Yes?" I managed to croak.

"I don't make studio deals on my pictures. At least, not in production. Distribution deal, that's something else. But a production deal, no way. Any picture of mine, I raise the money, I produce it myself."

I didn't want to appear totally ignorant. "Yes, I know," I said.

"Do you know *why* I do it?"

On the other hand, I didn't want to appear a know-it-all

wise ass, either. And that sounded like a rhetorical question to me.

It was. Sidney Garfellow leaned back in his chair, cocked his head, and gazed off into the distance—or what would have been the distance were it not for the wall and ceiling of his apartment—the posture of one obviously about to pontificate. "The reason I do that," he said, "is so I don't have to deal with Hollywood. If I had to point to one thing wrong with the motion-picture industry today, it's the major studios. Run by people who can barely let down their own trousers. Staffed with executives who were potty trained yesterday. And who worked for *another* studio the day *before* yesterday. And they're on their fourth studio now, and their only concern is not getting fired so they have to look for their fifth. 'Cause they're dealing with so much goddamned money that every decision they make could be their job. Which creates a breed of people ten percent of their job is making movies, and ninety percent of their job is protecting their backsides. Now how the hell you gonna make a decent movie like that?"

That struck me as halfway between a rhetorical question and one where a response might be required. I had just opted for the latter and opened my mouth to say, "You can't," when Sidney Garfellow said it for me.

"You can't. Obviously. All you can do is grind out carbon copies of last year's successes. And hope like hell they're competent enough someone will shell out money to see them in the event that trend hasn't run its course yet." He shook his head. "It's a sad and sorry business."

In the pause that followed that, I was at a loss as to what to say next. If I wanted to be absolutely honest with the man, what I would have said was, "Sidney, I'll agree with anything you want as long as you make my movie." But maybe it wasn't quite the time to be that honest.

Fortunately, Sidney forged ahead. "No," he said. "Studios are out. When I make a movie, it's gotta be the movie I want to make. I raise the money myself, and answer to no one but me. The only drawback is, that means working with a smaller budget. But it's worth it in order to make something of quality. And in the long run it pays off. If a two-million-dollar picture does the same business as a twenty-million-dollar picture, who makes money? You see what I mean?"

That was *not* a rhetorical question. I came in smoothly with, "Of course," feeling proud of myself for recognizing it instantly.

Sidney Garfellow nodded. "Good," he said. "Then you understand what I'm about to say. I think you're a fine writer. I would love to pay you a hundred thousand dollars for this project. Unfortunately, it is not in the budget."

I felt an incredible rush of adrenaline. And I suddenly found myself in the grip of half-a-dozen conflicting emotions.

First, there were the words *a hundred thousand.* That triggered alarm bells in my head. Well, not *alarm,* really. More like ecstasy. A hundred thousand, you see, was just in the range of the magical phrase *six figure,* as in six-figure sum, six-figure advance, six-figure salary. "Yes, I'm making six figures." "Damn, I had a six-figure tax year." "No, I couldn't consider less than six figures."

Yeah, yeah, I understand. He was saying he *couldn't* pay me six figures. But that didn't matter. He had mentioned it in terms of a payment, even if it was one I could not have. I could envision myself describing this conference later. "Well, a six-figure fee *was* mentioned."

But never mind that. *The guy wanted my screenplay!* Even if he only wanted to pay me a buck ninety-five, it didn't matter. *My screenplay was going to be made!* All this was just business, bargaining. So I'd been told I can't have a hundred thousand dollars. What *can* I have? Whatever it is, I'll take it. Oh, my god, I'm no good at these business things, what should I do?

And then the sudden huge rush of relief. I don't have to do anything. My agent's sitting right here.

I turned to Manny, a little guy with a thin mustache and a

sensitive, twitchy nose, who always reminded me of a rat—
though, to be fair to him, maybe that's just because he dealt
in the movie business.

Manny put up his hands and jumped right in, his beady
eyes gleaming and rat nose twitching, smelling the ten percent. "Hey, Sidney," he said. "You don't have to spell it out.
We know how it is. And I have to tell you, from a creative
point of view, Stanley's pretty damn happy Hollywood
won't be involved." He shrugged. "Still, the man has to eat."

I tuned out. Let them haggle over money. I really couldn't
care. Well, yes of course I did, but it was really so secondary.
The guy was going to make my movie. Sidney Oscar-nomi-
nee Garfellow was going to make my movie. The characters
I'd created were going to come to life and dance across the
silver screen spouting my dialogue. And be seen by millions
of people. Reviewed by critics. Who, were they rational
human beings, would have to agree with Sidney Garfellow
that it was head-and-shoulders above the usual Hollywood
drivel.

So, yes, the money would be nice, but it sort of paled into
insignificance in the light of a dream come true.

I crashed back to earth amid a torrent of such terms as
*Writers Guild scale, low-budget minimums, deferred pay-
ments,* and *union waivers.* All of that sounded like a hell of a
lot less than a hundred grand.

It was.

But when the dust had cleared, and when my agent Manny
Ratface Ten-percent had signed me up for what sounded akin
to penal servitude—the bottom line of which was, not only
would I not be able to quit my day job, I'd be lucky to afford
a leave of absence while they filmed the movie—nonetheless, there was not a happier man on this planet.

"So," Sidney Garfellow said, "now that we've got the sor-
did money stuff out of the way, the only possible obstacle to
our working together is whether we can agree artistically."

"I'm sure we can," I said.

"I'm glad to hear it," Sidney said. "To begin with, how much do you know about karate?"

I blinked. "Karate?"

"Yes. What's your background in karate? What do you know?"

I took a breath. Artistic agreement, indeed. There were no karate scenes in my courtroom drama, nor did I wish there to be.

Still, it's amazing what one will do when one does not yet have a screen credit. "Well," I said, "as a matter of fact, my son Tommie is taking karate lessons in the neighborhood and just got his blue belt."

He waved it away. "No, no. I don't mean *real* karate. I mean motion-picture stuff. What karate movies have you seen?"

Good lord. I racked my brain for the title of a karate movie. Came up empty.

"No problem," he said. "You can rent the video cassettes. Bruce Lee. Jean-Claude Van Damme. Watch a bunch of 'em, get some background."

"I'm sorry. Jean-Claude who?"

"Jean-Claude Van Damme." He looked at me. "You've never heard of him? He's the hottest thing going." He frowned. "We really should talk after you've seen the movies. No sense going over old ground. I'd like to have you on my wavelength when we start this. How's next Tuesday? Let's get together again next Tuesday. In the meantime, think about the women."

"The women?"

"Yeah. We're gonna need hot babes in this. At least four, maybe five. Young, big tits, look like they stepped out of a centerfold. But it can't read that way in the script. They gotta have separate personalities. Like there was some point to their being in this movie aside from how they look. You follow?"

No, I didn't. "I'm sorry," I said. "But . . . well, you read my screenplay. There's nothing in it about karate or four hot babes."

"Of course not," he said. "But that doesn't mean you couldn't write it."

"Well, I could," I said. "But . . ."

"But what? So write it."

"Yes, but—" I jerked my thumb at the screenplay. "That's a very tightly plotted script. I just don't see how I can add all that."

Sidney Garfellow frowned. "Add? What do you mean, add? Who's asking you to add? I'm asking you to write a karate movie with four hot babes."

I still didn't get it. Or maybe I just didn't want to. "But," I said, "what about my screenplay?"

He looked at me. Made a face. "What, are you nuts? A courtroom drama? The country's fed up to here with Perry Mason and Matlock. We gotta give 'em something that *sells.*"

Which is how I came to write the screenplay for *Hands of Havoc, Flesh of Fire.*

2.

Six months later we went into preproduction. Which, believe me, is pretty damn fast. Especially considering I had to write the screenplay first. I finished the first draft in two and a half months, which was pretty amazing considering I did it in my spare time while working full time for Rosenberg and Stone.

And considering the interference of Sidney Garfellow, who was constantly calling me up and wanting to give me input. And practically every time he did, it knocked something I'd just written into a cocked hat and I'd have to tear it up and start over. Eventually, this produced a Pavlovian response where every time the phone rang I cringed.

Still and all, somehow I managed to get it done.

I must say, I had very mixed feelings about it. A karate movie with four hot babes is not the sort of thing I would ever write. Still, having been forced into it, I had done the best job possible. Which allowed me to take a certain amount of pride in my work. It was, in my humble estimation, the best damn karate movie with four hot babes in it ever written.

Only you wouldn't have known it to talk to Sidney Garfellow. When he read my first draft, he had an amazing number of things he wanted changed.

In a way, I was pleased to hear it. Because my Writers Guild contract did have a provision for a second draft, if Sid-

ney Garfellow wished to pay for it. Since my contract wasn't
that lucrative, I could use all the money I could get.

Only I couldn't get it. See, Sidney Garfellow didn't want a
second draft. He wanted changes made in *this* draft.

I hemmed, I hawed, I begged, I pleaded, I called my agent,
but Sidney said it was a low-budget production and there
was no money, and in the end the bottom line was, if you're
a writer and you don't have a screen credit, you'll do just
about anything to get one.

Anyway, I wrote the revisions, the revisions of the revisions, and the fine tuning of the revisions of the revisions,
etcetera, etcetera, and if the truth be known, I was still fiddling
with it when we went into preproduction six months later.

If you're not in the movie business, preproduction is the
time just before principal photography. If you're in preproduction, it means your movie is a *go project,* you have a *start
date,* you're about to film the movie, and you're setting up
everything necessary for doing so. Preproduction can take
anywhere from two to six months, and on some big-budget
pictures can take as much as two years.

Preproduction for our movie was scheduled for three
weeks. There was a reason for this. The reason was, we were
a low-budget picture, and during preproduction some people
are on salary.

No, not me.

In our case, the people on salary included the production
manager, the director of photography, the gaffer, the first assistant director, the art director, the sound mixer, and four
teamsters.

The production manager was there to hire the crew, nego-
tiate with the unions, approve all purchases and equipment
rental, and work out the shooting schedule.

The assistant director was there to scout locations for filming.

The director of photography was there to plan camera angles and lighting.

The gaffer, or head electrician, was there to see that all locations had sufficient power to shoot.

The art director was there to see what needed to be designed and built.

The sound mixer was there to make sure no locations had any sound problems.

The teamsters were there because no one had the guts to tell them they weren't needed. Which was not that unusual. Teamsters are the backbone of the movie industry. They are to be treated with utmost respect, because if they are not happy, they won't move their fucking trucks. And if the teamsters strike, no union will cross their picket line, which means you can't shoot. So we had four teamsters on salary, even though we couldn't possibly need a truck for weeks. They drove in from Long Island each day, and hung out in the office playing cards.

I guess I wouldn't have resented this so much if it weren't for the fact that they were on salary and I wasn't, and I was working very hard on this movie while still working full time for Rosenberg and Stone.

Anyway, we were in preproduction and I was in a project in Harlem signing up Darnell Coles, who had fallen in a subway and broken his leg, when my beeper went off. I called the office and got either Wendy or Janet, one of Richard Rosenberg's two switchboard girls, who happened to have identical voices. Whichever it was, I was glad she'd beeped me. It was a slow day, and I could use another assignment.

Only there wasn't one.

"Oh, Stanley," Wendy/Janet said. "That was quick. Glad I caught you. You're in Harlem, right?"

"Yeah. Darnell Coles. I'm there now."

"Good. Your producer called."

"What?"

"That's right. Sidney Garfellow. They're doing a location scout in Harlem and they want you to check out a set."

"What?"

"That's right. Hang on and I'll give you the address."

She did. A warehouse on West 138th, not ten blocks from where I was.

I drove there shaking my head. Unbelievable, the power of

the motion-picture industry. Anybody else, Wendy/Janet
would have told them to get lost. "He's workin' for Rosenberg and Stone, buddy. Who the hell are you?" But Sidney
Motion-Picture Garfellow calls, and they fall all over themselves to cooperate.

I had the sudden paranoid flash that if there *had* been an
assignment for me, Wendy/Janet would have withheld it or
given it to some other investigator, just to accommodate Sidney Garfellow. So I was in a foul mood driving over there.

I was also in a foul mood because when I got to the warehouse there was no one there. Just a big empty warehouse
with a big chain and padlock on the front door. The chain
and padlock were conclusive—unless there was another entrance I didn't know about, no one was inside.

Which did not bode well. See, besides their voices, Wendy
and Janet also shared an amazing propensity for inaccuracy.
So there was no way for me to tell if this was even the right
warehouse.

It was.

The crew came tooling up a half hour later in a Ford station wagon driven as usual by a twenty-year-old production
assistant. They could have had a teamster drive, since there
were four on the payroll, but then they would have been subject to his whim. Whereas, the twenty-year-old kid, desperate
to please, did whatever he was told.

The crew piled out of the car.

Though I had met him before, I was always somewhat
awed by Jake Decker, the production manager. He stood six-
foot-six, two hundred and seventy pounds, all muscle. He had
curly dark hair, a full black beard, and the most hostile eyes
you ever saw. His forte was negotiation, and his speciality
was squeezing concessions out of unions. His success rate
was phenomenal—people just didn't want to deal with him.

Next was the director of photography, Eric Stoltz, a small,
wizened, wiry German, with an accent so thick I could never
understand a word he said. He was reputedly brilliant,
though, at least according to Sidney Garfellow. Sidney was
evasive as to his credits, however, and when I asked around

the industry, most of my friends had never heard of him, except for one writer who thought he might have been involved in, of all things, a spaghetti western.

Next was our first assistant director, who happened to be a rather attractive woman. So much so that I had to wonder why she'd been hired. Was it because Sidney Garfellow had the hots for her, or did she just happen to be the best available person for the job?

Then there was the gaffer, a middle-aged man with a wart on his nose and a chip on his shoulder. The wart was the type that was prominent enough you wondered why the hell the guy didn't take it off. The chip on his shoulder was due to the fact that as the head electrician he felt he didn't get as much respect as the DP. In this presumption he was absolutely correct. The director of photography is the artist who designs the lighting of the set—the gaffer is the functionary who carries it out. The only odd thing about his attitude was, he'd either been sitting on it for twenty to thirty years or else it had taken him that long to work it out.

Next up was the artistic director, a tall, thin black man with a high wide forehead and a smaller nose than Michael Jackson. If I had to describe the man in one phrase, it would be *perfectly pleased.* He seemed perfectly pleased with his lot as artistic director, and perfectly pleased with everything else with which he came in contact. His favorite expression was, "This will do nicely."

Last, but not least, was the sound man, Murky Doyle. I'm generally terrible with names, but his I remembered because there was a story that went with it. His real name was Vincent, but he'd been dubbed Murky as a comment on the quality of his sound recordings. The joke of the industry was that Murky had embraced the nickname gladly, thinking people were kidding, when in fact they were dead serious.

It was a good thing he had, because aside from that, Murky was a downright unpleasant fellow. As much as the art director was sweet, Murky was sour. He complained bitterly about everything, perhaps as a defense mechanism to prepare people for the dismal quality of his sound recording.

Anyhow, when Sidney Garfellow and the gang emerged from the station wagon, it was somewhat like clowns getting out of a circus car.

Sidney looked around and spotted me. "Stanley. There you are. Good. We wanted you here, but we didn't want to wait for you. Time's money and we can't afford to wait."

Since I'd beaten them there by a good half hour, that didn't make any sense at all, but one doesn't argue with a producer. I said nothing, waited for Sidney's attention to shift to something else.

Which it immediately did. "Good god, it's locked," he said, pointing to the warehouse door. "Why is it locked? Why isn't someone here to open up for us?"

"I have the keys," the production manager said. He held them up, jingled them in front of Sidney Garfellow. The action and attitude seemed to convey the fact that, in Sidney's case, a simple, bald statement would not suffice, and one would be smart to resort to visual aids. In this judgment, he was probably correct.

"Well, fine," Sidney said. "That's all well and good. But who's going to show us around?"

"I am," the production manager said. Jake Decker. The other name I could remember.

"You've seen it before?"

"No, but I discussed it on the phone."

"They should have sent someone."

"I didn't want them to."

"Why?"

"It would have cost us money."

"Money? Nonsense. We're renting the place. They *want* to show it off."

"In the negotiation, I mean," Jake said evenly. "I'll do better in the negotiation if we make our own independent investigation without their representative present. I'll be able to claim things are poor, even if some of these bozos say they're good."

"Who are you calling *bozos?*" the sound man demanded.

"Not you, Murky," Jake said. "We *know* you're not gonna think it's good."

"Can we get on with it?" the gaffer said. "I got a union meeting."

Jake Decker looked at him. "When?"

The gaffer stuck out his chin. "What's it to do with you?"

"You're on the payroll today. You telling me you're going to a union meeting instead?"

The gaffer's chin extended even more. Then drew back. "No, later tonight."

"Then no big deal," Jake said. "Come on. Let's look at the place."

He unlocked the padlock, took off the chain. The door itself was also locked. In fact, twice, with a regular lock and a police lock. Jake unlocked those, slid the door wide.

We walked into what appeared to be a large, dark room.

"Any lights in this place?" Sidney Garfellow said.

"There must be," Jake said. He fumbled on the wall. "No, not here."

"Great. No lights," Sidney said. He managed to give the impression it was a personal affront.

"There's gotta be lights."

Sidney laughed. "Great, great. I got a DP and a gaffer here, you'd think someone could turn on the lights."

There was a click and the lights went on.

"Got 'em," cried a triumphant voice. It was the young production assistant, who looked absolutely thrilled at having been able to help.

He got no thanks for it. Sidney Garfellow turned to the gorgeous assistant director, whispered, "What's his name?"

"Dan."

"Dan," he said, "what are you doing here? You're supposed to be with the car."

"I found a spot."

Sidney shook his head. "You can't leave the car in this neighborhood. It'll be stolen. Go back and wait in the car."

Dan had sandy red hair and freckles and wide, eager eyes. His spirits were obviously dampened, but he wasn't about to argue with the producer. "Yes, sir," he said. "Don't worry about a thing." He went out the door.

"All right," Sidney said. "What have we got here?"

What we had was a large empty space with a cement floor and a twenty-foot ceiling.

"Okay," Sidney said. "And this is for what? Our sound stage, right?"

Jake shook his head. "No, sir."

"Why not? It's perfect. Wide open, high ceiling."

"Yeah, but cement floor. You can't hammer into it." Jake jerked his thumb. "Upstairs, I'm told, same setup, but the floor's wood."

"Sounds good," the art director said.

"Yeah, but second floor," Sidney said. "What about getting the stuff up there?"

Jake jerked his thumb again. "Freight elevator on the other end. We can check it out, but I'm told it's huge."

"How do *we* get up there?"

"Stairs in the corner."

We filed up the stairs to another dark floor and played the game of find-the-light-switch. Without Dan, it took a little longer, with a lot of cursing and thumping and bumbling around, and once the attractive AD said, "Do that again, so help me," and a voice that sounded like the gaffer's grunted, "Sorry," but eventually the lights came on.

Revealing exactly what Jake Decker had predicted. A huge space, similar to that downstairs, except with a wooden floor.

"This will do nicely," the art director said.

The production manager looked around critically before declaring, "Yeah, this should be fine."

"Fine for you," Murky said. "You hear how you sound? I mean, Jesus Christ, do you just *hear* how you sound?"

It occurred to me to wonder if Murky ever heard how *he* sounded. The acoustics seemed perfectly good to me, but then what did I know?

My attention was captured by a loud, peremptory voice saying, "Stanley."

I didn't have to guess who that was. "Yes, Sidney?"

I turned and found him pointing to a far corner of the loft where huge cartons were stacked. Some of them were rectangular, but others were tall cylinders.

"Stanley," Sidney said. "Whaddya think. Wouldn't this be perfect for the big warehouse fight?"

I blinked. "Sidney, there *is* no warehouse fight."

"Yeah, but there *could* be. And this would be perfect for it. Those boxes and cylinders. We could move 'em around. Shoot wonderful angles going in and out."

"Sidney—"

"I don't expect you to do it now. Think it out tonight, let me see it tomorrow."

The DP stuck his nose in. "Sidney, a major fight sequence is going to be tough to light," he said. At least that's what I *deduce* he said from Sidney Garfellow's answer. With his thick German accent, I couldn't catch a word. Apparently, Sidney could. If so, it was just another indication of the man's genius.

Anyway, Sidney said, "Are you telling me you can't light a fight scene?"

The DP told Sidney Garfellow either that he *could* light a fight scene but it would take time, or that his shorts were on too tight.

Sidney turned to me and said, "It's no problem. Write it, Stanley. Write it. I'll look at it tomorrow."

I'm glad it was no problem for *him*. From my point of view, I couldn't imagine where in the script I was going to cram a warehouse fight. I knew if I asked Sidney, he would respond, as he always did when faced with a tough logistics problem, "You're the writer," as if that were some sainted profession on which he dared not intrude. Of course, once I had written it, it would turn out I was *only* the writer, and what the hell did *I* know?

Do I sound cynical? Get a screenplay produced sometime.

The gaffer broke in about then, complaining that there weren't enough outlets on the floor, and he'd have to run power up from downstairs. That didn't seem like that huge an imposition—it was what he'd been hired for—but the guy had a lot to say on the subject, which ended the script conference.

The discussion of how to get power upstairs segued into a discussion of how to get equipment upstairs, which led to a search for the freight elevator. It was discovered in the back corner of the side wall, which led to a fresh round of speculation and griping: Did it open onto the side alley? If so, was there room in there to turn the trucks around? Could you back up and unload flush, or did you have to do it catty-corner? Was the elevator wide enough, deep enough, high enough, and did the damn thing even work?

It did.

The production manager located a huge button on the wall and pressed it, and with a clang that could have been heard from the Bronx to Brooklyn, the elevator lurched into motion. There came the sound of huge chains clanking through gears and pulleys, as the elevator descended from some higher floor.

As we watched, the floor of the elevator came into view some twenty feet above, visible through the floor-to-ceiling steel-mesh door. When the elevator reached our floor and stopped with a mighty thoomb, the steel-mesh door split in two halfway up, the top ten feet rising up into the ceiling, the bottom ten sinking into the floor, and we surged forward to inspect the interior of the freight elevator.

It was almost perfect. It was huge—high, wide, and deep. You could load anything you wanted onto it and bring it upstairs. Hell, you could drive the truck itself on it and bring it upstairs, if you wanted to. Even the grumpiest crew member alive would be hard pressed to complain. The elevator was all they could have asked for.

The only possible drawback was the dead body lying in the middle of the floor.

3.

"You really piss me off," MacAullif said.

"Oh, yeah? Then why are you here?"

Sergeant MacAullif was here—in the warehouse with the dead body—because I'd called him up and asked him to come. I'd done it because we were a movie crew and I didn't want the situation to get out of hand. It's tough enough shooting movies in New York City. Industry loves it, but residents don't. Movie crews are disruptive—they take up parking spaces and block streets, intrude on the daily routine. They also generate a lot of publicity, the wrong type of which can make a lot of people's lives miserable. Still, the city wants them there because the city's damn near bankrupt, and needs the money.

So calling MacAullif was sort of in the nature of a gesture—the shit's hit the fan, is there anything you'd like to do in terms of damage control?

To my surprise, there was. MacAullif told me to skip 911, he'd handle it himself.

Which he had. The medical examiner had arrived, the crime-scene unit was going over the elevator, and MacAullif was here in person. To debrief the movie crew and send them on their way.

Or so I hoped.

"What do you mean, why am I here? You called me, schmuck."

"Yes. And I know you jump when I call."

"Fuck you."

"That's not an answer."

"It's as good as any."

We were in the far corner of the warehouse. MacAullif jerked his thumb at the other side, where a couple of officers were riding herd on the crew. "And these jokers here—these are all technical people?"

"That's right."

"The tall guy with the curly hair—the one who wouldn't shut up when I came in—that's this whiz-kid producer-director?"

"Yeah. That's him."

"Looks like an asshole."

"It's an occupational hazard."

MacAullif looked at me. "You don't like the guy?"

"He hired me six months ago. At the time I was grateful."

"You're really writing the guy's movie?"

"That's debatable."

"Oh?"

"Sometimes I feel like I'm hired as a typist. He tells me what he wants and I type it."

"Is that true?"

"No."

"Then how *is* it?"

I took a breath. "He tells me what he wants, and it's so fucking stupid I can't imagine it. But I got twenty-four hours to figure out how to make it work and stick it in the script. If I can, *he's* a genius. If I can't, *I* fucked up."

"Shit. Makes ambulance chasing sound almost respectable."

"Did you come here to discuss my screen career?"

"I came here because I thought there was a problem. Apparently, there's not."

What MacAullif was referring to was the fact the dead body had turned out to be a John Doe. A derelict dressed in rags with no identification on him. Obviously a homeless man who'd somehow wandered into the building and expired. While violence hadn't been ruled out, the man hadn't been shot or stabbed, so it was possible his demise had been from natural causes. At any rate, the man appeared to be associated with the building rather than the movie crew, which made him less of a priority.

"If there's really no problem," I said, "why are you pissed off?"

"It's no problem for *you*," MacAullif said. "For *me*, it's still a potential homicide. One I wouldn't have caught if you hadn't called."

"You saying I shouldn't have called?"

"No, damn it," MacAullif said. He grimaced, shook his head. "See, that's where you piss me off. You put me in a no-win situation. Here's a piece-of-shit case you saddled me with, and you get to be a wise ass and say, 'Well, would you rather I didn't tell you?' "

"Well, would you?"

"Fuck you."

"I'm sorry, MacAullif. But how was I to know it was a John Doe?"

"Does the guy look like a bank president to you?"

I let my eyes widen. "What's that? Are you saying the poor don't have the same rights as the rich?"

"What was that you asked me before? *Why* you pissed me off?"

"Guilty as charged," I said. "Look, if this is really routine, you wanna let the crew go before they get testy?"

MacAullif looked over at where the officers were holding the crew, then back at me. "They were *born* testy. What the fuck do *you* care?"

"Hey," I said. "I suggested to them that I call you. They'll be pissed at me if it turns out to have been a bad idea."

"Well, I certainly wouldn't want anyone else pissed at you."

"Come on. I didn't hit you over the head and say come down here. I apprised you of the situation. I considered it almost a courtesy."

"You're a regular Emily Post." MacAullif sighed and shook his head. "All right, I'll cut you a break. Let's have 'em one at a time and I'll let 'em go."

MacAullif looked at me, rubbed his hands together.

"Okay. Bring on the whiz kid."

4.

Sidney Garfellow acted as if he were in charge, as if it were still his show.

"Thanks for coming, Sergeant," he said. "I really appreciate it."

MacAullif blinked. I could practically see his mind going, trying to choose an adequate response—the number of devastating rejoinders that sprang to mind must have been overwhelming.

He opted to ignore it. "You're the producer-director?" he said.

"That's right. Sidney Garfellow."

MacAullif jerked his thumb. "Then you can thank this guy for calling me for you. I'll try to make this as painless as possible and get you out of here. If these questions sound stupid, they're just routine. You'll find it's a lot faster to just answer them than get all huffy and want to know why the fuck I'm askin'."

Sidney Garfellow smiled. "Well put, Sergeant. What do you need to know?"

"This warehouse—you ever been here before?"

"No."

"You're renting it for the movie?"

23

"No. We were looking at it to see if we *wanted* to rent it."

"You came here this afternoon to look at it?"

"That's right."

"You all came together?"

"That's right. All of us. Oh." Sidney nodded to me. "Except him."

"He met you here?"

"That's right."

"Who came first?"

"He did."

"How's that?"

"When we drove up, he was here."

"Where's here?"

"Right out front."

"The main door?"

"Yes. If that's the *main* door. It's the only door I know."

"The door was locked?"

"Yes, it was."

"How?"

"With a chain and padlock."

"Was that the only lock?"

"Actually, I think the door was locked too. You'd have to ask Jake."

"Jake?"

"Jake Decker. The production manager. He opened the door."

"He had the keys?"

"Yes." Sidney smiled. "Well, if you want to be technically correct, Sergeant, I didn't *see* the keys. But I assume he had them, since he opened the door."

"Which one is Jake?"

"You can't miss him. He's the size of a small truck."

"Right," MacAullif said. "So he opened the door and you all went in?"

"That's right."

"What happened then?"

"First we couldn't find the lights. Then someone turned them on."

"Who?"

"The production assistant. I don't know his name."

"He found the lights?"

"Yeah."

MacAullif jerked his thumb. "Which one is he?"

Sidney looked, said, "Oh, actually, he isn't here."

"Oh?"

"I sent him outside to wait in the car. In this neighborhood, you know."

"Right," MacAullif said. "Anyway, you got the lights on. What happened then?"

"So we looked around."

"What were you looking for?"

"Shooting space. We were looking to rent this place for a movie studio. Build sets in. Shoot scenes in."

"I see," MacAullif said. "Now, that was downstairs. Why'd you come up here?"

"The wood floor."

MacAullif frowned. "What?"

"The floor downstairs is concrete. You can't hammer into it. You're building sets, you want to hammer into the floor. Now, we can lay down a floor, but it costs money. But up here's wood."

MacAullif nodded. "I see. Did you know that?"

Sidney frowned. "What?"

"When you came—did you know the floor up here was wood?"

"No, I didn't, actually," Sidney said. He added, "Not my business to know. In fact, I thought the space downstairs looked pretty good, before Jake told me up here was wood."

"Jake?"

"Yeah. Like I said, the production manager."

"He told you this was wood?"

"Yeah."

"While you were still downstairs?"

"Yeah. That's why we came up here."

"I see," MacAullif said. "And how did you get up here?"

"The stairs."

"And who found the stairs?"

"I don't know. I think it was Jake. It wasn't important at the time. Is it important now?"

MacAullif shrugged. "Too early to tell what's important and what isn't."

"Then you'll have to ask Jake."

"Don't worry, I will," MacAullif said. "So you got up here, and what happened?"

"We looked for the lights. That took a while. I don't remember who finally turned 'em on. Then we looked around." Sidney broke off, put up his hand, and looked at MacAullif. "The place is perfect for filming. I know this is terrible to say, Sergeant. But I'd really hate to lose this space. I know you have a dead man here, and it's tragic and all that. But I hope it's not gonna shut down this building."

"I don't see why it should," MacAullif said. "Go on. You were saying. You got the lights on, you looked around."

"I think there was some discussion of where we could shoot. Some scenes I want Stanley to write. The acoustics, and running power upstairs. And how we're going to get the equipment in. And that's when we went to check out the elevator."

"You all went to check it out?"

"Oh, sure. All together."

"And what happened?"

"Well, we all went over there. And someone, I think Jake, pressed the button, and the elevator came down." Sidney shrugged. "And there he was."

"Right there in the elevator?"

"That's right."

"Right where we found him?"

"Absolutely. Right like that."

"Did anyone go *in* the elevator?"

"No."

"Are you sure?"

"Absolutely. Actually, someone tried to and he stopped 'em."

I tried to look modest.

Sergeant MacAullif wasn't impressed. "So no one actually went in?"

"That's right."

"Because he stopped you?"

"Not me personally. He just stopped anyone from going in there."

"Right," MacAullif said. "Of course, he was the one called and got me over here."

"Yeah. So?"

"So what about then? Who kept people out of the elevator then?"

"I did," Sidney said.

"You'll vouch for the fact no one went near the body during the time Stanley wasn't present?"

"Absolutely," Sidney said. "No one went near it."

"Glad to hear it," MacAullif said. "And the dead man— had you ever seen him before?"

"No, of course not. Why would I?"

"Why, indeed?" MacAullif said. "Okay, that will do for now. Stanley, you wanna run him over there and bring me that, what's his name, the giant?"

"You want me to stick around, Sergeant?" Sidney said. "In case his recollection needs prompting."

"Thanks all the same," MacAullif said. "In these cases we prefer independent testimony."

"You're letting *him* stay," Sidney said, indicating me.

"He's a detective," MacAullif said, as if that was any explanation.

It wasn't, but Sidney accepted it as such and said, "Suit yourself."

I figured Sidney Garfellow would be pissed off by MacAullif's attitude. But as I led him back over to the others to fetch the production manager, he tugged at my arm, jerked his thumb in MacAullif's direction, and said, "I *like* him."

5.

Seeing Jake Decker next to Sergeant MacAullif was the first time I realized just how huge the production manager actually was. MacAullif was a big, beefy cop. But next to Jake Decker he looked small.

"Now, then," MacAullif said. "Your name is?"

"Jake Decker."

"You're the production manager?"

"That's right."

"As I understand it, you came with the others, you all came together except him, when you got here he was waiting outside and the door to the warehouse was locked?"

"That's right."

"How was it locked?"

"With a chain and padlock. Also, the door was locked with a regular lock and a police lock."

"You had keys to those locks?"

"Yes, I did."

"Where'd you get 'em?"

"From the rental agent."

"When did you get 'em?"

"Yesterday."

"Yesterday?"

28

"Yes. Yesterday afternoon."

"How'd you get 'em."

"Actually, I sent a gofer for 'em."

"Gofer?"

"Production assistant. Kid who drives the car. I called up the rental agent, told 'em we wanted to see the place, they should give me the keys. I sent the kid over to get 'em."

"They just gave you the keys?"

"Sure."

"Why didn't they show you the place themselves?"

"They wanted to. I said no. I don't like those guys around when I'm lookin' at property. It inhibits discussion. So I told 'em to give me the keys."

"And they gave 'em to you?"

"Sure."

"Just like that?"

"Hey, it's not like I *asked* if I could have the keys. I told 'em I *wanted* 'em."

"Yeah," MacAullif said. "But it's not standard procedure for a real-estate agent to just give out the keys."

Jake what's-his-name looked at MacAullif as if he were a total idiot. "Sergeant," he said. "We're the *movies.*"

Funny. It was just like MacAullif's explanation to Sidney Garfellow about me being a detective. Except that explanation was bullshit and this one meant something. Jake was right. We were the movies, and people do things for movie people they wouldn't ordinarily do for anybody else. And even MacAullif, who'd never worked in the movies, took that as an explanation.

He nodded. "Right," he said. "So they gave you the keys. Now, this production assistant you sent for them—is that the same one who's here today? The gofer?"

"Oh, yeah. It was Dan."

"Dan is the production assistant? Do you know his last name?"

"Not offhand."

"Anyway, you sent him for the keys, he brought them back, he gave them to you when?"

"Yesterday afternoon."

"What time was that?"

Jake frowned. "Is it important?"

"Well, now," MacAullif said. "I'm just starting this investigation, so I don't know what's important and what isn't. So I have to ask my questions in order to find that out."

"Right. Well, it happens I was out yesterday afternoon. So I didn't actually get the keys till about six o'clock."

"When you got back to the office?"

"Right."

"This production assistant gave them to you?"

"No. He wasn't there."

"Then how'd you get the keys?"

"He left them on my desk."

MacAullif's eyes narrowed. "Oh, yeah? Is that what you told him to do?"

"No, but I wasn't around, so that's what he did."

"And you just happened to look on your desk and found the keys."

"No. I got back to the office and said, 'Where's Dan?' And the girl there, the secretary who runs the office—Grace, her name is—said he went out but he left the keys on my desk."

"She knew about the keys?"

"Of course. She works there. She made some of the calls to the rental agent for me."

"I see. And do you remember what time it was when you asked Dan to get the keys for you?"

"Not really. It was earlier that day. I think right after lunch."

"So he went and got the keys. When he came back and dropped them off you were out. He left them on your desk, and they sat there until six o'clock when you came back and picked them up? Do you have any idea when it was he left them on your desk?"

The production manager blinked. He cocked his head, squinted sideways at MacAullif. "Do you mean to imply that yesterday afternoon someone took those keys from my desk so they could get in here and kill that bum?"

MacAullif sighed. "I don't mean to imply anything. I just gotta get my facts straight. So I'm wondering how long those keys were lying on your desk."

"I wouldn't know."

"At any rate, you picked them up around six o'clock last night?"

"That's right."

"Did you come over here then?"

"Certainly not."

"How about this morning? Did you come over here this morning?"

"No, I did not."

"You didn't decide to scout out the place on your own ahead of the crew?"

"No."

"Why not? Wouldn't that be a help? To know where things are. To anticipate their questions. Wouldn't that save time?"

Jake nodded approvingly. "You're good. I like the way you think."

"That makes sense to you?"

"Absolutely."

"But you didn't do that?"

"No. In a perfect world, I would. But this is a skeleton crew. A three-week preproduction schedule. You ever work in the movies, Sergeant?"

"No."

"Well, trust me, that's short. There's a million things gotta be done in those three weeks, and I got no one to help me do them. No unit manager, no location manager. None of the people you'd have on a big-budget movie crew. Independent low-budget means you do a lot of stuff yourself. So I don't have time to prescout locations. I got the girl in the office calling around for me lining things up, and I go out and see 'em with everybody else."

"So this was the first time you'd ever been here, the first time you'd seen the place?"

"That's right."

"And the dead man—that was the first time you'd ever seen him too?"

"Absolutely."

"You have no idea who he is?"

"No, I do not. If you want a theory, I'd assume he's a homeless guy broke in here looking for a place to sleep, and was unlucky enough to drop dead in the elevator." Jake shrugged. "But that's just how it looks to me."

I had a feeling that was how it looked to MacAullif too, but he just nodded and said, "Thank you, Mr. Decker. Now this production assistant—the gofer—I believe he's waiting outside in the car?"

"He should be."

"You wanna run outside and get him for me, please? There's a few details I'd like to tie up."

Jake jerked his thumb at the cops. "They gonna let me go?"

"Good point," MacAullif said. He waved one of the cops over. "Stanford," he said. "Pass this man out. He's gonna fetch a kid for me. When he gets back, park him with the others and bring me the kid."

"Is that wise?" I said to MacAullif as they went off.

MacAullif frowned. "What do you mean?"

"Letting him fetch the production assistant. Gives them a chance to synchronize their stories."

MacAullif looked at me. He blinked. "Stories?" he said. "Are you kidding me? Stories? You know, what this guy just said—about some bum broke in here and died—that's what happened. All the rest of this stuff is bullshit. I do it 'cause it's my job. But ninety-nine percent of the investigative work you do is bullshit. You know why I talk to the kid? So no one can say I didn't. Odds are, no one ever gives a shit, but if someone does, it ain't my ass. And the one per-cent of the time it does pan out, I'm a fucking hero.

"Now, this doesn't happen to be one of those times. But you got your movie people here, you called me special, and I'm gonna do a real job. I'm sorry that don't mean kissin' their ass and lettin' them all go right away."

"Of course not," I said. "On the other hand, you don't have to bend over backwards the other way, keep them here when there's no need, just to show the motion-picture indus-try don't cut no ice with you."

"Did I happen to mention you're a real pain in the ass?"

"I believe the subject came up."

Before we could pursue that topic at any length, Jake re-turned with the production assistant.

Dan had always seemed young, but intimidated by the po-lice he looked about three.

"You wanted to see me?" he said.

"That's right," MacAullif said. "What's your name?"

"Dan Mayfield."

"Well, Dan," MacAullif said. He jerked his thumb across the room to where the production manager was just joining the others. "Did Jake happen to tell you what I wanted to talk to you about?"

"Someone got killed."

"That's right. Someone did. Did he mention why I wanted to talk to *you?*"

"About the keys?" Dan said.

I flashed a triumphant look at MacAullif.

He pretended not to see it. "That's right, about the keys. Did Jake say I wanted to ask you about the keys?"

"No, he just asked me when I picked them up."

"I see," MacAullif said. "And when *did* you pick them up?"

"Right away. When he asked me."

"And when was that?"

"Right after lunch."

"What time of day was that?"

"Around one-thirty."

"You picked up the keys then?"

"Sure."

"Where was the real-estate office?"

"Madison Avenue. Around Forty-fifth Street."

"You picked up the keys from there?"

"That's right."

"There's no parking Midtown. How'd you park the car?"

"I didn't take the car."

"Oh?"

"I went on the subway."

"Where'd you leave the car?"

"At the office."

"So you picked up the keys, then went back to the office to get the car?"

"That's right."

"So you picked up the car, you dropped off the keys then?"

Dan hesitated. "Actually, no."

"No?"

"I had another errand to run. So when I picked up the car, there was no reason to go up to the office. Except to drop off the keys. Frankly, I forgot. Anyway, it wasn't like he *needed* the keys. I knew they weren't going to use them till the next day. Still, I *should* have dropped off the keys. But the fact is, I just got in the car and took off. So, actually, I didn't drop off the keys until a couple of hours later."

"And when would that be?"

"I'm not sure. Say around four o'clock."

I tuned out. Not that the bit about the keys wasn't interesting as all hell. But with MacAullif admitting he was just going through the motions, it was hard to give a damn.

I'd actually wandered away from MacAullif and the production assistant and was surveying the stacks of crates and cartons and working out warehouse fight sequences in my head, when I felt a hand on my shoulder.

It was Sidney Garfellow, in the company of a rather exas-

perated-looking cop. I felt sorry for him—the cop, I mean.
Sidney was obviously accustomed to riding roughshod over
everyone.

"Stanley," Sidney said. "I gotta ask you something."

"I'm working on it now, Sidney," I told him. "I don't
know why we need it, but I'll fit it in somewhere."

"What? Oh, that." He waved it away. "No problem. I have
confidence you'll write a good scene. No, I want to ask you
about the cop."

I frowned. "Huh?"

He jerked his thumb. "Your buddy. The cop. You guys go
back a bit, huh?"

"You could say that. Why?"

"I'm thinkin' of hirin' him."

I blinked. "What?"

"For the movie. When we're shooting. The mayor's office
supplies cops for traffic control and shit like that. But it's
new guys every day, and they're not workin' for you. Be
nice to have our own man on board."

"Are you serious?"

"Absolutely. You think he'd go for it?"

The answer, *Not in a million years,* sprang to mind. But I
opted for diplomacy.

"Sidney, he's a homicide cop. He's here 'cause someone
died."

"Yeah, but that's no big deal. And it's got nothing to do
with us. If he's got the time, I'd like to sign him on." Sidney
shrugged. "Hell, he even looks like a cop. Maybe I'll stick
him in a scene."

"As a cop?"

"Why not?"

I could think of a lot of answers, but what the hey, it had
nothing to do with me.

"Well," I said, "can't hurt to ask."

"That's what I thought," Sidney said. "Thanks for your
input."

With an imperious gesture to the cop, he strode back to the

group. I turned my attention back to MacAullif and the production assistant. Only, now the production assistant had turned into the assistant director. That was, in my opinion, a bit of an improvement. But she could have been a bag of cement for all MacAullif cared. From where I stood I could see him grunting out questions and nodding his head gloomily at each response.

He was interrupted by the medical examiner, who'd apparently finished with the body. They stepped off to one side and conferred in low tones, after which the medical examiner headed back toward the freight elevator, and MacAullif sent the attractive assistant director back to her group.

He caught my eye and gestured me over.

"Find out the cause of death?" I asked.

"Yeah."

"Natural causes, I hope?"

"Yeah," MacAullif said. "Wouldn't that be nice? The fact is, he died of a blow to the back of the head."

"Son of a bitch. Any chance it was accidental?"

"Doc says no. Not where the body's lyin'. Of course, you're such a pain in the ass, I should have figured." MacAullif shook his head. "Just had to be murder."

6.

Alice was all ears. "Murder?"

I flopped down at the kitchen table, rubbed my head with my hands.

"Yeah," I said. "But it really has nothing to do with me."

"With you?"

"With us. With the movies, I mean. It's like they say, co-incidental and not to be inferred."

"Stanley."

Alice was at the stove preparing a sauce. I had no idea what it was, but Alice is a terrific cook, and I wouldn't have disturbed her for the world.

Only it's hard not to mention a murder.

I told Alice about scouting the warehouse and finding the body.

"A bum?" Alice said.

"We don't say *bum* anymore. It's politically incorrect. We say *homeless.*"

"Say whatever you like. The man was murdered in the elevator?"

"Apparently. I suppose he could have been killed elsewhere and dragged there, but I doubt it."

"What killed him?"

"A blow to the back of the head."

"Any chance it was accidental?"

"Medical examiner said no."

"They find the murder weapon?"

"Not when I left. Maybe they have by now."

"Cops are still there?"

"Far as I know."

"But you say it has nothing to do with the movie crew?"

"I don't see how it could."

"Why not?"

I was saved from having to answer by my son, Tommie, who came bouncing into the kitchen for help with his homework.

"I need a joke," Tommie said.

"Hey, Dad, good to see you, how's your day?" I said.

Tommie made a face. "Come on, Dad, this is serious."

"A serious joke?"

"It's for homework. We gotta write a joke."

Good lord. I must say I like the East Side Day School in most respects. Except for the homework. I can't recall *getting* homework in grade school. Not before junior high. But it seemed like Tommie got it every night. It was also often something like this—something the kids couldn't possibly do and the parents had to do for them.

"I'm not sure I understand the assignment," I told Tommie. "Is it Write a Joke, or Have Your Parents Write a Joke?"

"Dad," Tommie said. He had already mastered the preadolescent trick of making it a two-syllable word. "Come on, I need a joke."

"What about this?" Alice said. "What has eighteen legs and catches flies? . . . A baseball team."

"Mom," Tommie said. Also a two-syllable word. "That's an old joke."

"What has *twenty* legs and catches flies?" I said.

Tommie frowned. Thought. "What?"

"Two and a half spiders."

Tommie gave me such a look. He rolled his eyes, shook his head, and bounced out the door.

"Everyone's a critic," I said.

"Go on," Alice said. "Tell me about the murder."

"What about it?"

"You were telling me why the movie crew couldn't be involved."

"Oh. Because it wasn't our place. We just happened to be there. We went to scout it as a location and found the guy."

"And no one could have killed him then?"

"No. We were all together. And he looked like he'd been dead for some time."

"What did the medical examiner say?"

"I don't know."

"You know he was hit on the head."

"I heard the *cause* of death. I didn't hear what he said about the *time* of death."

"Why not?"

"I didn't stick around. We had work to do, and as soon as they let us go, we took off."

"So who do the cops figure did it?"

"Another bum. Most likely a couple of homeless guys broke into the warehouse looking for a place to stay, one of them wound up killing the other."

"Was there any sign of a break-in?"

"Yeah. There was. The basement window in the back was smashed. The cops figure they got in through there."

Alice nodded. "So it's really nothing."

"It doesn't seem to be."

"So there's no reason to call MacAullif."

I blinked.

"What is it?"

"I called MacAullif."

"Oh?"

"He was there. Took charge of the whole thing."

"You didn't tell me that."

"No, I guess I didn't."

"Why didn't you tell me that?"

I didn't know until Alice asked me, but as soon as she said that, I knew why. I'd been avoiding mentioning MacAullif because I didn't want to bring up the part about Sidney Garfellow offering him a job on the movie.

This was because Sergeant MacAullif had dumbfounded me by accepting it.

It's hard to explain why that bothered me, but it did. It really did. So much so I hadn't wanted to talk about it. Had left MacAullif's name out of the discussion of the murder.

No, it wasn't just that this was *my* motion picture, *my* chance for fame and glory, and I didn't want anyone to share in it. At least, I didn't think it was that. In fact, I think if MacAullif had been excited about working on my movie I probably would have been pleased.

But it wasn't like that. Because Sidney Garfellow worked on him. And for all of Sidney Garfellow's I-am-an-independent-producer-the-studios-don't-cut-no-ice-with-me, he fed MacAullif the straight Hollywood line.

See, it happened that just today he'd locked up a star for the picture.

The guy's name was Jason Clairemont. And he was a nobody, a twenty-two-year-old kid lucky to have a job. Only, last year Jason Clairemont had done an action picture with Clint Eastwood. Besides racking up an impressive body count, the picture had done a hundred and seventy-five million at the box office. And suddenly Jason Clairemont was a star.

You'll pardon me, but I just couldn't see it. From where I sat, *Clint Eastwood* was a star, and Jason Clairemont was just lucky enough to have been in his movie.

Only, a hundred and seventy-five million translates into a lot of theater tickets. A lot of people saw that movie.

One of them happened to be Sergeant MacAullif of the NYPD. MacAullif had actually gotten a silly look on his face when Sidney Garfellow mentioned Jason Clairemont.

"The kid?" MacAullif said. "Clint Eastwood's sidekick? *To Shoot the Tiger*?"

And MacAullif was in.

Which shouldn't bother me, but it did. Sergeant MacAullif hadn't agreed to work on a Sidney Garfellow movie. Or a Stanley Hastings movie. He'd agreed to work on a Jason Clairemont movie.

So I had to backtrack and explain to Alice about Mac-Aullif being there. Then I explained about Sidney Garfellow offering him a job.

"And he took it?" Alice said. "I find that hard to believe."

"Turns out he had some vacation time coming. Shooting schedule's only four weeks. Guess he figured he could spare the time."

"Did Sidney offer him a lot of money?"

"There *isn't* a lot of money. I think he offered something like five hundred a week."

"Why would he do it for that?"

I sighed. "Actually, I think what sold him was when he found out Jason Clairemont was in it."

Alice's mouth dropped open. "What?"

"Yeah. Just happened this morning. Sidney locked up Jason Clairemont to play the lead in the movie."

Alice had a silly look on her face. "You're writing a *Jason Clairemont* movie?"

Jesus.

Even Alice.

7.

"This won't do."

"I beg your pardon?"

"I'm sorry. This simply won't do."

The person making that statement was Sidney Garfellow. The thing that wouldn't do was the warehouse fight scene.

I didn't want to hear it. I'd stayed up most of the night writing the damn scene, and what I wanted to hear was, "It's perfect, it's just what I wanted, thank you very much."

"Sidney," I protested. "It's just what you asked for."

"No, it isn't."

"Sure, it is. A warehouse fight scene."

"Yes, but not *this* one."

"And what's wrong with this one?"

"It's from out of left field. It comes from nowhere. It has no business in the script."

I took a breath. That was just what I told him yesterday, and he told me to write it anyway. I paused, trying to think of a suitable rejoinder. One that wouldn't get me bounced off the picture.

From below there came the sound of hammering, as there had been periodically during the conversation.

Sidney and I were standing in the second floor of the

42

warehouse, staring at the stack of boxes, the ones that had failed to inspire me to write the definitive warehouse fight scene. The hammering came from carpenters on the first floor, throwing up temporary walls to create office space for the motion-picture production company. This had been facilitated by the fact that late last night the police had released the premises as a crime scene, and Sidney Garfellow had been able to rent the building.

It occurred to me to wonder if that was in any part due to the fact that Sidney Garfellow had given Sergeant MacAullif a job.

"Sidney," I said. "If you want something else, you'll have to be more specific. All I ~an say is, I tried to give you what you asked for."

Sidney didn't get angry. That wasn't his style. Instead, he put his arm around my shoulders as if we were the best of pals.

"Stanley, Stanley," he said. "Let me explain you the facts of life. Now, to start off, why is that scene in the script?"

"What?"

"Come on, Stanley. This isn't that hard. Tell me, why is that scene in the script?"

"Because you wanted it there."

Sidney smiled. "Exactly," he said. "That's *exactly* why it's there. It's the *only* reason it's there. You know it. I know it." He smiled again. "But we don't want *them* to know it. We don't want Joe-fucking-Public sitting in the theater saying, 'Gee, the director must have wanted to have a warehouse fight.' We want him sittin' there diggin' it. So there's got to be a logical *excuse* for the warehouse fight, to cover up the fact that there *isn't* one.

"Now, if the warehouse fight doesn't integrate with some of the other stuff in the script, obviously the other stuff has to go."

"You're kidding."

"Why should I kid about a thing like that?"

"Sidney. We're two weeks away from shooting."

"Stanley, grow up. You'll be rewriting *while* we're shooting. So take another crack at this."

I put up my hand. "Sidney, let me get this straight. It isn't the *scene* you object to, it's the way it's integrated in the script? So you don't want me to rewrite the scene, you want me to rewrite the connecting material?"

"No, rewrite the scene too. Some of the action's all right, but look at the dialogue. Is there any line you're in love with? I wouldn't think so. So throw it out, and give me something else. And when you write it, consider who's doing it. I mean, these lines are okay, but not for Jason Clairemont."

That was too much. I looked at him. "You want me to tailor the lines to this actor?"

Sidney looked at me in surprise. "What, are you nuts? Of course I do. And that's a good point. The rest of the movie—you've got to give it a dialogue polish. Think Jason Clairemont, and make it sound like him."

"Oh yeah? What the hell does he sound like?"

"Didn't you see *To Shoot the Tiger*?"

"Yeah."

"Like that."

"That's one movie. Does he always sound the same?"

"A kid like him? I should think so."

"He's just going to play himself?"

"What would be the point of havin' him if he didn't play himself? Look, you are not dealing with Dustin Hoffman here. Consider you got a one-trick pony. *To Shoot the Tiger*'s out on video cassette. Get a copy, watch it, make him sound like that. Well, hello."

I turned, looked over my shoulder to see Sergeant MacAullif bearing down on us.

"This is an unexpected pleasure, Sergeant," Sidney said. "We don't start shooting for two weeks."

"Yeah, I know," MacAullif said. "In the meantime, I do have this murder investigation."

"Oh? What's new?"

"Well, there's the autopsy results. Death was a blow to the

back of the head—you know that. But we got the time of death pinned down now. At least, narrowed the field. According to the medical examiner, it could have happened day before yesterday any time between noon and six o'clock."

"That's a fairly broad range."

"Best we could do," MacAullif said. "So what were you doin' Monday afternoon between twelve and six?"

"I love it," Sidney said. "Hot damn, I love it. Just like in the movies. What were you doin' between the hours of twelve and six. Sergeant, I'm going to work you a cameo, I swear."

"And I appreciate it. Meanwhile, you thought of an answer?"

"Are you serious?"

"Just doin' my job."

"Good lord," Sidney said. "Well, that's a tough one. And such a broad range. Two days ago. Let me think. Ah, twelve o'clock I'd be at lunch. Monday, what did I do for lunch? Oh yes. I had lunch with Pam."

"Who?"

"The assistant director. I took her out to lunch."

"And just where was that?"

"I don't remember offhand. Yes, I do. It was a deli on Fifty-seventh Street. I'm not sure of the name, but I could take you there."

"I doubt if that will be necessary. When did you finish lunch?"

"I imagine around two."

"And where did you go after that?"

"I think I went back to the office."

"Did the assistant director go with you?"

"I don't think she did. In fact, I'm sure she didn't. She had some errand to run at the guild office."

"And what time did you get back to the office?"

"I'm not sure. Is it important?"

"Absolutely. It's crucial," MacAullif said. "It's the fact I need to crack the case."

Sidney Garfellow looked up sharply, saw MacAullif's deadpan, and smiled. "You have an interesting way of making a point. I like that. Okay, I would say I got back to my office around two-fifteen or two-thirty."

"Who was there?"

"Grace, of course."

"Anyone else?"

"I don't think so."

"How long were you there?"

"Hold on a minute," Sidney said. He reached in his jacket pocket, pulled out what proved to be an appointment book. He opened it, flipped the pages. "Here we are. Aha. No, I was not there long. I had a meeting with my lawyer at three."

"Lawyer? Nothing wrong, I hope?"

"No. I'm producing a movie. You ever produce a movie? Well, before you start shooting, ninety percent of it is contracts."

"So how long did the meeting last?"

"I would say I was back in the office by at least four-fifteen."

"What makes you think so?"

"Frankly, I can't stand listening to lawyers. I get out of there as quick as I can."

"Who's your lawyer, by the way?"

"Fenton, Westpaul, and Klein. My man's Westpaul. They have offices on Madison Avenue. Around Forty-eighth Street."

"Uh-huh," MacAullif said. "And after that?"

Sidney shrugged. "I have nothing in my book. I'm trying to remember."

"So you're not sure how long you stayed at the office?"

"No."

"Are you sure you went back at all?"

"I think I did. But I can't be sure. You might check with Grace."

"Thanks. I will," MacAullif said. "And after you left your

lawyers, you have no idea where you were until six o'clock?"

"At the moment, I can't remember."

"Perhaps if you thought about it? . . ."

"I will certainly try," Sidney said. "Particularly since I see how crucially important it is."

We were interrupted by a voice calling, "Mr. Garfellow."

It was Dan the gofer. He came hurrying from the far end of the warehouse, waving his hand.

"Sorry to interrupt," he said, "but Mr. Westpaul called. He said it was important. The phones aren't in yet, so they sent me over."

"Good. You can run me back." Sidney looked at MacAullif. "Unless you have something else urgent, Sergeant?"

"Not just now," MacAullif said.

"Right. Come on, uh, then."

I could see Sidney hesitate on addressing the gopher, unable to come up with his name. If Dan was hurt, he didn't show it, just turned and accompanied Sidney out the door.

Leaving me alone with MacAullif. For the first time since he'd signed onto the project.

"So," I said. "Why are you really back here. Just a taste for show business?"

"Not at all," MacAullif said. "I gotta tie this up before I pass it on to the next guy."

"Pass it on?"

"Just between you and me, it's not the type of thing gets solved. Probably be on the books for a while. Before I pass it over, I gotta tie up all the loose ends."

"I thought you did that yesterday."

"I thought I did too. Let everyone go." MacAullif shrugged. "Sometimes you make a mistake."

I frowned. "Mistake?"

"Yeah. Cops found a busted window, report to me it's just routine—bums break in, one kills the other. That sounds good to me, the movie crew's answered enough stupid questions, I say fuck it, let 'em go. Now I say to myself, what kind of cop are you, lettin' those people walk just 'cause they're movie folk?"

"Glad to hear it," I said. "Equal justice under the law and all that crap. And what brings on this startling burst of conscience?"

"You're the one called me, fuckface. You're the one asked me to smooth this out."

"Guilty as charged," I said. "Anyway, what's the punch line? How come you're back?"

"The window. The stupid fucking window. I check it out myself and guess what? Your two-bum theory goes right out the window—no pun intended."

"How come?"

"Where the glass fell."

"Huh?"

"Yeah. And I gotta tell you, I chewed 'em out over it."

"What about the glass?"

"It fell outside the window. Not inside the window. Like it would have if someone had smashed the glass from outside to get in. There's no doubt about it. The glass was smashed from inside."

8.

Grace Jenkins blinked up at MacAullif over the top of her steel-rimmed glasses. "I don't understand," she said.

That was not surprising. Grace was a simple tool at best. And when Sidney Garfellow had hired the poor girl straight out of secretarial school two months ago to hold down his newly rented production office, I'm not sure what he gave her in terms of a job description, but I'd be willing to bet being grilled in a homicide wasn't included in it. But that's what Sergeant MacAullif was up to, and why he'd driven back to the East Eighty-sixth Street production office.

I understood the principle. If the bums didn't get in by breaking the window they must have got in somehow, hence it became necessary to trace the key. Still, I have to tell you, I wasn't that impressed. The phrase that came to mind was, big fucking deal. In my opinion, if the bums didn't get in through the window they got in some other way and the key had nothing to do with it.

Of course, MacAullif wasn't asking my opinion.

"Listen carefully," MacAullif said. "I want you to understand the principle."

Grace blinked. "Yes?"

"I'm investigating a murder. You know that."

"Yes. Of course."

"Well, I have to know how the victim got into the building. You can see that, can't you."

"Yes. Of course."

"So I have to keep track of the key. Because you open a building with a key."

"I'm not stupid," Grace said.

It was the type of remark that must have killed him. He couldn't say anything, but I knew he had one hell of a rejoinder.

"Fine," MacAullif said. "Then help me trace the key. You knew Jake Decker was having keys picked up from the real-estate company?"

"Of course," she said. "I made the call."

"What call?"

"The call saying we were picking up the keys. Jake told me to call, say Dan was going over to pick them up."

"Why didn't Dan call?"

"They didn't know Dan. I'd talked to them before. So I called, telling them to expect Dan."

"What time was that?"

"Around lunch."

"That's what everyone says," MacAullif said. "Did you go out for lunch?"

"No, I had a sandwich sent in."

"It was around then you called?"

"Yes."

"What time of day would that be?"

"Around one."

"And when did Dan go for the keys?"

"Then."

"Right after you called?"

"Yeah. He was there when I called. I wrote out the address for him, and he left."

"And when did he get back?"

"I don't know. It was later that afternoon."

"How much later?"

"I really couldn't say."

"Three o'clock? Four o'clock? Five o'clock?"

She shook her head. "I don't know."

"Six o'clock?"

"Before then."

"How do you know?"

"I went home then."

"And he'd dropped off the keys?"

"Yes."

"How do you know?"

"Because I remember telling Jake that he had."

"Jake wasn't in the office when Dan dropped off the keys?"

"No. If I remember, Dan came back, asked me where Jake was. I said he was out, Dan said, 'What should I do with the keys?' and I told him to leave 'em on his desk."

"Who was here then?"

"No one. Just me and Dan."

"What about the boss?"

"Sidney wasn't here either. I don't know where he was."

"At his lawyer, perhaps?"

"Yeah, I think he was."

"Then it must have been early."

"What?"

"When Dan dropped off the keys."

"Why?"

"Because Sidney was back by four-fifteen. At least that's how he remembers it."

"Oh."

"Is that how you remember it?"

"This was two days ago."

"I know that. I know it's hard. This is the same day you called about the keys. And Dan brought them back and left them on the production manager's desk. Sidney wasn't there then. But do you remember when he got back?"

"No."

"Well, maybe I can help you. You remember the production manager getting back?"

"Huh?"

"Because you told him about the keys being on his desk."

"Oh, that's right."

"Now what time was that?"

She made a face. "I'm not good with time."

How MacAullif resisted saying, What *are* you good at? was beyond me. But he just nodded and said, "Well, we know it was before six o'clock because that's when you went home."

"That's right."

"Anyway, whatever time it was Jake Decker came in— was he alone, by the way?"

"I beg your pardon?"

"When he came in and you told him about the keys—was he alone?"

"Yes, he was."

"Did he say anything else. Like, 'Boy, was that a long meeting,' or 'That guy gave me a hard time,' or anything like that?"

She shook her head. "No. He came in and he said, 'Where's Dan?' "

"Just like that?"

"Yeah. He was looking for Dan. To get the keys, you know."

"What did you say?"

"I said, 'Dan went out, but the keys are on your desk.' "

"You said Dan went out?"

"Yes."

"You didn't say something like, 'Oh, you just missed him'?"

She frowned. "I don't think so."

"But you might have?"

"I *might* have said anything. But I don't *recall* saying that."

"So the production manager probably didn't get back to

the office until sometime after Dan left. Or you probably would have said something like, 'Oh, you just missed him'."

She crinkled up her nose. "I guess so."

"Anyway, you told Jake Decker the keys were on his desk. Did you tell him anything else?"

"Like what?"

"Like anything. If you were all alone in the office, you must have been answering the phone. Did you have any messages for him?"

"Phone messages? No. Oh, but Sidney wanted him to make sure he spoke to the art director to confirm the location scout."

"You told him Sidney wanted him to do that."

"Yes."

"But that wasn't a phone message?"

"No. He told me to tell him."

"*When* did he tell you to tell him?"

"I don't know. It must have been . . ." Her eyes widened slightly.

"After he got back from the lawyer?" MacAullif said.

"Of course," she said. "That's when it was." For the first time, her face looked animated. "I remember now. That's why I couldn't remember him coming back from his lawyers. I didn't *see* him coming back from the lawyers. He came out of his office, he said he was leaving for the day and to make sure Jake got hold of Lance—that's the art director—to confirm the location scout."

"He didn't ask about the key?"

"No."

"This was after Dan had dropped it off."

"It must have been. In fact, I know it was. Because it occurred to me if Jake didn't get back before I left, I'd have to leave a note telling him that, on his desk under the keys."

MacAullif smiled. "Well, you've got a pretty good memory after all. So Dan dropped off the keys. Sometime after that Sidney came out of his office—but you never saw him go in—and told you he was leaving for the day and to tell

Jake to tell the art director about the location scout. And sometime after that Jake came by and you gave him the keys and the message."

"I didn't *give* him the keys," Grace corrected. "I just told him where they were."

"Right," MacAullif said. "And those were the only people in the office that afternoon."

She frowned. "What?"

"Dan, Sidney, and Jake. Aside from you, they were the only people here."

"Who told you that?"

MacAullif frowned. "You mean they weren't?"

"No, of course not."

"Well, why didn't you say so?"

"You didn't ask me."

MacAullif took a breath. "No, I suppose I didn't. I'm asking now. Who was here that afternoon?"

"Oh, practically everybody."

"Oh?"

"Yes, all the department heads. The assistant director. And the art director. And the electrician. And the cameraman. And that awful sound man."

"All of them?" MacAullif said. "Why were they here?"

"They came by to pick up the script changes."

"Script changes?"

I could see it coming. Prompted by the words *script changes,* her eyes shifted to me.

"Oh," she said. She pointed. "And him, of course."

9.

Rehearsals began the following Monday, the first day of the third and final week of preproduction.

The start of rehearsals marked a change for me in terms of my participation in the movie. Prior to rehearsal, my involvement had been akin to attempting the impossible while being pestered by swarms of bees. When rehearsals began, it was more like being drawn and quartered.

I'll never forget that first day of rehearsal. It was on the ground floor of the warehouse, where the art director had laid out floor plans with masking tape and set out folding chairs and tables to represent Blaire's apartment, the set for which was being constructed upstairs by the set crew even as we rehearsed.

But you don't know who Blaire is. It's happening to me again. I'm getting all crazy and telling this wrong. Movies do that to you.

Anyway, the plot of *Hands of Havoc, Flesh of Fire,* give or take a warehouse fight scene or two, was essentially this: Our hero, Rick Dalton, while in jail—for a crime he didn't commit, natch—is tutored in karate by his cell mate, a strangely endearing aging Japanese serial killer, who takes an interest in the boy. On his release, Rick uses his newfound skill to track down the men who framed him.

Hey, now don't blame me. The premise was Sidney's. My job was to make it as plausible as possible. Which wasn't easy, having to throw in four hot babes.

Blaire was one of them. A girlfriend of one of the men involved in the frame. Rick goes to her to try to convince her of his innocence, and to persuade her to help him. The theory in operation here—and I fought this out with Sidney, to no avail—was that women like Blaire are essentially good, and only go along with their boyfriends because it hasn't occurred to them that they are evil, but turn against them as soon as someone clues them in.

I pointed out to Sidney that this made women look like mindless sex objects incapable of independent thought. His response, "Who gives a flying fuck?" was uttered with a warm smile and grand good will, as was Sidney's habit when doing something utterly ruthless, obnoxious, or mean in his role of producer, sort of like winking and saying, Aren't we movie people wicked?

Anyway, that was the scene I was lumbered with—to have Rick Dalton talk Blaire Gangster-Girlfriend into helping him, without either of them coming across as total nitwits. Kind of like Mission Impossible.

Only I'd done a good job with it. I really had. In fact, some of my best work in the movie had gone into that scene. Even Sidney, who was quick to find fault with everything, was impressed. So I was eager to find out how it played.

Only I didn't get to for nearly an hour. First there was more farbling around than one could have imagined.

For one thing, Sidney was buffeted by an endless string of department heads and crew members. Of which there were many more, now that we were into our final week of preproduction. In addition to the set crew, laboring industriously and noisily upstairs, there were also two more electricians, the best boy and first electric, brought in to assist the gaffer in running power to the set.

In addition to the director of photography, there was now the first assistant cameraman, who was serving as the camera operator during rehearsals, a concession Jake Decker had negotiated from the union. For our movie, there was no camera operator—when we actually began filming, the DP would shoot, a second assistant would come on to load film, and the first assistant would pull focus.

We had also picked up a key grip and his best boy, who were responsible for moving things on the set. While there was nothing much to move on this set, there was still the camera, and on our skeleton crew, even the key grip would work the camera dolly.

Another new arrival was the script supervisor, a young woman by the name of Clarity Gray. Poor as I am with names, I caught hers, because Clarity struck me as such as appropriate one for a script supervisor, and also because she was the one person on the crew in whom I took a keen interest. The script she would be keeping track of happened to be mine.

In addition to all these, there were two more young gofer types, one tall and awkward, one short and nerdy, who apparently were all Jake Decker was able to get for what he was willing to pay, i.e., nothing. But even for unpaid college kids doing it for the experience, they looked bad. So much so it occurred to me to wonder if Dan had dug them up somewhere just to make *him* look good.

Anyway, all these people were constantly pestering Sidney, which I guess was an occupational hazard on a movie if you happened to be both producer and director. And what made this take much longer than it should have was the fact that Sidney wasn't paying any attention to them.

That was because the poor man was preoccupied with our other new arrival, a willowy blonde with a disproportionately enormous bosom, whom I assumed was the actress playing the part of Blair. I had to assume this, because Sidney wasn't taking time off from drooling over her long enough to introduce me.

Did I say drooling? I beg your pardon. I wouldn't wish to impugn the man. To be perfectly honest, I cannot specifically recall saliva dripping from his mouth. I think it *would* be safe to say his eyes were bugging slightly out of his head.

I think it would also be safe to say that this was not just my opinion, but was also shared by the attractive assistant director. I should say the *previously* attractive assistant director, because she might have been a wet dishrag for all Sidney Garfellow seemed to care now.

Anyway, you know what it's like to have tremendously selfish motives? To have a stake in something and be so personally involved in it you can't really focus on anything else? Well, that's how I felt that morning. My script was about to be read. For the first time. A major breakthrough in my life. Yeah, I'd had a few magazine articles published before. But nothing like this. My lines were going to come to life. My wit was going to be displayed. If there was a laugh from the cast or crew, it would be my writing that got it.

If you're not in the arts, I can't begin to explain what that meant to me. All I can say is it crowded everything else out of my mind. Which is why I didn't really realize what was happening for a while. All I knew was that we weren't rehearsing and I wanted to be. So it was a while before I realized the *reason* we weren't rehearsing was because our young star wasn't there.

When I finally *did* realize it, it pissed me off. We had only one week of rehearsal scheduled, which was tight, very tight. And here was this arrogant kid, fresh from his Hollywood success, too big to show up on time and rehearse with us. It occurred to me he'd probably come sailing in around noon, either hung over or stoned, with a pair of voluptuous teenage groupies on his arm. So even before I met him, I really resented him. Son of a bitch. Where the hell does he get off taking drugs and banging young girls all morning when he should be doing my script?

Anyway, somewhere in all this Jake Decker wandered in, noticed that we weren't rehearsing and that Sidney Garfellow had been rendered almost catatonic by a silicone overdose. Jake took him by the arm and said something in his ear.

I must say, Jake certainly had a way about him, because Sidney immediately sprang into action. He stepped out, clapped his hands, and said, "All right. Listen up, everyone. Rehearsal time. Let's clear the set and get ready to roll." He turned to the script supervisor, snapped his fingers imperiously, and said, "Clarity. What's the first scene up?"

"Page forty-six, scene one-oh-nine. Interior, Blaire's Apartment. Day. Rick and Blaire."

"Fine," Sidney said. "Places, please."

He took the young starlet by the shoulders and piloted her toward the set.

I was right in their path, so I realized he was going to introduce me, and I made a mental note not to stare. It was prudent, considering the extent of the cleavage and the bounty it revealed.

However, this personal admonition turned out to be unnecessary. Sidney steered the young lady around me as if I weren't there. As I watched him usher her onto the set, two thoughts occurred to me. One was that Sidney Garfellow really *was* an unpleasant, arrogant, fucking son of a bitch.

The other was, how the hell was he going to rehearse without Jason Clairemont?

I'd just had that thought when the two new young dorky gofers walked out on stage.

I blinked. Good Lord, it couldn't be. I'd seen *To Shoot the Tiger* myself. Even with a stunt double covering up the awkwardness, this tall, goofy dork couldn't be him.

He wasn't.

The short nerd was.

10.

I stared at the assistant director in disbelief—she was the one who'd just told me that. "Come on," I said. "It couldn't be."

The AD, obviously still very hassled by Sidney Garfellow, said, "Why should I kid about a thing like that?"

"Of course not," I said. "But I saw *To Shoot the Tiger*. The guy's almost as tall as Eastwood."

She gave me a look. "That's movies."

"Huh?"

"Movie magic. It's a camera angle, or they stand him on a chair. I heard Al Pacino once played with some tall actress, they dug a ditch for her to walk in."

"Yeah, but . . ."

"But what?"

"I can see why they'd do that, him bein' Al Pacino. I mean, you want him in the movie, so you do something like that. But the Eastwood film. The kid's a nobody. Why don't you get a kid who's right for the part?"

She smiled at me, a superior, condescending smile. "That film made a hundred and seventy-five million dollars," she said.

That was a conversation killer. And lowered my opinion of the assistant director a notch. Right. In hindsight, we know it did. But there was not one studio executive, one Hollywood producer who *knew* it was *going* to make a hundred and seventy-five million dollars. No one knows that on any project, no matter what director, no matter what star. It's all a crap shoot.

And gambling on this kid? What a long shot that was. Particularly considering how nerdy he looked. So finding out he was Jason Clairemont was quite a shock.

But nothing compared to the shock I got when rehearsal began.

Let me set the stage. This is, as you'll recall, the scene where our hero, having escaped from prison, attempts to elicit the help of the girlfriend of one of the men who framed him. The way I wrote it was, if I must say so myself, rather neat. See, when he goes to jail, our hero is young and naive, the type of guy who'd let himself get framed. When he comes out of jail, aside from having learned karate, he's street smart, and knows all these underworld tricks he picked up from other prisoners.

So here's how I wrote the scene of him calling on this gangster's girlfriend. We see a shot of her, returning to her apartment with a bag of groceries from the supermarket. At the apartment door, she balances it on one hip and fumbles with her keys, unlocking one huge police lock and then the regular double-locked door. She opens the door, walks in, and stops short. We cut to her point of view, and see a shot of our hero, sitting calmly on the living-room couch.

Which is a nice payoff, after the setup of her police lock— all the security in the world couldn't keep this guy out.

But as I watched the opening scene, it wasn't her pantomiming unlocking the apartment. No, instead, it's *him*, pantomiming picking the lock.

I went over, tugged Sidney Garfellow by the sleeve. "Sidney," I whispered. "What the hell's he doing?"

"Improvising."

"But what for? This isn't in the script."

"In the script he got in by picking the lock."

"Right. We *discover* him there."

"Right. But to get there, he must have picked the lock. So he'd like to try picking the lock."

"If we see that, there's no surprise."

"What do you mean?"

"When she comes home and finds him there."

Sidney gave me his condescending smile. "Stanley," he said. "Just 'cause we shoot it don't mean we use it. It doesn't work, we lose it in the edit. What's the harm?"

I took a breath. "Yeah," I said. "Sorry. I know you got other things on your mind."

I went over, poured myself a cup of coffee. I drank it while Jason Clairemont improvised several scenes of picking the front-door lock. Since there was no door and no lock to pick, and he was pantomiming the whole thing anyway, and since the scene wasn't in the script and was destined for the cutting-room floor, this had to be one of the most useless, futile, and boring endeavors one could have imagined.

Finally, when Jason Clairemont was through screwing around, we were able to get on with the scene. Hot Babe Number One pantomimed opening the front door with her bag of groceries. As she did, I realized Sidney was right. If we just cut the scene of Jason breaking in, the rest of the scene could play exactly as written.

Or so I thought.

Here's how the scene I wrote works. As I said, the bimbo opens the door, turns around and stops, shocked, and from her point of view we see our hero sitting on the couch. She looks at him in utter terror. She has no idea who this is or why he's here. He could be a rapist, a murderer, what have you. After all, this is New York City. Her first line is, "Who are you?"

So. The bimbo opens the door, turns around, sees him, and says, "Rick! What are you doing here?" And our hero says, so help me god, "Just couldn't stay away from your charms."

I blinked.

What the fuck?

I threw my half-full coffee in the garbage, went over and grabbed Sidney by the arm.

"Sidney," I said. "What the hell is that?"

"What?" he said. "They're doing the scene."

"No, they're not," I said. "Those aren't the lines."

"Stanley," Sidney said. "I told you. He can't *say* the lines. We gotta change 'em to fit him."

"I *did* change 'em."

"Obviously not enough. If he can't say the lines, he's gonna say something else."

And he *was* saying something else, even as we were talking. He was saying something juvenile and idiotic, having to do with their past relationship, which she has besmirched by her allegiance to this gangster.

"Sidney," I said. "He's killing the scene."

"Oh, come on," Sidney said. "Such a fuss over a few words."

"It's not just words," I said. "It's the whole damn concept. *She doesn't know him.* That's the whole premise. That's why the scene works. Take that away, and you got nothing. If they have a previous relationship, it's clichéd and predictable. What I wrote was subtle."

That's when Sidney turned on me. I'll never forget the look he gave me then. It was as if I were some loathsome bug.

"Subtle?" he said. *"Subtle? We are making an action film, not The Brothers Karamazov. The shark in Jaws isn't subtle. It bites."*

The thing is, I'm not quick on my feet. In terms of arguments, I mean. I'd be worthless on a debate team. By the time I think of a comeback, the moment has passed. I'm the type of guy who goes home grumbling to himself, and then thinks of what he *should* have said.

Which is what happened to me then. When Sidney Garfellow told me the shark in *Jaws* bites. I was dumbfounded. First by the fact he'd turned on me, and second by the statement itself. The shark bites? What could I say to that? Particularly when the line that ran through my head was, "When the shark bites with his teeth, dear." Which is of course from

Threepenny Opera, a play I acted in back in college, the song from which also became a number-one Bobby Darin hit.

See the problem? None of that was particularly relevant to the current situation, was a suitable comeback to what Sidney Garfellow had just said. It was not until Sidney had moved off, and I stood there seething in helpless fury, that I was able to frame a response.

Right, Sidney. The shark in *Jaws* bites. And that same shark was in all the *Jaws* sequels, and *they* bite. The sequels, I mean. *Jaws* was a great movie, and the sequels suck. Why? They all have the shark. The one that bites. So I guess that wasn't it. Maybe there was something about the *quality* of the movie. Maybe Steven Speilberg had something other than just the special effect of the mechanical shark going for him. Maybe who the characters are matters too. And what they say. And whether we give a flying fuck about them.

Naturally, I said none of this. I just stood and watched in impotent frustration as the nerdy twerp and the busty bimbo improvised the scene. Even with no stake in the matter, it would have been enough to make me throw up. Since I saw it as the end of my career, I can't tell you how excruciating it was.

And what made it worse—which was funny, because how could it possibly be worse?—was that of all the cast and crew members looking on, none of them *knew* it was bad. Or *why* it was bad. Because none of them were as familiar with the script as I was. Had worked with it for the past six months and knew every detail, every nuance. And realized, as I did, that what this schmuck was doing was not only ruining the scene they were working on, but was fucking up half-a-dozen scenes later on. The ripple effect—you change one thing, it effects everything else. If these two had a prior relationship, the scenes of them *getting to know each other* won't play. So some pretty neat dialogue plus a couple of comic bits go out the window.

Am I rambling? I bet I am. Am I saying something self-centered and defensive? Probably. Did I feel totally victimized? You'd better believe it. After all, I was doing this for the screen credit. Not for the money. I was, as I've said, working for the bare minimum, the least Sidney could possibly pay. That and a deferred payment—which it occurred to me right then, if the movie was this bad, I would never see. I was doing it for the screen credit on the theory that once other producers and directors saw my work, I could *get* work. Because most movies of this type were absolute shit. So if one came out with characters who were witty and likeable, and a plot that had a few surprises and at least made sense, people would sit up and take notice.

But this?

No one in his right mind was going to hire me because of this. This was exactly the type of mindless trash I had expected my movie to stand out from.

Oh boy.

I tell you, from that moment on things did not improve—if anything, they got worse. Sidney did not apologize for what I felt was a gutless betrayal. Instead, he passed it off just the way I should have imagined he would. With a shit-eating grin and his boy-aren't-we-movie-producers-ruthless bit.

Meanwhile, Jason the Wonder Nerd continued ignoring the script and saying any damn thing he felt like, and not only the dialogue but also the plot of the movie went right out the window.

And as for me, I just watched. I was still nominally the writer of the piece, though any resemblance between me and a screenwriter was coincidental and not to be inferred. Clarity, wielding script, pad, and notebook, would pencil in whatever lines Jason Clairemont and the various hot babes and gangster types would come up with, and deliver it to me to render into script form. So not only was I forced to hear this garbage, I had to type it too. And, I realized with a shudder, ultimately put my name on it.

How devastating was this? I've tried to give you an idea. I doubt if I've done it. I think it can be best summed up as this: From the time Jason Clairemont first opened his mouth, I was so preoccupied with what was happening to the script that, throughout the whole week of rehearsals, I never once had a single thought about the man who had been murdered in the very building where we were rehearsing.

11.

Early Monday morning Jason Clairemont, nerdy twerp superstar, walked into a brownstone on East Eighty-fourth Street.

"Cut!" yelled Sidney Garfellow. "And that's a print."

This was greeted by a burst of applause from all those assembled in the street.

All but MacAullif, who nudged me with his elbow. "What they clapping for?"

"They got the first shot."

"Yeah. So? Guy walked into a building. Big deal."

"Yeah, but it's seven-fifteen. Crew had a seven o'clock call. They got the first shot in fifteen minutes. Makes 'em feel good. Sets a tone for the production."

"You mean this crew's very efficient?"

"Not at all. It's a setup."

MacAullif frowned. "What do you mean?"

"For the first shot they set up something very simple. Schmuck walking into a building. An exterior day shot. No lighting required. No sound sync. Just set up your camera and shoot. If the moron don't fall on his face, you got a shot."

"You're a cynical son of a bitch, aren't you?"

I was indeed. I also knew everything I'd said was absolutely true, 'cause that's the way Jake Decker had outlined it when we'd gone over the shooting schedule. I saw no reason to quote my sources to MacAullif, however.

MacAullif and I were standing on the sidewalk across the street from the brownstone where Sidney Garfellow had just nailed down his first shot. We could have been standing on the other side of the street where most of the crew were, but MacAullif had chosen this position, probably due to its proximity to the catering truck, where coffee and doughnuts had been set out. MacAullif practically mainlined coffee—he had filled his Styrofoam cup twice since we'd been there.

"I can tell you something worse than that," I said.

."What's that?"

"The crew may be clapping, but they don't want it smooth and efficient."

MacAullif frowned. "Why not?"

"There's a lot of money to be made in movies, and the further behind schedule they run, the more they make."

"Are you saying this crew would do that?"

"Of course not," I said. "I'm sure they're above it. Just like I know there're no cops on the take."

"Fuck you," MacAullif said. "Tell me something."

"What?"

"That's really Jason Clairemont?"

"Yeah. Why?"

"He's tiny."

"He'll look big on the screen."

"Yeah. Maybe. I just can't believe it's him."

"Well, it is. Play your cards right, you might get an autograph."

MacAullif gave me a look. "What's with you?"

I hadn't seen MacAullif since we started rehearsal, so he knew nothing about the situation regarding Jason Clairemont and the script. And I wasn't about to get into it.

"What's with your murder?" I said.

"Oh, that? Nothing. It's a John Doe, just like we thought. Some bum got killed. I did the work, turned it over, and that's that. I'm on vacation."

"There's nothing to it?"

"What could there be?"

"I thought the glass indicated the window had been broken from the inside."

"It did. But so what? All that means is the guy got in sometime when it was open, busted the window to get out. After that he could go in and out the window as he pleased, which he did up until the time he was killed."

"By whom?"

"Person or persons unknown," MacAullif said. He shrugged. "I know you civilians hate to hear that, but a large percentage of homicides fall into that category. They're unsolved and they'll stay unsolved until somebody cops to 'em. Which doesn't mean the guy who cops actually did 'em, either. Sometimes a perp will confess to something just because the cops want him to. Cooperating, you know? The case is cleared, but we've still got no idea who actually did it."

The shrill squawk of, "Quiet on the set," pierced our eardrums. That was the attractive AD, who turned out to have a less-than-attractive voice, particularly when amplified by a bullhorn.

However, it certainly got your attention. MacAullif and I shut up and looked over toward the set where Jason Clairemont was back in position and about to go into the building again.

"Roll camera," the AD yelped into the bullhorn.

Seconds later, the German cameraman yelped something back. Unaided by a bullhorn, his voice didn't carry, and even if it had, no one would have understood him anyway, but what he should have said was, "Rolling." I presume that's what he did, because seconds later Sidney Garfellow shouted, "Action!"

And Jason Clairemont walked into the building again.

"Cut!" Sidney cried. He turned immediately to confer with his cameraman. He must have liked what he heard, because he cried, "That's a print. New setup."

"It's a camera move," the AD squawked on the bullhorn.

"New setup. A camera move." She turned to the script supervisor. "Clarity, what's the scene number?"

"One twenty-two, Blaire's entrance."

I looked up at MacAullif. "Wait till you see this," I said.

MacAullif had seen no rehearsals, and had arrived just before shooting, so he hadn't seen the actress playing Blaire.

"See what?" he said.

Before I could answer, a voice said, "Well, well, Sergeant. What do you think?"

We both looked up to find Sidney Garfellow standing there.

MacAullif said, "You're moving pretty fast."

Sidney nodded. "Got a four-week shooting schedule."

"What would be normal?" MacAullif said.

"On an average, ten. You got a hundred-page script, you shoot two pages a day. That's ten weeks. We gotta do five a day. So we gotta move fast. You check in?"

MacAullif nodded. "With Jake. He told me to hang out and watch the shoot. I also checked in with the two cops here from the mayor's office. I don't want to be steppin' on anybody's toes."

"Fine," Sidney said. "You got a script?"

"Me? No."

"Stanley, see that he gets a script. Ask Clarity to issue him one on my say-so."

Before either of us could say anything, Sidney slapped MacAullif on the back, said, "Good to have you on board," and hustled back across the street.

There came the distant roll of thunder, and I noticed the sky had gotten darker.

"Son of a bitch," I said. "Looks like rain."

"Yeah," MacAullif said. "What do you do then?"

What we did was move indoors to the cover set. That's why you always shoot your exteriors first on a movie—if it rains, you got somewhere to go.

It poured, and we went.

Suddenly crew members were rushing every which way,

packing up equipment. And the teamsters, after three weeks of nothing at all, finally got to move their trucks.

The crew piled into whatever vehicles were available. Some had brought their own cars. Some rode with gofers.

Jason Clairemont rode alone. The tall, gawky kid who'd been with him, when I'd mistaken both of them for gofers, actually was. But not an ordinary gofer. He was Jason Clairemont's personal gofer. To satisfy his every whim, and drive him wherever he wanted to go.

I rode with MacAullif. I hadn't brought my car, and he'd brought his. We hopped in and headed back to the warehouse. MacAullif pulled in next to a fire plug—handy being a cop—and we hopped out and sprinted inside.

We'd beaten everyone back except the VIP van, Dan's station wagon, which had nosed us out by pulling up right to the door to unload. The VIPs were Sidney Garfellow, natch, and most of the department heads, basically the same group who'd been on that ill-fated location scout.

In fact, the only one not present was sound man Murky Doyle. That was because this morning's street shots were MOS, which, so help me, stands for *mit out sound.* He wasn't on the call sheet for that location, and today his place in the car was taken by the script supervisor, who darted into the building just ahead of us.

Which reminded me. MacAullif needed a script.

We caught up with her in the office, where she was drying her hair with paper towels. It seemed a poor time to tell her MacAullif needed a script, but then, I wanted him to have one. I mean, the damn thing had my name on it.

"Excuse me, Clarity," I said.

She looked up. "Yes?"

"This is Sergeant MacAullif," I said. "He's a technical advisor on the show. I know it's a bad time, but when you get a chance, Sidney said to issue him a script."

Clarity smiled. "It couldn't be a better time. They're right here."

She pulled open a cabinet on the wall, revealing a pile of

scripts. She took the top one off the pile, flipped the cover open, and looked at the number on the first page.

"One twenty-seven," she said. "One moment, please."

She reached in her book bag and pulled out a huge three-ring binder. She searched the tabs, found the one marked *script*, and flipped it open. Balancing the heavy notebook in the crook of one arm, she pulled a pen from her shirt pocket and said, "Your name again?"

"Sergeant MacAullif."

She smiled at him. "Your first name is Sergeant?"

MacAullif smiled. I think he almost blushed. I guess movies make people crazy. "My name is William, ma'am," he said.

I knew that. I'd never used it, but I knew it. To me, MacAullif's first name was sort of like a trivia answer.

Clarity wrote MacAullif's name in her notebook, then handed him the script. "Here, William," she said.

"By the way," I said, "what are we shooting?"

Clarity looked up. "Huh?"

"What's the cover set?"

"Oh. Blaire's apartment, of course."

Silly me. Of course. If you call actors, you have to pay 'em, whether you use 'em or not. So whenever possible, the cover set uses the same actors who would have worked anyway. Since that was Jason Clairemont and the bimbo, today's cover set had to be Blaire's apartment. Which meant we were going to shoot the same scenes we'd worked on the first day of rehearsal.

Shit. What a kick in the teeth. Suddenly I didn't *want* MacAullif to have a script. Because it wasn't *my* lines he was going to read. No, the script in MacAullif's hand was a rainbow of blue, yellow, and pink replacement pages, each one representing the amateurish improvisations of our illustrious star. On second thought, I didn't even want MacAullif to have that script at all.

That was such a depressing thought, it was almost a relief when my musings were interrupted by the arrival of Murky Doyle, dripping wet and mad as hell. Murky strode up to

Jake Decker and said, "This is most irregular. I had a two-o'clock call."

"On the set, yes," Jake said. "But this morning you're on standby."

"There's no such thing as standby," Murky said. "I'm either on the clock or I'm not."

"You're *on* the clock, Murky," Jake said. "I let you stay home as a favor."

"Some favor," Murky grumbled. "Those street shots should have sound. What are you going to do, lay in foleys later?"

"I'd have to anyway," Jake said.

Murky stuck out his chin. "What is that, an insult?"

"Not at all," Jake said. "Any scene like that, the sound editor's going to supply extra sound for the mix. The real sound only matters if there's something specific."

"Better with it," Murky said.

"This morning it wasn't necessary."

I smiled. I'm sure MacAullif had no idea what the argument was about, but I tuned right in, and it was kind of funny. Jake, wanting to insure that Sidney grabbed his first shot in record time, had elected to shoot the scene MOS, and considering the personality of our sound mixer, I couldn't blame him. Murky would undoubtedly have putzed around, screwed up, and made the shoot take longer. Jake was paying Murky for the time anyway, figuring that should appease him. But Murky, ever the grouch, was arguing for his *right* to have been present for the shoot, fucking up the sound, making things take longer, and doubtless, in the back of his mind, piling up some overtime at the end of the day.

It was sort of what I needed to hear at that moment. Yeah, your script gets mangled and the movie sucks, but life goes on as usual.

Jake Decker rather firmly suggested that Murky shut up and set up his sound equipment. Murky responded with a haughty, "Sound is *always* ready," and stalked out to comply.

MacAullif and I trailed along behind to see how the crew was coming on the set.

Actually, not bad. The freight elevator, when it wasn't delivering dead bodies, worked just fine. As Jake had suggested, the trucks had been driven onto it and brought up to the second floor, so the crew could unload directly onto the set. By the time we got there, the camera, grip, and electric trucks were parked in a line.

So was the catering truck, which MacAullif made a beeline for. While he dumped cream and sugar into his coffee, I watched the crew.

The gaffer, whose name I couldn't remember, was standing near the truck, barking orders at his best boy and assistants, who kept emerging from the back of the truck with lights and coils of electrical cable.

The key grip, whose name I also couldn't recall, was supervising the unloading of sandbags. As I recalled from my work in the movies, on the set they always used lots of sandbags—I was never quite sure why.

On the back of the camera truck the assistant cameraman sat, his arms immersed in a black changing bag, loading film magazines.

The camera truck was also serving for sound, one of the few concessions Jake Decker had been able to squeeze out of the teamsters union, and while I watched, Murky Doyle and a short dumpy man with horn-rimmed glasses who must have been his assistant unloaded a large laundry hamper they were using for a sound table, one of those huge bins with a wooden top. I could tell by the way they were lifting it that it was heavy. It occurred to me it would contain most of Murky's sound equipment—microphones, cables, and so forth—and maybe even his Nagra, the tape recorder sound mixers use.

Murky's assistant climbed back up in the truck and emerged a minute later with the long boom mike, which reminded me who he was. Right. The assistant sound man wasn't called the assistant sound man. He was the boom man. Responsible for holding the boom mike just outside of camera range during each shot. It occurred to me it had been a while since I'd worked in films.

I turned back to find MacAullif looking in the script. In fact, at the very scene we were about to shoot.

He looked up at me. "You wrote this?" he said.

There was no avoiding it. I took a breath. "Originally," I said.

"What does that mean?"

"Yeah, originally I wrote it. But your golden boy Jason Clairemont changes anything he feels like."

MacAullif frowned. "And they let him?"

"They have no choice. He's a star."

"That's stupid," MacAullif said.

"Tell me about it."

I had a feeling MacAullif didn't quite believe me. On the other hand, MacAullif was a good cop, but he was still a cop. What I mean is, I wonder if he knew the scene he just read was bad. That's not to say cops have no taste, it's just—aw, hell. I'm sorry. I'm just not rational on this subject.

I'm not sure how the conversation might have gone, but at that moment MacAullif murmured, "Holy shit!"

I looked. As usual, MacAullif was right. Holy shit described the situation quite aptly.

The bimbo playing Blaire Kessington had just bellied up for a cup of coffee. She had obviously just come from her dressing room, where she had decided to relax during the setup by removing her costume. She paraded out for coffee attired in bra, panties, and robe. The robe was diaphanous; the underclothes were skimpy at best. That which they supposedly concealed was not. The effect was quite stunning.

The young lady jiggled up to the table, poured a cup of coffee, dumped in cream.

"No sugar," she said with a smile. "Gotta watch my figure."

"Son of a bitch," MacAullif said as she made her way back to the dressing room.

I tapped the script he was holding. "Read on," I said. "There's three more like her."

I steered MacAullif away from the coffee to the other end of the warehouse, where the carpenters had erected the Blaire set. It was your basic living room with movable walls. A nice set.

Simple. Functional. One wall had been removed now and was leaning against the far wall of the warehouse. The camera had been set up in its place. Electricians, grips, prop men, and set dressers swarmed over the set, getting it ready for the shoot.

The AD poked her head in, said, "How long?" and received varying estimates, including, "Almost set," from the art director, "Give me a break," from the gaffer, either "A half hour," or "A hot flower," from the DP, "Ready when you are," from the key grip, and, "Get real. They won't be ready for hours," from everyone's favorite sound mixer.

It was actually forty-five minutes later when they began to rehearse. And, wouldn't you know it, the scene they began with was the one I hadn't even written at all, the one of Jason Clairemont picking the front-door lock.

Before, he'd just pantomimed the damn thing. Now, with an actual door and lock in place, he was attempting to pick it open, inserting two thin strips of metal into the keyhole and twisting them around.

Beside me, MacAullif said, "Shit."

I looked up. "I beg your pardon?"

MacAullif shook his head. "That ain't right."

"What?"

"That's a police lock on that door. No way he gets in with that shit."

"You sure?"

"Absolutely. Any cop sees that'll laugh his ass off."

"Well," I said, "you're the technical advisor."

MacAullif looked at me. "Damned if I ain't." He turned and walked over to the other side of the set, where Sidney Garfellow was conferring with the DP.

He was back a minute later.

"Well?" I said.

"Well, I told him."

"And what did he say?"

"I think his exact words were, Who gives a flying fuck?"

"Just like that?"

"Well, not that abrupt. But he said, who's gonna care but

cops like me, and the moviegoing public likes to see guys pick locks."

"Aha," I said.

Sidney's response was absolutely typical. It was also an out-and-out contradiction of what he told me in rehearsal. So, the moviegoing public likes to see people pick locks, Sidney? I thought we were going to cut this scene out in the edit.

I was not in the best of moods twenty minutes later when the scene began to shoot. Even so, I had to admit it was exciting. First off, you got all your crew members standing around watching. Plus you got lights on tripods all over the place, illuminating the scene. Then you got your camera dolly in place, with DP aboard and two grips ready to roll it sideways during the shot to reveal the lock. Then you got crotchety sound man Murky Doyle sitting at his laundry hamper with his earphones on, ready to record the sound. And the boom man standing near the edge of the set, trying to sneak the boom mike in just above the top of the door jamb. Then you got Sidney Garfellow overlooking all this like a proud papa, and nerdy twerp superstar standing by ready to pick the door lock with two strips of metal MacAullif assured me couldn't open a cigar box.

And finally it happened. The attractive AD said, "Lock it up." At his laundry hamper, Murky Doyle pressed a button, and a sound like a loud doorbell rang three times. We were now what was referred to in the industry as being *on bells*, that is, locked up, dead quiet, ready to shoot.

From her position next to the camera the assistant director yelled, "Roll it!" which is the way every shooting sequence began. Next, Murky Doyle would shout, "Speed!" to indicate the tape was rolling and tell the assistant cameraman he could slate the scene. Then he would say, "Scene one thirty-seven, take one," and clack the slate. And Sidney would say, "Action!"

Not this time.

The AD said, "Roll it!" all right. But before Murky Doyle could say, "Speed!" there came a sound like the crackle of lightning, and Murky Doyle's boom man flipped in the air, dropped the boom, and crashed to the floor in a heap.

12.

"It's sabotage."

"Yeah, sure, Murky," Jake Decker said. "It's a personal vendetta."

"Damn it, someone screwed with the machine."

"Why would they do that?"

"How the hell should I know? Maybe someone's got it in for me."

"I'm sure they do, Murky, but I don't think they'd take it out on your equipment."

"Yeah, well, someone did. I'm going to take this apart and find out."

"On your own time, Murky. Right now we gotta shoot."

I should explain, the reason for Jake Decker's cavalier attitude was that the boom man wasn't seriously hurt. He'd had a minor shock and a major scare, which left him shaken but unharmed. Which meant the show must go on.

"Come on, Murky," Jake said. "Break out the backup machine and let's go."

"I want to know what went wrong," Murky insisted.

"We all do, Murky. But right now we got a crew standing around and we're already behind schedule because of the
78

rain delay. So either break out the backup machine, or I'm going to go ahead and shoot this MOS."

"That would be a violation," Murky said.

"File a grievance," Jake snapped.

Cursing, Murky unplugged his Nagra, took it off the top of the laundry hamper, opened it up, and took out another.

MacAullif and I, who had been watching, moved away.

"What do you make of that?" I said.

MacAullif shrugged. "Frankly, the man does not inspire confidence."

"No shit."

"On the other hand, that's an expensive piece of equipment, why should it just short out?"

"Maybe it got wet in the rain."

"I thought the sound crew wasn't out this morning."

"Good point. But the equipment was."

"How's that?"

"The sound equipment's on the camera truck. So it was on location. When it started raining and they had to load up the truck, the sound hamper's in the way and they had to lift it down off the truck to get the camera dolly on."

"Did that happen?"

"How the hell should I know? We hopped in your car and took off. I'm just saying that's how it could have happened."

"Yeah, maybe," MacAullif said.

Son of a bitch. MacAullif suspected foul play.

I didn't. I'd seen enough of Murky Doyle over the past two weeks, I'd have been surprised if the sound *hadn't* fucked up.

Anyway, after stalling as much as possible, Murky finally got his act together and we started filming again. This time, the scene of picking the lock went off without a hitch. Sidney shot the master four times in rapid succession, then moved in for the close-up of the picks being inserted into the lock. We grabbed that shot and broke for lunch with minutes to spare—if we'd gone over, we'd have had to pay the crew meal penalty. As it was, we fed them in the nick of time.

Lunch was served right there on the set by the caterers, an older couple everyone called Mama and Papa and a young girl assistant. The three of them had set up folding tables and chairs from the truck and now stood behind a row of steam trays ready to serve a hot buffet.

MacAullif and I went through the lunch line and found ourselves at a table with the attractive AD and Clarity, whether by accident or design, I don't know. Anyway, to my surprise, I found MacAullif actually making small talk with the young ladies.

"What's that?" he asked, pointing to the black-plastic object hanging from Clarity's neck.

She lifted it up, turned it around where he could see. "Stopwatch," she said. "For timing the scenes."

"That's part of your job?"

"Sure. I record the length of each take in my script notes."

"Then what do you do with it?"

"Log it, and type it up at the end of the day. We need to know what we shot, what we printed, how many takes we have, and how long they were."

"That's very interesting," MacAullif said.

The attractive AD, who had been looking at MacAullif, said abruptly, "You're a cop?"

"Yes, ma'am."

"Why are you here?"

"Sidney hired me."

She frowned. "Oh? What for?"

"As a technical advisor. Didn't he tell you?"

"Sidney forgets to mention things," the AD said.

It was a particularly barbed comment. None of us wanted to touch it.

After a pause, she said, "Then you're not still investigating the murder?"

"No."

"Is it solved, then?"

"It happens to be one of those killings that is likely to go unsolved. Particularly common in the case of street people. Which is what this man apparently was."

"You never even identified him?"

"No," MacAullif said. "How could we?"

"Fingerprints, of course."

MacAullif smiled. "You watch too many movies."

The AD gave him a look, said, "Yeah," took her plate, got up and walked off.

"Don't mind her," Clarity said. "She's just pissed off at Sidney and taking it out on everybody else."

"What for?" MacAullif said.

Clarity shrugged. "The usual. Sidney gave her a big rush, now he's making a play for the girl playing Blaire."

"Oh."

"So don't take it personally." She smiled. "Wait till we start shooting the scene this afternoon. You'll see."

Indeed we did. The way Sidney fondled Blaire while directing her in the scene of unlocking her door with the bag of groceries was enough to make you sick.

But it was nothing compared to the next scene. The scene where Blaire enters and finds young hero Rick sitting on the couch. It was the first dialogue scene to be shot, as well as the first scene of any length. It was also the first scene requiring a complicated camera move. In the final cut, Blaire would walk in, register surprise, and then we would cut to a shot of Rick sitting on the couch. In the master—the continuous shot of the whole scene that the other shots are to be cut into—the plan called for the camera to pull back from the shot of Blaire, and dolly around to include a two-shot of her and Rick.

During the rehearsal of this camera move, MacAullif nudged me with his elbow and whispered, "She's not very good, is she?"

"No, she's not," I said. "But it's not entirely her fault."

"Oh?"

"No actress is going to look good saying those lines."

"You didn't write that?"

"I should hope not."

"Wanna show me what you wrote sometime?"

I suddenly realized MacAullif was one hell of a good guy.

"In her case it probably wouldn't help," I said. "But what she's saying is particularly stupid."

"He's not so bad, though," MacAullif said.

I suddenly realized MacAullif wasn't that great a guy after all.

But, damn it, he was right. Jason Clairemont, nerdy twerp superstar, despite his many failings, still came across pretty well, even saying his stupid lines.

Which really wasn't fair. The guy was making me look bad—he should look bad too.

But, no, the kid could act. Even with the bad material he'd provided himself with. He had a way of presenting it that was going to get by. Leaving everyone else decimated in his wake.

It went that way for the rest of the afternoon. Take after rotten take. This being a long dialogue scene with a camera move, when we shot it they managed to screw up somewhere seven times running. If the camera move was right, they'd blow the lines. And if they got the lines, the sound would be off. If the sound was right, the lighting would be wrong. Once, so help me, everything was going right except someone farted and the actors broke up. For all that, they were damn lucky to get it on the eighth try.

They got it again on the twelfth. I think they would have gone again, but Jake Decker stepped in, whispered something in Sidney's ear. The next announcement was a new setup and a camera move to shoot close-ups for the same scene, which they did for the rest of the afternoon.

Imagine, if you will, your own private hell. You've written something you think is good. A moron has changed it to something you think is bad. And you're forced to watch this new version repeated again and again and again, all day long.

As I rode the subway home, the only consoling thought was, it couldn't get any worse.

Wrong again.

13.

Tuesday morning was more of the same. The rain did not let up, and we were once again on the cover set. Not wanting to be totally drenched, I arrived at the warehouse by cab and sprinted in the door. In the office I found the script supervisor and Sidney's secretary manning the Xerox machine, which was spewing out a seemingly endless succession of pink pages.

"What's this?" I said.

"The scenes for today," Clarity said. "And I think Sidney's got some more for you."

"Oh?"

"Yeah. Here he is."

I looked around as Sidney came walking in.

"Oh, Stanley, there you are," he said. He detached two pages from his clipboard, handed them to me.

I saw they were script pages with new lines penciled in. "What's this?" I said.

"Please revise this for Grace and Clarity," Sidney said. "Revisions for the Veronica scene. If it rains, it's tomorrow's cover set. Type it up so the girls can run it off."

"Sidney," I said. "You didn't even rehearse that scene."

"I know. But Jason had a few changes to suggest."

84

I looked at the first page. "Sidney, he's not even *in* this scene."

"Yes. He's in the next one."

"Is he going to rewrite the whole damn movie?"

"Stanley," Sidney said. "You think these words are set in stone. You ever see a movie they didn't rewrite every day? Clarity, you ever on a picture you didn't have a rainbow script?"

Clarity either didn't hear or pretended not to, just went on working the Xerox.

Sidney couldn't have cared. I'd learned by now most of his questions were rhetorical anyway.

"Just work it up," Sidney said. "You can use that typewriter there."

And with a nod and a grin he was gone.

What the hell. I pulled up a chair and proceeded to type.

It was bad, as expected. I typed it anyway. And as I did, it dawned on me, Jason Clairemont wasn't in this scene. He wouldn't be around, making at least some of the bad lines seem good. If the other actors couldn't, it was going to seem bloody awful. Well. Not my problem.

"What are you grinning about?" Clarity said.

I looked up. I hadn't realized I was grinning. It occurred to me what a strange profession I was in. Here I was, making my script bad and being thrilled by the prospect people might notice.

I was still typing when Murky Doyle and Jake Decker breezed in, arguing about the accident. Which struck me as funny. It was the same argument they'd been having yesterday, which made it seem as if the conversation was continuous, as if they'd been arguing all night.

"It was deliberate," Murky said. "Someone took the Nagra apart and crossed the wires."

"You mean a wire came loose," Jake Decker said.

"No, a wire didn't come loose. Someone crossed them."

"So a wire came loose and they got crossed."

Murky shook his head. "Couldn't have happened."

"Happens all the time."

"No way. Someone unscrewed the case and crossed the wires."

"Why?"

"To be a prick, that's why. You think people don't do things just to be a prick?"

"Are you saying the Nagra's fixed?" Jake said.

"Fixed? It wasn't broken. Someone crossed the wires."

"But the point is, it's functioning now?"

"Of course."

"So we can shoot today. I'm pleased to hear it."

They went out again, still arguing.

I finished typing, gave the pages to Clarity, and went out to check out the set.

MacAullif was—where else?—hanging out by the catering truck. I told him what Murky said about someone taking the Nagra apart and crossing the wires.

MacAullif wasn't impressed. "The guy's got a couple of wires crossed himself."

"I know that," I said. "That still doesn't make him wrong."

"Right, right. Paranoid people have enemies too. I am on the set, ever vigilant."

"Right," I said.

It occurred to me when he said that, maybe that was why Sidney Garfellow had really hired him.

At any rate, shooting today was uneventful. Not to mention dull and painful. More Jason Clairemont and the bimbo scenes, each more scintillating than the last. By the end of the day, I had really had enough.

Only it wasn't over.

Instant replay. Today we had the dailies. All the footage we shot yesterday had to be viewed. Every excruciating, agonizing moment from yesterday had to be relived.

I could have just gone home. But that would have been so ignominious. I mean, this was my picture, damn it. At least, it used to be. This was the first footage from my first movie and, come hell or high water, I was going to see it.

I did.

And I suffered. The torments of the damned.

We screened the dailies right there in the warehouse. Screening-room time was expensive, it was cheaper to rent a machine. The dailies were shown on a thirty-five-millimeter interlock projector, where the film reels and sound reels were threaded up and synchronized by the multitalented gofer, Dan. Since there was only one projector, we had to wait while he threaded up each reel, which made the dailies last forever. Or maybe it just seemed that way.

At any rate, MacAullif, who'd stayed because it was a novelty for him, left after the first reel.

I stayed till the bitter end.

As I watched take after sickening take, it occurred to me that this would never end, because tomorrow night I'd get to watch the garbage we shot today. Like hell, I told myself. Tomorrow I won't stay.

Only I knew I would.

Because some part of me wouldn't let go. Wouldn't let me admit to myself what I knew for certain, that what I was watching was bad. Every now and then a faint glimmer of hope would flash through. That maybe Sidney was right—that the dialogue and plot *didn't* matter. That all that mattered was that we were making a Jason Clairemont flick. That what we were doing was good, and everything would be all right.

These moments, fueled by desperate hope, though fleeting, were nonetheless there. Needless to say, they did nothing to cheer me. Just the opposite. If anything, they turned me into a paranoid schizophrenic. As I watched the dailies I kept thinking: *It's garbage.* No, it's all right. *What are you, nuts? You call that all right?* Relax, they'll fix it in the mix. *You can't fix bad dialogue.* No one cares about dialogue—screenplays are structure. *He's fucked with the structure.* Nothing you can't fix, and his performance is good. *Just*

*what the reviews will say—a good performance despite a
rotten script.* It doesn't matter, you'll get work from this. *Are
you kidding? Who would hire me? It's the end of my career.*
It's the beginning of your career. *It's both, and you know it.
Oh, good god, where did he get her? It's like he put a casting
call in Back Stage—"Big Tits, Can't Act." Damn it, I am not
staying tomorrow.*

See what I mean?

Granted, I am not the sanest of individuals. I have always
been a little crazy.

Even so, I was relatively stable before I wrote *Hands of
Havoc, Flesh of Fire.*

14.

Wednesday morning found me one hundred feet up in the air, swaying in the breeze on a six-foot catwalk. The rain had stopped and the sun had broken through and we were on the road again.

Or, rather, on the balance beam. Jake Decker, in what had to be a major coup, had locked up the location for us, an actual high-rise construction site on Amsterdam Avenue. It was perfect for our purpose. The construction had reached eight stories high, with scaffolding all around, creating a veritable jungle gym, ideal to film an action sequence. There are hundreds of such locations in New York, but what made this one special was Jake happened to know the owner of the construction company and was able to work a deal where the guy would shut down for a day and assign his crew to other sites so we could film.

"Jesus Christ," MacAullif said when we pulled up next to it. He pointed. "You shooting up there?"

"Why? You got fear of heights?"

"Heights, no. But I'm not crazy. I mean, just look at that. You sending Jason Clairemont up there?"

"I should hope so. It's his scene."

"This is an action sequence, right? Not much dialogue?"

"Yeah. So?"

"The script pages are blue. The kid rewrite this too?"

"No, I did."

"Oh?"

"See, I scouted the location with Jake. Then I rewrote the scene to tailor-make it to the site." I jerked my thumb in the direction of the construction elevator. "Come on. Let's go."

"You kidding me?"

"Don't you want to see it?"

"I'm not sure I do."

"Some technical advice you're gonna give."

"You have a point," MacAullif said. "All right, let's take a look."

We walked over to the construction elevator. One of the new gofers, not Dan, was waiting next to it. "You guys going up?"

"Yeah."

"Then wear these." He fished two hard hats out of a bin, handed them to us."

"Do we have to?" I said.

"It's the rule."

With a clank the construction elevator touched down and the metal grill in front of it went up. Inside, Dan was running it. What that would do for our insurance I had no idea, but that was Jake Decker's problem, not mine. MacAullif and I got in, Dan pulled the lever, and up we went.

The thing clanked and swayed, and of course there were no walls, only grillwork. I didn't mind that much, having been up before, but MacAullif looked rather green.

The first six floors we passed were more or less completed—at least cement slabs had been poured. But the last two were open air—just the bare beams.

We reached the top and emerged onto a catwalk on top of the scaffolding. It had railings and seemed sturdy. Still, MacAullif was mighty reluctant to step out.

"Come on," I said. "It's perfectly safe."

I don't think MacAullif was entirely convinced. Still he

came, perhaps shamed into it by the fact that there were already about a dozen people on the catwalk. We stepped out and walked down to the other end, where we found Sidney Garfellow taking the attractive assistant director to task.

"What do you *mean*, he's not here?" Sidney said. "It's your *job* to see he's here."

The AD was having none of it. "It's my job to call him," she snapped. "It's not my job to drag him out of bed."

"Did you call him?"

"Yes."

"What did he say?"

"He didn't answer his phone."

"Fantastic. So how can you say you called him? It's not a call if he doesn't answer his phone."

"It's not my *fault* if he doesn't answer his phone. When I couldn't get him, I called his agent."

"What does he say?"

"He's got a call for eleven, he'll *be here* at eleven."

"Who the fuck gave him a call for eleven?"

"You did."

Sidney blinked twice, obviously about to explode. He was saved from the eruption by the arrival of the camera dolly, which came clanking out of the construction elevator pushed by two strong grips.

To recap the Sidney Garfellow–first AD dispute, the construction site was actually our second location of the day. First thing, we'd gone over to the East Side to pick up the shot of the bimbo entering her apartment that got washed out on day one. That was where the camera dolly was arriving from. And that was why Jason Clairemont had been given a later call. The bone of contention was why that would have been eleven o'clock. It was nine-fifteen now. There was no set to dress and virtually nothing to light. Even with a worst-case scenario, we'd be shooting by ten.

Without Jason Clairemont.

During the interruption Sidney Garfellow regained his

composure. "All right," he said. "Let's make the best of this. What's the first shot?"

"One eighty-seven F, Rick and Wickem, dialogue master," Clarity said.

Sidney frowned. "There's dialogue in this scene?"

"Six-lines. Mid-fight, when Wickem has Rick pinned to the rail."

"Why is that scheduled first?"

"Because that's the only time your camera's set up there. The initial fight's the other end. Then there's the breakaway, and the run with the camera pan. Then the two-shot on the rail. Then Rick slips away, and we're back to the other end for the rest of the fight. The idea was to shoot this first, so we only move the camera once."

"But we can't shoot this without Jason, can we?" Sidney said. No one said anything to that. Sidney turned on the assistant director. "Can we?" he snapped.

"No, we can't," she said through clenched teeth.

"Then there's no fucking point setting it up, is there?" Sidney said. "So let's pick a shot, move the camera, and find something we *can* shoot."

"That's going to be a neat trick," I murmured to MacAullif. "Jason Clairemont's in every shot."

Clarity looked up from her script, said, "How about the spin kick leading into it?"

Sidney looked over her shoulder at the script. "Rick spins, kicking gun out of Wickem's hand. Wickem lunges, knocking Rick out of frame. We pick them up on the rail. Fine. Good. So move the camera over here, we set up for the spin kick."

I frowned. "Sidney," I said, stepping forward. "I don't understand. The spin kick's Jason Clairemont too."

"What?" Sidney said. "No, no, it's not. It's the stunt double."

"Huh?"

"Assuming *he's* here." He turned on the assistant director. "How about it? You manage to get the stunt double here?"

"He's down on the bus with the other actors."

"Fine. Well, you better go down there, tell him his call's been moved up. We're starting with the spin kick. Clarity, change the schedule, make sure everybody knows. I'm going for coffee." Sidney stomped onto the construction elevator. "Assuming *the coffee* got here."

The AD looked ready to explode. She took a breath, then marched onto the elevator, stood there stone-faced as it went down.

"Clarity," I said. "What's with this stunt double?"

She looked up, saw me and MacAullif for the first time. "Oh, hi," she said. "Stunt double? Well, Jason's not here yet, so we're gonna shoot the stunt double."

"Yeah, I heard," I said. "I was just wondering why. I mean, why a stunt double? It's not a stunt, it's just a lousy karate kick."

"Yeah, but he can't do it."

"What?"

"He doesn't know how to do it. You may not have noticed, but our star is not that athletic."

"Yeah, but anyone can learn a simple move."

Clarity smiled. "Sure. But he doesn't have to."

"Wait a minute," MacAullif said. "Are you telling me? . . ."

"Telling you what?" Clarity said.

"That fight in *To Shoot the Tiger*—you mean that wasn't him?"

"Of course not," Clarity said. "He can't fight."

MacAullif blinked. "Son of a bitch."

"Hey, could be worse," Clarity said.

"What do you mean?"

"We're lucky to get him up here at all." She shrugged. "He could be afraid of heights."

At that point the construction elevator delivered sound man Murky Doyle, who'd just heard the first shot had been changed and took it as a personal affront.

"I'm set up for the dialogue scene," he said. He jerked his

thumb over his shoulder at the laundry hamper on the catwalk. "I've *been* set up for over an hour. Since I *wasn't* called for the street shot, but I *was* called here as early as they were."

"The crew was called here, Murky. The street shot was a pickup."

"Right. And my call was here, set up for the dialogue scene. Which I am, except for the body mikes, because you can't put a body mike on an actor who isn't here."

"You can body-mike the stunt double. That's who we're starting with."

Murky looked at her witheringly. "Stunt doubles don't *need* body mikes. They don't *say* anything. They're *stunt doubles.*"

"How about fight sounds?"

"Not with a body mike. All you'll get is clothing rustling. We'll catch it with the boom."

With a final withering glance and a shake of his head, Murky stalked to his laundry hamper and proceeded to push it from one end of the catwalk to the other. It took thirty seconds, tops.

Next up was the DP, who emerged from the elevator as Murky was getting on it. He strode straight up to Clarity and took her to task, talking animatedly for about five straight minutes. Then he turned on his heel, stalked back into the elevator, and went down.

"Good lord," MacAullif said. "What was all that?"

"Yeah," I said. "What did he say?"

Clarity said, "I haven't the faintest idea," and all three of us broke out laughing.

About twenty minutes, five grumbles, three bitches, and two pissings and moanings later, we were almost ready to shoot. There were now nearly twenty people on the catwalk, and I sure hoped it was strong enough. That was MacAullif's feeling too. I could tell by the way he kept close to the construction elevator. Anyway, by that time the following people were in place: the DP, the first assistant cameraman and the dolly grips; Murky Doyle and the boom man; Sidney Garfellow, Clarity, and the first AD; the second AD and his cadre of six stunt men; the production manager; the writer and the technical advisor; and Jason Clairemont's stunt double.

Boy, was he a surprise. I wouldn't have known he was Jason Clairemont's stunt double. In fact, when he came up in the construction elevator, I thought he was a grip.

Maybe it was just the sequence. Usually, when you think of a stunt double, you think of the star doing a scene to a certain point, and then the double steps in for him. That didn't happen in this case. We hadn't shot any part of this. We'd never seen Jason Clairemont do it. So the stunt double didn't appear dressed *as* Jason Clairemont—I mean, I assume he was dressed the way Jason Clairemont was *going* to be dressed, but I'd never *seen* Jason Clairemont dressed that way. See what I mean?

The other thing was, this guy was muscular and big. I mean, hell, unlike Jason Clairemont, he looked like he *could* fight.

He was also a lot better looking than Jason Clairemont. And I couldn't help thinking, Jesus Christ, if someone would just bump Jason Clairemont off, this guy could do the part.

And maybe save my script.

Anyway, Sidney Garfellow took the guy aside and talked to him in low tones for a few minutes. I don't know what he told him, but afterwards the guy came out, took his place in front of the camera, and executed the dandiest little spin kick you ever did see.

"Great," Sidney said. "Where's Wickem?"

"Flying in," yelled the second AD and motioned to one of his actors, an ugly, burly type with few discernible features and no discernible neck, as if Sidney had cast a punching bag in the role. The guy shuffled forward, took his place holding a gun, and the stunt double spun kicked it out of his hand.

"Damn good," MacAullif said.

MacAullif was right. Much as I'd lost faith in the production, I had to admit that was a pretty nice move. Get that on film and it was gonna look good.

"Okay," Sidney said, clapping his hands together. "Camera ready? Can we shoot this?"

"All right, lock it up," the AD said.

At his laundry hamper, Murky Doyle pressed the button three times. From way below came the sound of the bells, warning the gofers not to send up the construction elevator.

"All right," the AD said. "Places, please. Very quiet. This is for picture. All right. Roll it."

Murky Doyle had just yelled, "Speed!" when the DP turned from the camera and said something.

"Cut!" the AD said. "Hold the roll!"

"What is it?" Sidney demanded.

The DP said something unintelligible, but it was obviously that he could see the boom mike in the shot, because Sidney immediately wheeled on the sound table and said, "Jesus Christ, can we get some makeup on the boom mike? I mean, if it's gonna be in the damn picture, it ought to look good."

The boom man had been lying down in front of the camera dolly, laying the boom on the catwalk and sticking the microphone up from the actor's feet. "Sorry," he said.

The DP gesticulated and talked animatedly and unintelligibly.

Sidney translated. "You can't mike this from below. It's a kicking shot, for Christ's sake. You gotta *see* the feet. You gotta go from overhead."

"Sorry," the boom man said, scrambling to his feet. "It's just there's no room."

"Make room," Sidney said.

Easy for him to say. On the narrow catwalk there *was* no room. The man had to squeeze himself between the camera dolly and the rail. Standing practically on tiptoe, he aimed the boom mike out over the actors.

"How's that?" Sidney asked the DP, who looked in the camera, then nodded. "Fine," Sidney said.

"Fine for you," Murky said. "Let me hear a level. You. Stunt man. Clap your hands."

The stunt double clapped his hands together.

"No good," Murky said. "You're too far back," he told the boom man. "Can you lean in some?"

"Fine, fine," Sidney said. "He can lean in on the shot. When we shoot it, you tell me how it sounds. Right now I'm running camera. We still on bells?"

"Yeah, but hit 'em again," the AD said. "Murky, three bells."

Grumpily, Murky pressed the bell three times.

"All right," said the first AD. "We were never slated, this is still take one. Let's roll it."

"Speed," Murky said grouchily.

"One eighty-seven D, take one," the assistant cameraman said, and clacked the slate.

The stunt double and the bull-necked actor playing Wickem waited.

The boom man, squeezed between the camera dolly and the rail, stood on tiptoe and raised the boom high above the actors.

Sidney Garfellow yelled, "Action!"

And the rail he was leaning on gave way, and the boom man fell eight stories straight down.

15.

Sidney Garfellow wanted to shoot.

Unbelievable. His boom man's lying dead in the middle of the street, and the guy wants to roll film.

The fact that his cast and crew were in a state of shock didn't seem to register. Nor did the fact that they were no longer on the catwalk but had been brought down to the street in the construction elevator. All Sidney cared about was not falling behind schedule.

MacAullif was having none of it. "Forget it," he said. "No one's doin' nothin' till the crime-scene unit gets here."

"Crime? What crime? It was an accident. The guy fell."

"Yeah. Sure." MacAullif jerked his thumb over his shoulder where the officers from two patrol cars were attempting to keep the crowd away from the body. "Until someone says otherwise, that's a suspicious death and we treat it like a homicide. And up there's a crime scene until someone says different."

"Then I'll shoot somewhere else." Sidney turned, yelled, "Clarity, what's the cover set?"

MacAullif shook his head. "You can't leave the scene."

"What?"

"You're witnesses to what happened. You all gotta make statements."

Sidney's eyes narrowed. "You're working for me."

"I'm a cop. I may be on vacation, but I'm still a cop."

Sidney Garfellow stuck out his chin, thrust his finger in MacAullif's face. "Hey," he said, "I'm paying you."

"Right," MacAullif said. "And you can fire me too. But no one's leavin', and no one's goin' up there, and that's how it is."

Sidney stared at him for a moment, then turned on his heel and stalked off.

MacAullif shook his head. "Is that guy for real?"

"I don't know. I think he works at being insensitive on the theory artistic geniuses are all pricks. So, what's keeping crime scene?"

They arrived just then, four plain-clothes officers in two cars. MacAullif stepped out, intercepted them, and talked to them where I couldn't hear. After that, two headed for the body and two for the construction elevator. I'd never seen them before, and I'd been at a few crime scenes in my day.

I walked over to MacAullif. "You going up with them?"

"No need. They'll find it okay."

"You really do have fear of heights?"

"No, there's just no fuckin' need."

I looked at MacAullif. "What you so touchy about?"

"I shouldn't be touchy—I'm on vacation, suddenly I'm a goddamned witness?"

"So am I."

"You're not a cop. I'm supposed to be a trained observer. Well, what the fuck do you think I saw?"

"Same as I did. The rail cracked and the guy fell."

"You're a civilian. That's all you're *supposed* to see. You won't have some sarcastic ADA wonderin' why you can't do better."

Yeah, that made sense. To an extent. It didn't explain why Sergeant MacAullif was so particularly cranky on the one hand, so particularly hostile to me on the other. Unless he blamed me for getting him the job in the first place—which I certainly hadn't—and getting him into this mess. But he was decidedly cranky, even defensively so, and—

Shit. Defensively. The minute I thought it, I knew.

The crime-scene unit was here, but the officer in charge hadn't shown up yet.

I turned to MacAullif. "Who'd you call?"

"What?"

"Who'd you phone this in to. You didn't just phone it in, did you? You gave it to someone."

MacAullif took a breath, exhaled noisily. "There's a previous homicide. The two things are probably unrelated, but still. I had to give it to the officer in charge."

"Who?" I said, but in my heart I knew.

All the officers I'd ever dealt with in the course of my detective work were intelligent, efficient men, well suited to their jobs.

Except one.

Sergeant Thurman.

You remember my description of the actor playing Wickem—with no discernible features and no neck? Well, he looked like a Rhodes scholar compared to Sergeant Thurman.

I met Sergeant Thurman in the course of three separate homicide investigations. They'd been solved, but that wasn't Sergeant Thurman's fault. The man didn't have a clue. He always had a theory—simple, obvious, and straightforward—from which he would not budge. Instead, he would twist all available facts to support it. He was, in short, exactly the sort of policeman who always turned up in detective novels—a bungling fool, desperately in need of the assistance of some private eye. To anyone who knew him, he was the last man on earth to whom you'd ever assign a case.

MacAullif had done that. And I couldn't really blame him. The murder of some old bum in an abandoned warehouse was exactly the sort of case you gave to Thurman. An unimportant case with no leads and little hope of ever being solved. MacAullif had done that, and now, with the death of the boom man, it had backfired in his face. Good god, Sergeant Thurman dealing with these movie folk? The mind boggled. No wonder MacAullif was so uptight.

When MacAullif didn't answer me, I said, "It's Thurman, isn't it? You gave the job to Thurman."

MacAullif took a deep breath, exhaled, then turned and looked at me. "No," he said. "I didn't."

I blinked. He didn't? Then what was all the fuss?

And a car pulled up and out stepped Sergeant Clark.

16.

I met Sergeant Clark back during the Rosenberg and Stone murders, when a number of Richard Rosenberg's clients began turning up dead. He'd solved that case, though I couldn't give him any credit for it. He'd solved it for all the wrong reasons. I mean, his theory was right in one respect and wrong in another. So it almost wasn't fair that he'd solved the case somehow. Even though I had to admit that his approach was fundamentally sound. Though flawed. And—

Aw, hell.

I just didn't like the man. Alice put her finger on it way back when. Everything else was a rationalization. The simple fact was I didn't like him.

Why? Well, because he wasn't a man so much as a machine. Sergeant Clark was a cold, efficient, methodical officer who did everything strictly by the book. He was short and slight for a cop, and, in my personal opinion, he saw this as a defect and went out of his way to overcompensate.

I also had the feeling he liked me about as much as I liked him.

I looked up at MacAullif. Jesus Christ, no wonder he'd been ill at ease. Sergeant-fucking-Clark.

Sergeant Clark emerged from his car and spotted Mac-Aullif. He must have spotted me at the same time, but he gave no sign, just strode up to MacAullif and without so much as a howdy-do said, "Where's the body?"

MacAullif pointed. "There."

"And the crime scene?"

"There."

"You holding the witnesses?"

"Absolutely."

"Segregated?"

"Not possible."

"I didn't say it was, I just asked if they were," Clark said. "I understand you're a witness yourself."

"That's right."

"Good. That'll make the others toe the line. Why is he here?"

The transition was so abrupt it took MacAullif a second to realize he was talking about me. "Oh," he said. "It's his movie."

"What do you mean by that?"

"He wrote it."

Sergeant Clark frowned. "I thought you were a private detective."

"That's a job-job. To pay the bills. I'm really a writer."

"No kidding," Clark said without enthusiasm. "Well, I guess I'd better see the body."

We went with him. Not that I wanted to. I'd already seen the body, which was a bloody, broken mess. But I wanted to see what Sergeant Clark would make of it.

Not much. He took one look, said, "Okay, hold him for the medical examiner." To MacAullif he added, "Not that it matters much. We know the cause of death. And I assume the time of death?"

"Nine fifty-four," MacAullif said.

"Noted," Clark said. "Who was he, by the way?"

"The boom man. That's the sound man who holds up the boom mike during a shot."

"I know what a boom man is," Clark said. "What's his name?"

"Charles Masterson," MacAullif said. "No one seemed to know that, by the way. The production manager did, 'cause he hired him. But the rest of the crew just knew him as the boom man."

If Sergeant Clark found the death of an unknown boom man ironic, he didn't say so. He merely nodded and said, "Anything else I should know about him?"

"Yeah," MacAullif said. "It's possible this was the second attempt on his life."

Clark raised his eyebrows. "Oh?"

"First day of filming he got a shock. From the boom mike itself. It wasn't serious, but I guess it could have been."

"Was the equipment tampered with?"

"According to the sound man it was. Someone crossed some wires. But that's just according to him, and he's the type of guy, no one listens to him."

Clark gave MacAullif a look. "You didn't inform me at the time?"

MacAullif exhaled. "Like I said, you gotta consider the source. Everyone, me included, figured the guy just fucked up."

"And now?"

"It's still a hell of a stretch. I just tell you for what it's worth."

"Noted," Clark said. "All right, let's go topside."

"Over here," MacAullif said, and led him to the construction elevator.

Dan and the gofer who had given us hard hats were accompanied by a police guard.

"Anyone up there?" Clark said.

The guard jerked his thumb. "Two guys from crime scene. Up there now."

Clark nodded. "They process the elevator?"

"Sir?"

"For prints. They dust it for prints?"

"Not that I know of."

"Then they didn't. Who ran 'em up there?"

"He did," the guard said, pointing to Dan.

"Is that right?" Clark said.

"Yes, sir."

Clark turned to the other gopher. "What about you?"

"Sir?"

"You ever run the elevator?"

"No, sir. My job was down here."

"That's fine, but we'll take your prints anyway."

"Prints?"

"Right." Clark turned back to Dan. "All right, we're going up, but I don't want you touching the controls. You got gloves?"

"Gloves? No."

"What about a handkerchief? Any piece of cloth?"

"No, sir."

"That's all right, I got one," Clark said. "Come on in and show me what to do."

Sergeant Clark stepped into the construction elevator. MacAullif and Dan followed. I stepped on, half expecting Clark to boot me out, but he didn't seem to mind. Either that or he was too preoccupied with the gofer.

"Don't touch the lever," Clark said. "Don't touch anything. Keep your hands to yourself. Now, then, I assume that lever's the control?"

"Yes, sir."

"Pull it back is *up?*"

"Yes."

"Fine," Clark said. "I'll do it."

He took a handkerchief out of his pocket, used it to pull the cage door closed, then to pull down the lever. The elevator clanked upward.

We reached the top, emerged on the catwalk. On the far end two plain-clothes detectives were inspecting the scene. One had a camera and was snapping pictures of the broken rail. When he saw Clark he stopped, stood up, and said, "Sir."

"Perkins," Clark said. "How are you coming?"

Perkins, a tall man with a drooping mustache, said, "Just about done. I can do better when we move the camera."

"That's where you found it?"

"Absolutely. I waited for you."

"Good man. Can we move it now?"

"Hang on a minute, let me get a picture first."

Sergeant Clark turned to MacAullif. "You were there and you saw it?"

"Yeah." MacAullif jerked his thumb at me. "Him too."

"So what happened?"

MacAullif pointed. "They were shooting right there. There wasn't much room, and they were having trouble getting the boom mike in. The boom man was squeezed between the camera and the rail. When they rolled the shot he leaned on the rail and it just gave way."

"Uh-huh," Clark said. He walked over and inspected the rail.

Before it had given way, the rail had appeared perfectly sound. It seemed standard for construction sites and must have conformed to some building code or other. It consisted of vertical metal posts with pockets for holding three two-by-four horizontal rails. The bottom rail was flush with the floor, probably to prevent tools from being kicked over. The middle rail was knee high. The top rail was waist high.

Only the top rail had given way, but that had been enough. The middle rail was too low to hold anyone up, and the boom man had flipped right over it.

Jesus.

I pushed the thought from my mind, forced myself to take a look.

As far as I could tell, everything was just as we'd left it. The wooden rail, broken in two, jutted out over empty space. It had snapped in the middle. The two remaining ends had been pushed outward away from the catwalk. The right-hand one was nearly level, but the left-hand one drooped about forty-five degrees. They were pushed out far enough that it was hard to see the crack where it had given way.

Clark turned to the detective named Perkins. "All your measurements completed?"

"Absolutely."

"You got all the pictures you need?"

"Till we move the camera."

"All right. Let's move it."

"Fingerprints?"

"On the camera? I doubt if that's an issue." Clark turned to us. "When and how did the camera get here?"

"This morning, after we did," MacAullif said. "They shot another scene across town and brought it from there. The camera came up in the elevator sometime around nine o'clock. A couple of grips brought it."

"And you were up here from then on?"

"That's right."

Clark nodded. "Then fingerprints are meaningless. Go ahead and move it."

The two crime-scene detectives rolled the camera dolly out of the way, revealing a rather chilling sight. No, not just the broken rail. It was the cord of the boom mike, which was still dangling over the side.

"Pull it in?" Perkins asked.

"Yeah, but don't handle it. Just lay it down."

Perkins pulled the boom mike up hand over hand by the cord, and laid it down on the catwalk in front of the sound hamper.

"All right," Clark said. "Let's bring in the rail."

Easier said than done. Neither of the detectives had brought a grappling hook, nor had any such object been brought topside by the crew.

This created what seemed an interminable delay, as first the elevator was processed for fingerprints before Dan was allowed to take Perkins down to look for a tool.

He returned with a broomstick with a hook taped to the

end of it with gaffer's tape. He went to the edge of the catwalk, reached down, hooked the end of the broken rail, and pulled up.

I marveled at the ease with which he did this. His toes were right up against the edge of the bottom two-by-four, and he had to lean over the middle one slightly to hook the rail. I was a good four or five feet farther back and feeling mighty brave to be there.

Perkins straightened, raising the beam to level, then hand over hand pulled it in.

"Look!" I said. And immediately kicked myself. I'd just been lecturing me to keep my mouth shut, and here I was crying *Look!* just like a kid. But I couldn't help myself.

There was a gap in the middle of the rail. It hadn't just snapped in two. There was a piece missing. You couldn't tell with the two pieces out at an angle and the one hanging down. But the minute Perkins pulled them together it was readily apparent. There was a gap of at least a foot.

"Anyone look for a piece on the ground?" Clark said.

Perkins shrugged. "I've been up here. But I would say probably not. There was no reason to think there was one."

"Well, let's see what's left."

Clark, cool as a cucumber, walked right up to the edge where Perkins was standing.

I saw no reason to crowd him. Neither did MacAullif. We stood, waited, while Sergeant Clark inspected both broken ends.

When he was finished he turned back to MacAullif. "You did well to call me."

"Oh?"

Clark nodded. "That's right. The rail was sawed halfway through."

17.

"What's *he* doing here?"

Sidney Garfellow meant me. We were back on solid ground, and Sergeant Clark was taking witness statements. For that purpose he had commandeered Jason Clairemont's Winnebago, and he, MacAullif, and I were sitting in the plush camper while Perkins ushered in the witnesses. First up was Sidney Garfellow, who took exception to my presence.

I could understand his point of view. Sergeant Clark and Sergeant MacAullif were cops, but who the hell was I?

"Who, Mr. Hastings?" Clark said. "He happens to be a private detective."

"What's that got to do with anything?"

Clark nodded. "A valid point. But I've worked with him before. And he happens to be a witness to what happened. As is Sergeant MacAullif. Which is a stroke of luck. It's not often you have trained observers witness a crime. Since it happened, I certainly intend to make use of it. I wasn't there, they were. I want them to listen carefully for anything that doesn't jibe with their recollection."

"Including *me?*" Sidney said. "You have them judging me?"

"Judging? Certainly not. More like compare and contrast. Now, then," Sergeant Clark said smoothly before Sidney could protest again, "you saw this happen?"

"Yes and no," Sidney said.

"What do you mean by that?"

"I didn't really *see* it happen. I mean, I *heard* it—the scream and the crack of the rail. Then I looked and the man was gone. But I didn't really see him go."

"Why not?"

"Why not? My attention was elsewhere. We'd just rolled camera. We were about to shoot a scene. I was watching the actors."

"Who were where?"

"In front of the camera, of course."

"Yes, but in relation to the catwalk and the place where the boom man fell."

"All right," Sidney said. "They were at the end of the cat-walk closer to the elevator."

"The end of the catwalk?"

"Not the *end* of the catwalk. They were in the *middle* of the catwalk. But they were closer to that end. Closer than we were. We were shooting in that direction."

"And you were behind the camera?"

"Of course."

"Where were you?"

"Like you said. Right behind the camera."

"Not to one side or the other?"

"Behind and to the right."

"Close behind?"

"Sure. So I could talk to the DP."

"That's director of photography?"

"Yes, of course."

"And Mr. Masterson was where?"

"Who?"

"Charles Masterson. The boom man."

"Oh."

"You didn't know his name?"

"Come on. He was the boom man."

"And the boom man was where?"

"To the left of the camera dolly."

"You know that for sure?"

"Yes, of course."

"Do you just know that because that's where he fell, or did you *see* him there?"

"No, I saw him there, I know for sure. Because we had problems with the boom mike on that shot."

"What kind of problems?"

"It was in the shot. The guy was trying to mike it from below, and Eric—that's the DP—could see it in the shot. I told the guy he'd have to mike it from above. The only way he could do that was to squeeze in between the camera dolly and the rail and hold the boom up high over the action."

"Which he did?"

"That's right."

"Which is why he leaned on the rail and fell?"

"I suppose so."

"If he'd miked the scene from below, he'd still be alive?"

"No, he wouldn't. Because I'd have killed him for getting the boom mike in the shot."

Sergeant Clark took a breath. MacAullif and I had neglected to warn him about Sidney Garfellow's celebrated calculated insensitivity. "At any rate," Clark said, "you didn't actually see him fall?"

"No," Sidney said. "When I looked, he was gone."

"But you were directly behind the camera. And to the right. There were other crew members who would have been behind you, is that right? And some of them presumably would have been on the left."

"Yes, of course," Sidney said. "The whole crew was behind me. Otherwise they'd have been in the shot."

"So I'll have to rely on an eyewitness account from someone else," Sergeant Clark said. Sidney frowned, but before he could say anything, Sergeant Clark pressed on with, "Now, with regard to the catwalk—was this morning the first time you'd been up there?"

"Of course not. We don't go into these things blind. I scouted it out first."

"When was that?"

"I don't know. Sometime the week before last."

"Do you recall which day?"

"No, I don't." Sidney jerked his thumb at me. "He might. He was there."

"I'll ask him," Clark said. "But I'm testing your recollection now."

"Well, I don't recall. It was someday the week before rehearsal. I think it was in the morning, but I could be wrong."

"But whatever day that was that you scouted the location—have you been back there since? Before this morning, I mean."

"No, of course not. What would be the point?"

"I wouldn't know," Clark said. "But the fact is, you weren't?"

"No, of course not."

"Who was present when you scouted the location?"

"God, I wouldn't know. We scouted so many." Sidney shrugged. "The usual suspects."

"Suspects?"

"Just a bit of movie humor."

"I've seen *Casablanca,*" Clark said dryly. "Could you identify these suspects for me?"

Sidney looked miffed at having his wit unappreciated. "I'll try," he said. "Jake Decker—that's our production manager—I know he was there. And of course our director of photography—that's Eric Stoltz. The first assistant director was there. And the gaffer. And me and him. Those I know for sure. The sound man might have been there, but I couldn't swear to it. He scouted some locations, not others. Frankly, the guy's a pain in the ass, we often try to leave him behind."

"I see," Clark said. "And on that occasion, did you notice anything significant? Anything that would have indicated the railing wasn't safe?"

"Of course not," Sidney said. "If I had, I wouldn't have filmed there."

"I understand," Clark said. "Very well. Do you have anything else to tell me about this incident? Aside from what we've covered, is there anything else that I should know?"

"What's to know? The guy fell. It's too damn bad, but nothing's gonna bring him back. And I got a movie to make.

I got a movie crew standing around with their thumb up their ass waiting for you to tell me I can make it. Now maybe I'm insured for this and maybe I'm not, but that's not the point. The point is, I got actors locked up for this low-budget feature, squeezing their appearances in between their regular gigs. If I run over and lose 'em, I got no film. If I seem callous and hardhearted about this whole thing, you're damned right I am. This is my livelihood and my career. So do what you gotta do, but please do it fast. Am I done?"

"For the time being," Clark said. "Perkins, take him back to the others and bring me the sound man."

Perkins and Sidney Garfellow exited.

Clark said, "Observations?"

"He didn't mention the boom man getting a shock," MacAullif said.

"That's right, he didn't," Clark said. "And you would think he would. Unless he figures the two events are trivial and unrelated. Even so, you'd think he'd mention it."

"You didn't mention it either," I said. "Why didn't you ask him?"

"I'm here to gather information, not give it out. If I ask him for the information, I deprive him of the opportunity of volunteering it. Without asking, I learn the man never intended to bring it up."

"Maybe he just didn't think of it," I said.

Clark shrugged. "Either way, the fact is, he didn't. Now you two, you're professionals, you immediately make the connection. If Sidney Garfellow doesn't, I'm not going to tell him, because he'd tell everyone else. And I don't want that, because I want to see if anyone else mentions it. And if there's anything to this, odds are someone will."

I smiled.

"What's so funny?" Clark said.

"Didn't you just ask for the sound man?"

"Yes. Why?"

"Then I'd say you've got a pretty safe bet."

18.

"It's the second time," Murky said.

"Second time?" Sergeant Clark said.

"That's right," Murky said. "Didn't they tell you? About the electrocution?"

"Electrocution?"

Murky waved his hands. "Not electrocution. It didn't work. *Attempted* electrocution. Someone crossed the wires in my Nagra, and he got zapped."

"That's Charles Masterson?" Sergeant Clark said.

"Charlie. Yeah. The boom man."

"You knew his name?"

"Of course I knew his name. He was my boom man."

"I'm glad to hear it," Clark said.

"Why's that?"

"Because no one else did. The production manager had his name—that figures, he hired him—but to the rest of the crew he was the boom man."

"Not surprising," Murky said. "Sound gets no respect. You think they wouldn't know the cameraman?"

Clark ignored the question. "So this Charles Masterson—the boom man—in your opinion, someone tried to kill him before?"

"Exactly," Murky said. "They screwed with my Nagra. They opened it up and crossed the wires. When I switched it on he got a shock."

"But it wasn't serious?"

"He screamed. He dropped the boom."

"But he wasn't hurt?"

"Just luck. If he'd been touching metal, I bet he would have been fried."

"When did this happen?"

"Monday. First day of shooting. First shot with sound. Of course, it would have to be."

"Why?"

"Because the Nagra was sabotaged. Someone crossed the wires. So the first time I used it, this would happen."

"And where did this happen?"

"On the set, of course. The stage set. At the studio."

"And this was first thing in the morning?"

"No."

"No? I thought you said this was the very first shot."

"No. The first shot with *sound.* They shot some other stuff first. Street shots. That *should* have had sound, but they chose to go without it. Sound wasn't called till the afternoon."

"So this happened in the afternoon?"

"No. In the morning. 'Cause it rained, so they went inside. Then called up all pissed off, wondering why I wasn't there."

"I see," Clark said. "So you came to the studio, set up your equipment, and the first time you used it your boom man got a shock."

"Exactly," Murky said. "That's exactly what happened."

"And it wasn't because the equipment got wet in the rain?"

"What rain?" Murky said. "Didn't you hear me? Sound wasn't *out* in the rain. They didn't call us. And rain or no rain, the fact is someone crossed the wires."

Clark nodded. "Let me be sure I understand this," he said.

"It's your opinion that someone was trying to kill your boom man, Charles Masterson?"

"Trying?" Murky said. "Hell, they *did*."

"I understand," Clark said. "What I mean is, this business with the tape recorder was the first attempt. When that failed, they tried again."

"Exactly," Murky said. "That's exactly what happened."

"And who do you think did this?"

Murky spread his arms. "I have no idea. I can't imagine why anyone would do such a thing."

"Me either," Clark said. "That's the problem. Apparently, no one knew the man. No one even knew his name. Why would anyone want to kill him?"

"How the hell should I know?"

"Well, you're the only one who knew him at all."

Murky blinked, then looked up at Sergeant Clark. "Are you implying that *I* killed him?"

"I'm just saying that you're the only one who seemed to know him. And I can't think of a reason why *anyone* would have wanted to kill him. Can you?"

"No."

"There you are," Clark said. "So, you come in here and tell me it's the second time, I'm all ears. I will certainly take your story into account. But you see the difficulty?"

Murky Doyle looked at Sergeant Clark. He frowned, cocked his head. "Hey, wait a minute. Are you telling me, if *I* can't explain why someone wanted to kill him there's no case? Who's the cop here? *I* don't have to explain what happened. I'm the sound man, for Christ's sake."

"Of course, you are," Sergeant Clark said. "I'm sorry I got the wrong impression. From the way you came in here telling me this was the second attempt on Mr. Masterson's life, I thought you knew something. Other than what you observed. You *are* merely telling me what you observed, aren't you? I mean, you have no other knowledge that this was a murder attempt, this business with your recorder? You conclude it was a murder attempt from the fact that it happened. But the fact that it happened is really all you know. Isn't it?"

Murky Doyle blinked. Once. Twice. "Could you repeat the question?"

"I don't think that will be necessary," Sergeant Clark said. "All I'm asking is, do you have any information other than what you've already given me?"

It was almost comical, the look on Murky Doyle's face. He obviously had nothing to add, but didn't want to admit it. After a long pause he said, "No."

"Fine," Sergeant Clark said. "Perkins, show Mr. Doyle out. Then let's have the director in again."

Perkins exited with Murky and was back minutes later, ushering in a very exasperated Sidney Garfellow.

At the first questioning, Sidney had been merely annoyed. Now he was fit to be tied.

"Again?" he said. "I told you all I knew the first time. Now you're having me again?"

"You neglected to mention there had been a previous attempt on the life of this boom man."

I had a feeling Sidney Garfellow was about to treat us to another example of unbridled insensitivity, and he did not disappoint.

"What, are you nuts?" Sidney said. "He's a boom man. He's not important. Who the hell would want to kill him?"

"According to Vincent Doyle—"

"Who?"

"Your sound man."

"Murky? Good god, are you listening to him?"

"He claims his equipment was sabotaged in a previous attempt on Mr. Masterson's life."

"Sure he does."

"Do you deny the incident happened?"

"No. The incident happened. It wasn't serious. I don't think it held us up for more than ten minutes."

"How nice for you," Clark said dryly. "The point is, it happened."

"Yeah, it happened. I'm not surprised. Hell, you talked to him. You can't imagine him making a mistake?"

"He says the wires were deliberately crossed."

"Sure. You think he's gonna say it's his fault?" Sidney smiled. "Look, Sergeant. In a perfect world my sound man wouldn't be Murky Doyle. I've worked with him before, I know he's not the best. But this is an independent low-budget production. I got big concessions from the unions. But I'm comin' to 'em hat in hand, so I don't get to pick and choose. See what I mean? They stick me with a sound man, I'm stuck with him. I went to the wall for the DP, got who I wanted, but that used up my bargaining chips. So I'm workin' with the sound man from hell. All right, it's a trade-off. I'd rather have picture than sound. You can fix sound in the mix. You can't fix picture."

Whether Sergeant Clark followed all that or not, it wasn't what he wanted. "You claim this business with the tape recorder is unrelated and of no importance?"

"Of course. Isn't that obvious?"

"No, it isn't. The man *was* killed."

"It was an accident. The guy fell."

Sergeant Clark shook his head. "No accident. The rail was sawed through."

"Then it was a prank."

"Is that your idea of a prank?"

"It could be someone's."

"Possibly," Clark said. "But it turns out there was this previous incident."

"Bullshit," Sidney said. "Give me a break. If someone wanted to kill the boom man, how the hell would they know he was gonna lean on that rail?"

Sergeant Clark held up one finger. "Now we're coming to it," he said. "Exactly. That's just the point. Working before, my premise was that someone weakened the rail so someone fell. Now it's suggested to me that the killer was actually after this particular individual. Based on this previous incident." As Sidney Garfellow was about to interrupt, Sergeant

Clark spread his hand, palm out. "I know, I know," he said. "You refuse to credit that. Let's not go around again. The point is, once it's brought up it must be dealt with. What I want to consider now is the question of, is there any way the killer could know it would be the boom man who would stand precisely there?"

"Absolutely not," Sidney said. "That's why the whole thing's ridiculous. Hell, we weren't even going to shoot that shot."

"Oh? Why not?"

"I mean, not then. It was scheduled for later in the day."

"Why'd you shoot it then?"

"The schedule got screwed up. The shot we were supposed to shoot, the actor wasn't there."

"Oh? Why not?"

"He wasn't called. Well, he *was* called, but for later on. It was a fuck-up, basically. He should have been here but he wasn't."

"Who gave him the later call?"

"I suppose indirectly I did."

"Indirectly?"

"I can't be responsible for all these things. I'm the producer and the director. People are shooting questions at me all day long. Every little thing. So what happens is, I'll have an assistant director say to me, 'Jason isn't in the street shots so I'll give him an eleven o'clock call at the construction site, all right?' And if I'm working out camera angles with the DP at the time, maybe I don't correct that 'cause I got fifty people runnin' around here, and I gotta assume some of 'em know their job." Sidney smiled, kicked shit. "On the other hand, I'm in charge, so if something goes wrong it's my fault."

"Is that what happened?" Sergeant Clark said. "Did an assistant director give this actor an eleven-o'clock call?"

"I don't recall. I was using that as an example."

"I don't want an example," Sergeant Clark said. "At the moment, it's rather important that you recall."

Sidney frowned, obviously displeased. "It's hard to remember, since it wasn't important—and I can't see that it's all that important now—but to the best of my recollection the conversation took place between the first assistant director and me. Though you might check with the script supervisor too."

"I'll do that," Clark said. "The point is, if this actor had had an earlier call, you would have shot a different shot. Is that right?"

"Absolutely. We changed the shot because he wasn't there."

"This actor—I believe you said *Jason?*"

"Yes. Jason Clairemont." When Sergeant Clark didn't fall over backwards, Sidney added, "He's the star of the show. Hot young actor. Starred in *To Shoot the Tiger*. That's why we're apt to make concessions to him, give him a later call. Another actor, we get him here eight in the morning, who gives a shit?"

"Who, indeed," Sergeant Clark said dryly. "If this actor *had* been there, what scene *would* you have shot."

"I don't know the number. You'd have to check with Clarity."

"The scene was on a schedule?"

"Yes. Of course."

"And everyone knew that schedule? The people on the crew, I mean?"

"Of course. They have to know what to set up for."

"Would that be a printed schedule?"

"Sure. There's a daily shooting schedule. I just don't happen to have it with me."

"Who would?"

"Everybody. They're handed out to the crew."

"When?"

"What?"

"When are they handed out?"

"Oh. The day before. In the afternoon. When we know pretty much what we'll finish today, we lock in the schedule for tomorrow. That gets typed up and run off, and before we wrap, one of the gofers hands it out to the crew."

"Wrap?"

"Finish for the day. In the industry it's called a *wrap.*"

"I see. And this schedule would list the first shot you were going to shoot today?"

"Yes. Of course. But actually, the first shot was a street scene on the East Side."

"It would also list your first shot up there?"

"Of course."

"What was that shot?"

"Like I say, you'd have to check with Clarity. That's the script supervisor. She'd have the number."

"Yes, I will. But generally speaking, do you know what that shot was?"

"Yes, of course. We were shooting the fight scene between Rick and Wickem. That's Jason Clairemont, our star, fighting one of the bad guys."

"What happens in the scene?"

"They fight. Jason breaks away, runs. The other guy catches him, pins him. They have a few lines of dialogue—in fact, *that* was the first shot."

"What was?"

"The dialogue part. When Wickem has Rick pinned against the rail."

"Against the rail?" Clark said.

Sidney's eyes widened. "Son of a bitch."

"Is that right?" Clark said. "Was it that rail?"

"Christ, I think it was," Sidney said.

"Wickem pins who against the rail?"

"Wickem pins Rick."

"And Rick is? . . ."

In what can only be described as a movie moment, Jason Clairemont, nerdy twerp superstar, stuck his head in the door and cheerfully announced, "Here I am."

19.

Jason Clairemont seemed rather confused.

"Where *I* was? Why do you want to know where *I* was?"

"Did I mention this was a homicide?" Sergeant Clark said.

He had indeed, about the same time he'd booted Sidney Garfellow's ass out of there, a fact the gentleman did not take kindly to, particularly since I got to stay.

"Yes, of course," Jason Clairemont said. "But I can't see that. You say this man fell, then he fell."

"He fell because the rail was sawed through."

"That couldn't be a mistake? A stupid workman builds the rail with a bad board? Didn't notice someone started sawing it in half?"

"Not just in half," Sergeant Clark said. "The board was deliberately weakened in two places so the middle section would snap out."

Jason Clairemont smiled what I had come to realize was his trademark smile, the endearing one that made the moviegoing public forget he was a nerdy twerp. "Now then, Sergeant, if I were playing a lawyer I think I would have to object to that on the grounds that it was purely a conclusion on the part of the witness. How do you know that's why the board was sawed like that?"

122

"One indication is the *way* it was sawed."

"I beg your pardon?"

"Both cuts were made from the bottom outer edge. In other words, the board was sawed in half *diagonally*. The only cuts were on the bottom and outside, where they wouldn't be seen. The top and inside were untouched. So to anyone standing on the catwalk, the rail would appear perfectly sound."

Jason pursed his lips. "I see."

"So," Clark said. "There's a strong possibility this was done deliberately. If so, I have to consider who it was intended for. In which case, there's a good chance it was you."

"Why do you say that?"

"Because according to the script, you lean on that rail."

Jason Clairemont frowned. "I do?"

"Yes, you do. And according to the shooting schedule, you leaning on the rail was the first scene to be shot."

Jason blinked. His frown deepened. He put up his hands. "Wait a minute. Wait a minute. What are you saying here? Are you trying to imply someone was trying to kill me?"

"I'm not trying to imply anything. I'm sorting out the facts. The facts are that rail was weakened in the middle, the scene of you pinned against the rail was the first scene scheduled to be shot up there, and if that scene had been shot first, it's entirely likely you'd have gone through that rail." Clark shrugged. "What do *you* think? Does that sound like someone's trying to kill you?"

"That's ridiculous," Jason said. "Who would want to kill me?"

"I have no idea," Clark said. "I was wondering if you did."

"Well, I don't," Jason said irritably. "The whole thing's absurd."

"Maybe so, but a man is dead."

"I can't understand that."

"I can't either," Clark said. "That's why I'm asking questions. Now, in terms of you, why are you here so late?"

"I have an eleven o'clock call."

"Who gave it to you?"

Jason frowned. "What do you mean?"

"Who told you you had an eleven o'clock call?"

"I think it was Phil."

"Who?"

"My driver. Phil. He keeps track of stuff like that."

"Your driver? Would that be a teamster?"

"No. Of course not."

"Why *of course not?*"

"They don't do anything, they just drive. Phil, he does what I ask. You know, like keep track of the paperwork. A pain in the ass, all the pages they hand you. Script revisions. Schedule changes. I'm an actor, I'm busy, I don't have time for that stuff. I'd lose 'em. Phil doesn't."

"I see," Sergeant Clark said. "And Phil was the one who told you you had an eleven-o'clock call?"

"I think so."

"Did he just tell you, or did he show you the schedule?"

"Why would he show me the schedule? I'm sure he gave it to me with everything else. But he wouldn't point it out to me, he'd just tell me that call."

"Are you saying he did?"

"I think he did." Jason shrugged. "He usually does."

"You understand, I'm not concerned with *usually*. I need to pin this down."

"I'm giving it to you the best I can. You can check with Phil."

"Thanks for the suggestion. Anyway, if Phil told you you had an eleven-o'clock call, that would be yesterday when he drove you home?"

"More or less."

Sergeant Clark frowned. "What do you mean, more or less?"

"That would be when he told me, but he didn't drive me home."

"Oh?"

"I went out to dinner. The Russian Tea Room. He dropped me off there."

"He didn't wait and drive you home after?"

"No. That would be ridiculous. After shooting, his day's done. He takes me where I want to go and he's through."

"How'd you get home after dinner?"

"I took a cab."

"Where to?"

"My hotel."

"What hotel?"

"The Plaza."

"So what time did you get back there?"

"Why?"

"A man's dead."

"Yeah, but what has this got to do with it?"

"I have no idea. I ask my questions and try to figure things out. Right now I'm trying to figure out if the person who killed this boom man was actually trying to kill you. I'd appreciate your cooperation."

"You got it. I'd say I got back to the hotel around eleven."

"Were you alone?"

"I beg your pardon?"

"When you got back to the hotel—were you alone?"

"Yes, I was."

"What about dinner?"

"What about it?"

"Who did you have dinner with?"

"Who said I had dinner with anyone?"

"Well, did you dine alone?"

Jason Clairemont frowned. "Actually, I had dinner with a young lady."

"And who might that be?"

"I see no reason to bring her into this."

"I'd like to confirm your story."

For the first time, Jason appeared angry. "Story? What story? What the hell difference does it make what I did last night?"

"That's what I'm trying to determine," Clark said evenly.

"Well," Jason said, "in point of fact, I dined with a young

woman who's got nothing to do with this, and that's all I have to say on the subject. If that's not satisfactory, talk to my agent. Also my publicist." He held up his finger. "But I would be very unhappy if you happened to mess me up with the tabloid press."

"That's not my intention," Sergeant Clark said. "But the fact is, you got home around eleven last night, you knew you had an eleven-o'clock call this morning, so you slept late, rolled out of bed, and got here just now."

"That's right."

"Who brought you here? Your driver, Phil?"

"Yes."

"Good. I'd like to talk to him."

Jason frowned. "Why him?"

"Didn't you say he was the one who gave you your call?"

"Yes, but—"

"Then I need to know who gave it to *him*. When I'm finished with you, I'd like to see this Phil. You say he brought you here, so he must be here now."

Jason frowned again. "Yeah, he's here."

"Fine. Then I'll talk to him next. Getting back to you, when did you come on the picture?"

"I beg your pardon?"

"When did you start work?"

"Oh. Well, this is the first week of shooting. I was here for rehearsals, of course."

"How long was that?"

"Just last week."

"I see. Are you from New York?"

"No, of course not. California."

"I see. So you're just here to do the picture?"

"That's right."

"You flew in when? The weekend before rehearsal?"

"Actually, the week before that. I came in with my agent, put the final touches on the contract. Firmed up the deal. I've been here since then."

"I see," Sergeant Clark said. "And had you ever been here

before? At this location? Did you rehearse up there, for in-stance? Or scout it out?"

Jason shook his head. "No."

"You've never been up there at all?"

"No."

"So any fingerprints we found up there could not be yours?"

"Say, what *is* this?" Jason said.

"I believe it's called the process of elimination," Sergeant Clark said. "If you've *never* been up there, it makes my job a little easier."

"I've never been up there."

"So how'd you know you could do it? Suppose you got off the construction elevator and said, Oh, my god, I'm not going out there?"

"I don't have fear of heights," Jason said.

"Even so. Suppose you took one look and said, I'm not doing this. What would happen then?"

"I assume they'd shoot somewhere else," Jason said.

I gritted my teeth. Arrogant schmuck. Yet, it occurred to me Jason was absolutely right—if he couldn't shoot up there they would simply cater to his whim and shoot somewhere else. Even if it meant me rewriting the whole fucking se-quence.

There came a knock on the door and Perkins stuck his head in.

"Found it, sir," he said.

He held up a large plastic evidence bag. In it was a huge chunk of wood, obviously part of the rail. Even through the bag it was easy to see that the ends had been sawed halfway through and then split.

"Where was it?" Clark said.

"Under a parked car. Must have bounced and skidded. That's why nobody found it."

"Come in here," Clark said.

Perkins came up the steps into the Winnebago.

Clark pointed. "Show it to him."

Perkins held the plastic bag out in front of Jason Clairemont.

When Jason put out his hand, Clark said, "No, don't touch
it. Just look. See there, how it's sawed in two, so that it
would give way? Do you see that?"

"Yes, of course," Jason said.

"And do you see how both cuts are the same, on the diagonal, so that from above they wouldn't show?"

"I suppose so."

"Fine. Thanks, Perkins. That will do."

Perkins went out with the evidence bag, closing the door
behind him.

Sergeant Clark was looking at Jason Clairemont. "I
wanted you to see that," he said. "Do you know what that
is?"

"Sure," Jason said. "A piece of the rail."

"Right," Clark said. "A piece of the rail. And do you know
what that piece of the rail is?"

Jason frowned. "No. What?"

"It's a murder weapon," Clark said. "That is the murder
weapon used to kill the boom man, Charles Masterson. I
wanted you to see it because, the way things look right now,
there are two possibilities. One, the boom man is dead because someone wanted to kill the boom man. And two, the
boom man's death was an accident, and someone was actually trying to kill you."

"I understand," Jason said.

"Do you?" Clark said. "Good. Then I hope you understand
this. If it's the second-case scenario, if someone was actually
trying to kill you . . ."

"Yes?"

"They might try again."

20.

They descended on us like locusts.

No, not the TV crews that had arrived en masse as soon as they found out someone was dead—the police had set up barricades and were doing an excellent job of keeping *them* back. But the cast and crew swarmed around us. There were two police officers supposedly riding herd over them, but the poor men never had a chance. When MacAullif and I emerged from Jason Clairemont's trailer, the movie crew pushed right by them and met us in the middle of the street.

"What's the story?" Sidney Garfellow demanded. "Is he letting us go?"

"Not just yet," MacAullif said.

"What do you mean, not just yet? You came out of there, he must be done."

"Can we move it out of the street, please?" one of the officers said. To MacAullif he added, "Sergeant, could you help me in getting them out of the street?"

"You heard the man. Back on the sidewalk," MacAullif bellowed. He moved forward, flapping his arms, moving the crowd ahead of him.

"Fine, look, here we are on the sidewalk," Sidney said,

hopping up onto it. "Now what the fuck's the story? Is the questioning over?"

"No."

"Then why are you out here?"

MacAullif frowned. We were out here because Sergeant Clark had decided he didn't need us anymore. From my point of view, on the one hand I was miffed, but on the other I had no right to be there anyway. But MacAullif was a cop. Sergeant Clark telling him to get lost had to be a kick in the face.

"He's doing individual interrogations now," MacAullif said. "One on one. Simple, straightforward, you don't have to read anything into it."

"What?" Sidney said. "What shouldn't I read into it?"

Everyone laughed. After the tension they'd been under, they needed to laugh. I'm sure Sidney hadn't expected it, but he covered well. Instead of acting embarrassed that they were laughing at him, he smiled and took credit as if he'd just made a joke.

The attractive first AD spoke up. "Is Jason still in there?"

"Yes, he is."

"Why? Is he a suspect?"

MacAullif shrugged. "No more than anyone else."

"But he wasn't even here when it happened. What does the sergeant want with him?"

"Maybe he just wants his autograph."

"It's not funny," Murky chimed in. "Charlie's dead."

"Right," Sidney said. "It's not funny. It's fucking tragic. Meanwhile, we're all trapped here like bugs in amber with nothing the fuck to do." He turned back on MacAullif. "How much longer is this going to go on?"

"You can judge for yourself. He's got to question everyone here."

"Everyone?" the art director said. "I wasn't even up there. I mean, why would he have to question me?"

I looked at him, wondered if it was true. About him not

being up there, I mean. If he had been, surely I would have noticed him; after all, he was black.

Isn't that a hell of a thing. It hadn't occurred to me before, but when I thought that, I realized Lancelot Xavier was the only black man on the crew. For a crew that size, that seemed hopelessly out of proportion. It also occurred to me that, poor as I am with names, I knew his. And I had to wonder, did I remember it because it was an exotic-sounding name, or did I remember it because he was black? If so, was the bleeding-heart liberal guilty of yet another form of unintentional discrimination?

Not that I had much time to dwell on it at the moment. Actually, what impressed me more was the fact that Mr. Agreeable-this-will-do-nicely was actually taking exception to something.

MacAullif didn't give him any satisfaction. "Of course, you'll be questioned," he said. "It doesn't matter if you were up there or not. The point is, someone weakened the rail. Didn't have to be done today. So naturally the cops have to ask."

"Ask what?" the gaffer said irritably. "If we sawed the damn rail? I mean, is that what's happening here? The guy's gonna ask us if we did it? Thinkin' if we did we'll say, Oh, sure, you got me?"

I had to suppress a smile. The gaffer—whose name I couldn't remember and wondered if it was because he was white—was not the swiftest of individuals, but he happened to have voiced a sentiment I secretly sometimes shared. I wondered what MacAullif would say to that.

I was not to find out. Because at that moment Jake Decker came pushing through the crowd.

"Okay, I called the union," he said.

Sidney frowned. "The union? Why?"

"To hire a new boom man."

Son of a bitch.

Life goes on.

Yeah, of course you have to hire a new boom man. A sim-

ple, obvious consequence. But I, like Sidney Garfellow, hadn't
even thought of it till Jake brought it up.

"What did they say?" Sidney asked.

"They'll have someone by tomorrow morning. I figure today's a wash. They're not gonna round him up in time, and it
doesn't look like the cops are gonna let us shoot anyway."
He spotted MacAullif. "Oh, you're out here. What's the
story? They windin' this up?"

" 'Fraid not," MacAullif said. "He's still taking statements. And there's a lot to go."

"Can you do anything about it?" Sidney said. He seemed
to have forgotten his outburst at MacAullif, and treated him
as his ally and conspirator again. "Can you hurry him
along?"

"I've done all I can. The man works at his own pace. I
agree with Jake. Today's a washout. The best I can do is try
to insure you can shoot tomorrow."

"Tomorrow?" Sidney said. "What the hell are you talking
about?"

"This is a murder investigation. It's not going to go away.
Assuming no one breaks down and confesses, it's not likely
to be solved this afternoon. That means Clark will be around
tomorrow. The best I can do for you—and what I'll try to
do—is let you go ahead and film, and have him just grabbin'
people off the shoot."

"You mean taking people away from the set?" Sidney
said. "How the hell am I supposed to make a picture with
that going on? I don't have to stand for this, do I? Jake, call
the mayor's office, tell 'em I'm trying to make a picture and
I'm gettin' lots of flak."

"That might not be a great idea," Jake said.

"What?" Sidney said. "What are you saying? Movies are a
big industry here in New York. You think they wanna lose
one?"

"We're low-budget independent," Jake said. "With a
twenty-million-dollar budget we'd have more clout."

"Clout, hell," Sidney said. "That's what you're hired for,

to make the numbers sound good. Talk to 'em, for Christ's sake. I mean, what the hell am I paying you for?"

"To bring the picture in under budget," Jake said. "Which we will do. Now, today's a washout, which means I gotta spend tomorrow on the phone with the insurance company. If you think about it, that's far more profitable than buttin' heads with the mayor's office. Meanwhile, we gotta shoot. I can stand one down day, I can't stand two. So let's get tomorrow's schedule set now. The way things stand, we're on location, exterior, Seventy-ninth Street boat basin."

"What about this?" Sidney said, jerking his thumb at the construction scaffold.

"We fit it in later on," Jake said. "Even if the cops let us use it, I gotta get permission all over again. We had it for one day. Tomorrow the construction crew's back here."

"Christ, what if they build up there?" Sidney said. "What if they build where we wanna film?"

"I gotta make some calls, make sure they don't. Even if they do, it's no big deal, they'll build the same thing. I mean, what's the difference if we film on the ninth-floor catwalk or the eighth-floor catwalk? The action's still the same."

"Yeah, I suppose," Sidney said.

"Anyway, tomorrow we're at the boat basin." He turned to the first AD. "And spread the word. 'Cause we may or may not get the daily shooting schedule."

"And why is that?" Sidney demanded.

"Because Dan was supposed to pick it up from the office, but he's being held here with everybody else."

"Shit."

"Yeah. I could have Grace hop in a cab, but then there'd be no one on the phones. With our luck, she'll get held here too. Maybe even interrogated."

As if on cue, a voice announced, "Clarity Gray." A loud, peremptory voice.

I looked, saw it was Perkins, who had just emerged from the Winnebago and was calling across the street.

"Who, me?" Clarity said. She looked alarmed. "Oh, my. What do I tell him?"

"Whatever you know."

"But I don't know anything."

"Then it should be brief."

She bit her lip. "Oh."

I couldn't help smiling. As script supervisor, Clarity Gray was the model of cool efficiency. And here she was, totally flustered at the thought of being questioned by a police officer.

While we were talking, Perkins caught a break in the traffic and crossed the street. "Has anybody seen Clarity Gray?" he demanded.

Clarity actually raised her hand. "Uh, that's me."

"Then why didn't you say so?" Perkins said. "Come on. You're next."

As Perkins led Clarity across the street, Jason Clairemont emerged from the Winnebago. He didn't cross the street to join us, however. Instead he walked down the street to where a limo was parked. As if by some sixth sense, Phil, his tall, gawky personal gofer, emerged from the driver's seat just in time to open the door. Jason paused just long enough to wave to the TV crews before he hopped in. Phil closed the door, got in, and the limo took off.

To a chorus of indignant remarks.

Mine included.

I mean, hell, Jason Clairemont might be the star of this movie, but he wasn't the star of this murder investigation. Where did *he* get off going home?

The more I thought about it, the more the iniquity impressed me. I decided I'd take it up with Sergeant Clark next time I got the chance.

Assuming that ever happened. As the afternoon wore on, and witness followed witness, it occurred to me I'd already talked to Sergeant Clark, so I wasn't going to be called. This notion seemed to be borne out when Sergeant Clark finished with every witness who had been up on the catwalk at the time of the incident, and began interviewing the crew members who hadn't. These included the art director, Dan and the other gofer who'd given us the hard hats, the caterers, and the teamsters. Even Phil, when he returned from dropping off Jason Clairemont, was taken in to be interrogated.

He appeared to be the last of the lot, and it was getting on to six o'clock, and a very exasperated crew was very ready to go home, as was I, when Perkins emerged from the trailer and announced, "Stanley Hastings."

21.

Sergeant Clark seemed in no hurry. He laced his fingers together, put his hands behind his head, leaned back in his seat, and stretched.

"If this is a ploy to make me crack, you can forget it," I said. "The problem is, I didn't do anything."

Sergeant Clark frowned and straightened up. "I beg your pardon?"

"I've been waiting all afternoon to see if you wanted to talk to me. Just when I decide you don't, you do. Then when I get in here you stall. It's a fine technique, but I don't happen to be guilty."

"Whoever said you were?"

"You'll pardon me, but I don't understand your attitude."

"Oh?"

"You start off having MacAullif and me sit in on the interrogation. Midway through Jason Clairemont you boot us out. Now, is that because he's a star so you cater to his whims?"

"Not at all."

"Oh, no? He goes home while the whole crew stays. Now, what's the reason for that?"

"I was done with him."

136

"You were done with the others. But when they came out of the trailer, they stayed."

Sergeant Clark frowned. "I can't believe I'm hearing this. You're actually angry this actor went home."

"I've been standing across the street all afternoon listening to the whole crew gripe. Believe me, it's been a prime topic of conversation."

"Eclipsing a murder?" Clark said. "That's what we have here. A murder. I'm amazed to find so many people unconcerned."

I took a breath.

Clark went on. "Well, for your information, I kept the crew here because I didn't know which of them I might need to see again. Like you, for instance. I sent Jason Clairemont home because I knew I was done with him. And because I needed to talk to his driver, who couldn't leave his limo. Or so Jason said. So I had the driver take him home, park the limo, and return it. If that ruffled people's feathers, it's unfortunate, but there you are.

"Now, then. To the matter at hand."

"Yes?"

Sergeant Clark sighed. "Oh, dear, how to bring it up? Well, how about what you just said. This whole thing about Jason Clairemont going home."

"What about it?"

"You express more animosity than the incident would seem to inspire."

"So? You try standing on a street corner all day long with a bunch of cranky crew members."

"We went through that," Clark said. "If I could offer another reason why I sent Jason Clairemont home."

"What's that?"

"What I said to him before. You were still there, weren't you? When I warned him. Maybe this was an accidental death. That the killer might actually be after him. In which case, he might try again."

"Were you serious?"

"But of course. Isn't that obvious? If someone was trying to kill Jason Clairemont, they're not going to stop just because they got the wrong man."

"So you're saying? . . ."

"I sent him home to get him out of harm's way."

I shook my head. "I can't really buy that."

"Oh?"

"It's a stretch."

"Be that as it may. For the time being, buy the premise. Charles Masterson's death was an accident, and someone was trying to kill Jason Clairemont."

"Yeah? So?"

"So the question is *why?* Motivation. Who would want to kill Jason Clairemont?"

"You got me."

"Exactly."

"What?"

"I've got you. When I asked the crew members who on this movie would want to kill Jason Clairemont, the majority named you."

"That's absurd."

"Is it? I understand he won't say the lines you wrote, he's rewriting your script, changing all the scenes. And you think he's messing things up, ruining the movie, and trashing your career. You're furious, and you'd like nothing better than to see him get hit by a truck."

"Oh, come on now."

"That's what they're saying. Then you come in here with a chip on your shoulder a mile wide because the guy got to go home. I look at you and I have to think they're right."

"You think I tried to kill him?"

Sergeant Clark put up his hand. "Please. Let's be rational. I'm telling you what I hear. I happen to know you, and I can't imagine for a minute you killing this guy."

"I'm glad to hear it."

"Though if you did, that's just the way you'd do it."

"I beg your pardon."

"Sawing the board in half. There's no way you'd stand up and shoot Jason Clairemont dead. You'll pardon me, but you haven't got the nerve. On the other hand, stealing out in the dead of night and sawing a board in two—it's not exactly the same thing. You're not doing it to him. Not really. It's a kind of hopeful murder. If he leans on this rail, he'll die. Even with the foreknowledge that he's *going* to lean on the rail, the act is still removed from the deed. By time and distance. He isn't there when you saw the board, and nothing happens when you do. Or will happen till the next day."

"Excuse me, excuse me," I said. I had both hands up, as if pushing his words back. "You'll pardon me, but you started off by telling me you don't believe I did this. Now you're telling me all the reasons you think I could."

"Not at all. I'm just saying, if you had, it would have been in this manner."

"I don't find that reassuring."

"Well, you should. Would you prefer it if I were accusing you of the crime?"

"At least I'd know where I stood."

Sergeant Clark took a breath. "You'll pardon me, but you are a difficult man. I know we've had our differences in the past. Since that matter came to a satisfactory resolution, I had hoped we could get around them. I find your attitude somewhat disappointing."

"Excuse me, but who's accusing who of murder?"

"Exactly my point," Clark said. "I just got through pointing out that I am *not* accusing you of murder." He shook his head. Then he reached in his jacket pocket, took out his glasses, put them on, and referred to his notebook. "If we could move along," he said, "the point I was making that got you so upset was that this murder did not happen on the spot. It was rigged, as much as an hour, a day, or even a week in advance. Which means anyone could have done it. The suspects are *not* limited to the people who were on the catwalk when the incident occurred."

"That's obvious," I said.

"Good," he said. "Then let me tell you the possibilities and see if your thinking is attuned to mine. We start with the fact that the boom man, Charles Masterson, is killed. Possibility one, Charles Masterson was the intended victim. In support of this is the previous incident where he got the electric shock. The stumbling block is, how could the murderer know he would be the one to lean on the rail?"

"True," I said. "Unless the murderer was Sidney Garfellow."

Sergeant Clark frowned. "Why do you say that?"

"I say that because I've been standing around all afternoon with nothing else to do but think it over. Now, frankly, I think it's a hell of a stretch. But if you take the premise these two incidents indicate someone was trying to kill the boom man, it's the only solution I can see."

"Tell me how you figure."

" 'Cause it was Sidney Garfellow who gave Jason Clairemont the eleven-o'clock call. He can say all he wants about how it was the assistant director suggested it, he merely approved it, so it was a mistake but he's got so much to think about so he relied on the advice of others, but the fact is, he's the one gave him the call. Which was way too late. So assume it's *not* a mistake, he gives him that call deliberately. So they *can't* shoot that shot, and they have to turn the camera around and shoot the reverse. Sidney was up there with the cameraman, laying out the shots, and knows the positions on the reverse and knows where to weaken the rail."

"And how does he know that's where the boom man's going to stand?"

"That's the whole point. He *told him* to stand there."

"As I understand it, that was only because the scene couldn't be miked from below."

"Exactly. Which Sidney would have known before he got up there. He *lets* the boom man mike the scene from below, of course the boom's in the shot, the DP says it's gotta move, and Sidney tells the boom man where to go."

Sergeant Clark frowned. "You really think Sidney Garfellow did that?"

"No, I don't. I think it's absurd. But you ask me how it could work out that Charles Masterson was actually the intended victim, that's the only way I see it."

"Interesting," Clark said. "And what if he wasn't? Possibility number two. What if Charles Masterson's death was an accident and the intended victim was Jason Clairemont?"

"Just the reverse," I said.

"What do you mean?"

"That would tend to indicate Sidney Garfellow was innocent. Why? Because he gave Jason Clairemont the eleven-o'clock call. Which saved his life."

"Right," Clark said.

"It would also tend to vindicate the assistant director."

"Oh?" Clark said. "Why is that?"

I frowned. "What do you mean, why? Same reason. She was involved in giving him the eleven-o'clock call."

"Involved?"

"Didn't Sidney say it was the AD who suggested eleven o'clock and he just went along?"

"As you'll recall, he said that *might* have been the case. He wasn't sure."

"Well, what did she say?"

Sergeant Clark raised his eyebrows.

I exhaled. "Jesus Christ," I said. "You wanna discuss this, or you wanna play games. How the hell can I discuss what people said if you're gonna give me the I'm-a-police-officer-I-just-gather-information-I-don't-give-it-out bit?"

One of Sergeant Clark's more infuriating traits was the fact that it was almost impossible to ruffle him. He nodded judiciously. "Quite right," he said. "In point of fact, she can't remember either."

"Are you kidding me?"

"Why should I kid about a thing like that? The fact is, she can't remember. Or so she says. And I have no real reason to doubt her."

"What does she think? I mean, where did the figure *eleven o'clock* come from?"

"That's where it gets tricky."

"How so?"

"The first AD refers to Clarity Gray, the script supervisor."

"She suggests the time of the call came from her?"

"No, but she names her as the person who ought to know where it came from."

"Does she?"

"She does not. Which I find somewhat strange. You would expect the script supervisor, someone in charge of keeping track of everything, to be particularly levelheaded and efficient. I found Miss Gray to be rather flustered and unsure of herself."

"Couldn't that be a natural reaction to being interrogated by a police officer?"

"Oh, of course. It's probably nothing more than that. But for whatever reason, her information is less than reliable."

"What *is* her information?"

"She seemed to think the suggestion for the eleven-o'clock call might have originated with Jason Clairemont himself."

I frowned.

"That bothers you?"

"Not at all. I find it very interesting."

"There again, it's either very interesting or basically irrelevant."

"What do the others say?"

"About what? The idea Jason asked for the eleven-o'clock call?" He shrugged. "Like I said before, they can't remember."

"That's Sidney and the first AD. What about Jason himself."

"Ah, there . . ."

"There," I said, "you haven't asked him because you let him go home."

"Are you going to keep coming back to that?"

"You said you let him go home because you didn't need him anymore. Turns out you did."

"You really *do* dislike the man," Sergeant Clark said. "So the next possibility should absolutely thrill you."

"Oh. Do you mean? . . ."

"Yes, of course. The possibility that Jason Clairemont was not the intended victim but actually the perpetrator of the crime."

"Are you kidding?"

"You hadn't considered the possibility?"

"Yes, but not seriously."

Sergeant Clark nodded. "I know what you mean. It occurred to you how nice that would be. But you never really thought it was true."

"Are you saying it might be?"

"Anything *might* be. We already discussed how *you* might have done it. Would you care to discuss how Jason Clairemont might have done it?"

"By all means."

"Well, then that's the first strike against him. If he asked for the eleven-o'clock call knowing they'd get to him before then, the whole thing could be deliberate on his part. He kills the boom man to make it look like someone's trying to kill him."

"Why?"

Sergeant Clark put up his hands. "Motive? It's far too early to guess at motive. We're only exploring possibilities now. Could this have happened? Take it as a premise, the way we did with you. Say Jason Clairemont wants to kill someone. Could he weaken the rail and then give himself an eleven-o'clock call so someone else dies?"

I thought that over, shook my head. "Huge stumbling block," I said.

"What's that?"

"Too iffy. How does he know someone's gonna lean on the rail? How does he know someone's gonna fall? Now, in

Sidney's case, he told the boom man to stand there. He could have engineered it, see? But Jason wasn't even there. Suppose no one leans on the rail?"

"I agree," Sergeant Clark said. "It's just like I said about you. In that case it would be a rather hopeful sort of crime."

"No," I said. "Entirely different."

"Why do you say that?"

"Because in my case, if no one falls down, tough luck. In Jason's case, if no one falls down, he shows up at eleven o'clock and has to go up there and lean on the damn rail."

Clark nodded. "This is true."

"Which means he couldn't have done it."

"No. It only means he must have had a plan to handle that contingency."

I opened my mouth to say something, closed it again. I cocked my head, looked at Sergeant Clark. "You really think Jason Clairemont did this?"

"No. I'm merely examining the things that indicate he might have. And you, quite rightly, are pointing out the flaws. The fact that he would have to lean on that rail himself is indeed a flaw and a valid point. It's not conclusive enough to exonerate him, because we don't know the extent of the plan. Do you see what I mean?"

"Yes. Of course."

"Good. Then keep going. You're Jason Clairemont's advocate. Can you think of anything else that would tend to indicate his innocence?"

I took a breath. "Not offhand," I said rather stiffly.

"Now, now," Clark said. "You may not appreciate the assignment, but that's no reason not to do it well."

I sighed. "I've had a long day. I'm not up to playing guessing games. What do you mean?"

"Well," Sergeant Clark said. "An obvious point in Jason Clairemont's favor is that he wasn't along on the original location scout."

"Oh."

"Well, was he?"

"No, he wasn't."

"Right," Clark said. "And you know that for sure because you *were* along on it."

I opened my mouth to speak and realized anything I said at that point could only sound defensive. I took a breath, said nothing.

"That's in Jason's favor," Clark said. "That he wasn't along on the scout. Which, to the best we can determine, was Thursday, the week before last.

"Now, then," Clark said. "In support of the other theory—that Jason Clairemont is guilty—we have the fact that he was in town two weeks ago."

I frowned. "What?"

"By his own admission," Clark said. "In fact, you were there when he said it. He and his agent arrived in town a week before rehearsals to conduct contract negotiations. So by his own admission he was here."

I put up my hand. "Wait a minute. I think you're going off on the wrong foot."

Clark frowned. "What do you mean?"

"This whole two-week business. I mean, yes, we scouted the location then. And, yes, the rail could have been weakened in advance. But not then."

"I never said it was."

"You said it could have been done in advance. And the point is, it couldn't have."

"Oh? And why not?"

"I can't believe no one's pointed this out," I said. "But this is an active construction site. That catwalk *wasn't there* two weeks ago. We scouted *a* catwalk, but not *that one*. That's the *eighth* floor. The catwalk we scouted was identical. But it was the *sixth* or *seventh* floor. Whatever they were up to. If you wanna know when that rail was weakened, you gotta get hold of the construction crew, find out when that eighth-floor catwalk was done."

"Yes, of course," Sergeant Clark said. "You're not the first one to point this out. Jake Decker said exactly the same thing."

I frowned. "Then I don't understand. What's all this about who went along on the location scout?"

"Those people would be familiar with the site and the workings of the construction elevator. Of course, they couldn't weaken the rail then. But they'd have the inside knowledge to do it when the time came."

"Yes," I said. "But Jason Clairemont wasn't *on* the location scout."

"Yes, of course," Sergeant Clark said. "I counted that as a point in his favor."

I shook my head as if to clear it. "Hold on," I said. "You just said a point against him was he was here two weeks ago."

"Yes. Of course."

"But the rail couldn't have been weakened then."

"The rail? Oh, no. Of course not. It has nothing to do with that. No, the point is Jason Clairemont was in town two weeks ago when the first murder occurred."

I blinked. "What?"

"It's a huge strike against him," Clark said.

"Wait a minute, wait a minute," I said. I smiled, shook my head. "Sergeant, I realize the man found in the freight elevator is the reason you're here to begin with. It's the reason you're on the scene. It's why you were called when the boom man was murdered. But that's really all there is to it. You have a homeless man killed in a warehouse and a crew member killed on a movie set. Isn't it obvious the two crimes are totally unrelated?"

Sergeant Clark looked at me in surprise. "Absolutely not," he said. "There's no doubt in my mind the same person killed both men."

22.

"Unbelievable!"

"Calm down."

"Absolutely unbelievable!"

"Please stop shouting."

"I'm not shouting."

"You're talking very loud. You want Tommie to get upset?"

"Alice—"

"Shhh."

"Don't shhh me!"

"Lower your voice."

"Don't you understand, Alice? He's doing it *again!*"

The *he* was Sergeant Clark. What he was doing again was making a mistake in a murder investigation.

If I had been slightly more rational, I wouldn't have been so upset about Alice not understanding that. After all, this was all news to her. Ten minutes ago, she didn't even know there'd been a murder. There was no pay phone near the construction site, so I hadn't been able to call her. And she hadn't watched the evening news. So first she had to relate to the fact the boom man had been killed, before she could comprehend the fact that the investigation of it was being botched.

It was her inability to assimilate this at lightning speed that was causing me to raise my voice. Which I admit was totally unfair. But I couldn't help it. The son of a bitch was doing it again.

"All right, slow down," Alice said. "Try to tell me again. So far all I know is there's been a murder and the officer in charge is Sergeant Clark. I understand why that's enough to set you off, but it doesn't tell me any of the specifics in the case. *What* is he doing again? And why is it tying you up in knots so bad you can't talk about it?"

What Sergeant Clark was doing again was, as I said, making a mistake in a murder case. What made it so infuriating was it was the *same* mistake he'd made in the first murder case. Remember how I said he'd solved the Rosenberg and Stone case, even though he'd made a faulty assumption? Well, it was the same damn faulty assumption. In the Rosenberg and Stone murders, he'd taken a homicide that had happened a year before and lumped it in with the group. And every time we wound up discussing the crimes, he kept harking back to that one. Which was enough to drive me nuts, since I knew *for a fact* it had nothing to do with it.

I knew that because, one, I'd solved the case, two, the murderer had been apprehended and was in jail, and, three, the only thing that linked that murder to the Rosenberg and Stone crimes was the fact the victim was apparently one of Richard Rosenberg's clients.

I use the word *apparently* for good reason. The victim was *not* one of Richard's Rosenberg's clients. He only appeared to be because I made it look like he was, in order to get me out of a jam. The man in question had actually no connection with Rosenberg and Stone whatsoever.

Of course, I couldn't tell Sergeant Clark that. All I could do was point out the absurdity of lumping him in with the others. To absolutely no avail. The man persisted, right up until the solving of the case, in considering the death of the man in question as a factor.

And here he was, doing it again.

"He's a *bum*, for Christ's sake," I said. "Alice, we're talking about a bum."

"Sergeant Clark?" Alice said.

"No, not Sergeant Clark," I said impatiently. "The *victim*. He was a *bum* who happened to get killed in the warehouse. Before we even *rented* it. *Before* we had anything to *do* with it. Some poor homeless man who happened to get killed by some other poor homeless man who probably wanted to steal his *wine*, for Christ's sake."

"You're shouting again."

"And what the *hell* has that got to do with some boom man falls off an eighth-story catwalk?"

"I have no idea."

"Of course you haven't. Because there's no connection whatsoever. It doesn't matter whether someone's trying to kill the boom man, or whether someone's trying to kill Jason Clairemont, or whether Jason Clairemont's trying to kill someone, or whether *I'm* the fucking murderer—none of those premises have the least to do with knocking off some bum in a warehouse."

"What's the harm?" Alice said.

I blinked. Gaped at her, mouth open. "The harm?" I said. "The harm is going off on a tangent and failing to solve the crime. That's the harm. The harm is blowing the investigation by getting hung up on something irrelevant."

"You sure *you're* not getting hung up on something irrelevant?"

"Damn it, Alice—"

"Stanley. Please. I understand. You've had a hard day. I mean, you were up there when it happened?"

"Yes."

"It's so frightening. I mean, *you* could have leaned on the rail."

That hadn't really occurred to me. I mean, it *had*, but not the same way as when she said it. I felt very mortal at that moment. Also very frustrated, exasperated, what have you.

"Right," I said. "It could have been me. It could have been

anyone. Which is the whole point, isn't it? I mean, if there's a killer running around loose, he might try again. Are the people on the movie safe? Is Jason Clairemont safe? Is Sidney Garfellow safe? Am *I* safe, for Christ's sake?"

"Stop. You're scaring the shit out of me."

"I should hope so," I said. And immediately wished I hadn't. "I'm sorry. I don't mean that."

We were in the kitchen and I had been pacing up and down. Now I sank into a chair at the kitchen table, put my head in my hands. "I'm sorry," I said. "I'm calming down. Really. But you gotta understand. This movie was my chance. I got a creepy kid actor who's ruining it for me, but it's still my chance. I still can't let go. I'm carrying all that emotional baggage around with me, then I get smacked in the face with a murder and kicked in the teeth by Sergeant Clark. It's enough to drive anybody around the bend."

Alice came over and put her arm around me. "I know," she said. "And I want to help. But I only can if you're rational."

I put my arm around her waist. "I'm rational."

"There's a difference between horny and rational," Alice pointed out. When that failed to amuse me, she added, "You're really upset, aren't you?"

"Am I finally getting through to you, Alice?"

"No. I understand. Sergeant Clark's on the scene, he has no leads, and he's barking up the wrong tree. Am I right?"

"That's it in a nutshell. Why?"

"Sure," Alice said. "With all that happening, I suppose you've forgotten."

"Forgotten what? Alice, don't do this to me."

"Sorry," she said. "Isn't tomorrow the day you invited Richard to the set?"

"Oh, my god."

23.

It once occurred to me an interesting experiment would be to lock Richard Rosenberg and Sergeant Clark in the same room together for a few days and see who lived.

To say the two men did not like each other would be putting it mildly. And their dislike was not without foundation. It was, in fact, very specific.

Sergeant Clark despised Richard for being a negligence lawyer, which he regarded as slightly lower than pond scum. But that was just in general. Specifically, he could point to one particular case where Richard had sued the city of New York on behalf of a client who was alleging police brutality.

Richard, on the other hand, could point to Sergeant Clark's not-so-veiled threats to shut down his law practice. Plus, he just naturally liked bopping cops around.

In short, I could not think of any two men I would have less preferred to see meet on the set of my first motion picture.

But sure enough, bright and early next morning, who should come striding onto the dock of the Seventy-ninth Street boat basin but everyone's favorite negligence lawyer, Richard Rosenberg.

He didn't meet up with Sergeant Clark though. Clark had

not yet put in an appearance. No, the first police officer he ran into was Sergeant MacAullif.

"You," Richard said. "What are you doing here? Are you in charge of the investigation?"

"What investigation?" MacAullif said.

"Are you kidding me? It was all over the evening news. Boom man goes boom. I'm surprised someone didn't use that. But there was no official statement. No interview with the officer in charge. So is that you?"

"Not this time."

"So what are you doing here?"

"Working."

"Oh?"

"On the movie. They hired me as a technical consultant."

"You're kidding," Richard said. He was grinning from ear to ear. "So you went Hollywood, huh? So who's in charge?"

"Well, as to that," MacAullif said. He looked over at me.

Richard frowned. "Stanley? What's the story?"

And who should come driving up but Sergeant Clark.

Ever since Alice had mentioned it the night before, I'd been anticipating the meeting of these two people. And I'd built it up so much in my mind that subconsciously I think I expected some kind of reversal—Richard and Sergeant Clark, unbeknownst to me, would have become golf buddies, or have served on the same election committee, or something, but whatever the case they would greet each other like long-lost friends.

Not quite.

Richard's face got as hard as I've ever seen it. "Son of a bitch," he murmured.

"I would have called you, Richard," I said, "but I don't have your home number."

"Are you telling me *he's* in charge?"

"Aw, hell." I sighed and said a silent prayer. Sergeant Clark wouldn't see him and he'd walk right by.

No such luck. As Clark came toward us, I could see his

eyes widen. He changed pace and direction, strode right up to Richard. The two men stood there, squared off, toe to toe.

It was quite a sight. They were both small men, scrappy, intense. And standing there, jaws jutted out, eye to eye, they looked like a pair of bantamweights who had just been told to shake hands and come out fighting.

"Well," Sergeant Clark said. He cocked his head at me. "So you've consulted an attorney. I wasn't aware we'd even reached the stage where I had to advise you you had that right."

"He's here for the movie," I said.

"Aren't we all?" Sergeant Clark said. "Amazing what one will do for the greater glory of the motion-picture industry."

"Am I to assume you're investigating this crime?" Richard said.

"You mean they haven't told you?"

"I just got here."

"Yes, I'm investigating the crime. As a matter of fact, I'm investigating them both."

I took a breath.

"Both?" Richard said.

"Yes. I have two homicides. One yesterday and one two weeks ago."

"Two weeks ago?" Richard frowned, looked at me. "Is that the one you told me about? The derelict in the warehouse?"

"That's it."

"I thought that was a John Doe. Had nothing to do with you."

"It doesn't," I said.

"So how'd you get stuck with that?"

"I don't consider myself stuck with that," Clark said. "I consider it a related case."

"Related?" Richard said. "Wait a minute. I thought this was something happened before the movie crew even got there."

"True. But while they were in possession of keys to the building."

Richard's eyebrows launched into orbit. "Keys to the building? You're saying the movie crew had not been inside yet, but they *had* taken possession of keys to the building?"

"That's right. On the day of the crime."

"Well, what are you waiting for? Lock them up. Good god, it's an open-and-shut case."

As I said, it's hard to ruffle Sergeant Clark. He merely cocked his head and said, "From your sarcasm I assume you know absolutely nothing about it."

"Actually," Richard said, "I assume *you* know absolutely nothing about it. Or am I misinformed? Are you telling me you *have* identified the body?"

"So far we have not."

"Pardon me, Sergeant," Richard said, "but wouldn't that tend to indicate the man was exactly what he appeared to be—a derelict looking for shelter? And most likely done in by another derelict?"

"At the present time, it's too early to tell."

"Too early to tell? Two weeks and you haven't identified the body. Doesn't that tend to indicate the body's not *going* to be identified?"

"Not at all," Clark said. "After all, this is not a case where the body was unrecognizable. The face was unmarked. We have a perfectly good photograph which is being circulated. It's only a matter of time before someone recognizes him."

Richard cocked his head, grinned. "And you believe when you do it's going to shed some light on the man who was killed yesterday?"

"I think so, yes."

"For how much?"

"I beg your pardon?"

"Put your money where your mouth is, Sergeant. How much you wanna bet if you identify the body it has anything to do with yesterday's murder?"

Sergeant Clark took a breath. "I'm not a gambler, I'm an officer of the law."

Richard put up his hands. "I quite agree, Sergeant. I wouldn't bet on that, either." He smiled and took a step toward me, turning his back on Sergeant Clark.

"Define your terms."

Richard stopped, turned back. MacAullif and I also turned to look.

Though still outwardly calm, Sergeant Clark's chin was set.

"I beg your pardon?" Richard said. "What did you say?"

"I said define your terms," Clark said. "You made some vague reference to a wager. But there were way too many variables in it. Were you betting whether the man would *be* identified? Or whether he would be identified as someone relating to the case? Was there only a bet in the event he was identified, or in other instances all bets were off?"

Richard cocked his head. "I hope you are more accurate in your investigation than you are in casual banter. What I said was quite specific. In the *event* the man is identified, I was willing to bet you it has absolutely nothing to do with the present case."

"I beg *your* pardon," Clark said. "But what I *thought* I heard you say was, in the event he was identified, that fact would *shed no light* on the present case."

"I don't want to get hung up on semantics on the one hand or technicalities on the other," Richard said. "But *shed light* is unacceptable. So is *clarify*. If the cases were *totally unrelated,* just *establishing* that fact would shed light or clarify the situation. See what I mean?"

"Of course I do," Clark said. "And while I don't expect you to believe it, I happen to be a reasonable man. I would consider it unsporting to take advantage of such a technicality. I said *shed light,* because those were your words. There are many ways to define them. Just as there are many ways to define the word *related.* You are an attorney-at-law. I have no doubt that whoever the man turns out to be, you would be able to argue your side of the case. I trust you as a gentleman not to do that and, in the event I am right, give in with good grace. Are you willing to extend me the same courtesy?"

"Absolutely," Richard said. "How much do you wish to bet?"

The mind boggled. I'm standing there watching this, and I can't imagine what Sergeant Clark is going to say. My mind started racing: How much does a policeman make? A cop, a homicide sergeant? Specifically, Sergeant Clark—did he have an outside source of income? How much would he be willing to risk just to make a point?

Sergeant Clark turned, looked out across the river. At the end of the dock, two electricians were setting up a huge reflector, angling it to catch the morning sun, aim it onto one of the yachts.

Clark turned back, looked at Richard. "Dinner," he said.

Richard blinked. "I beg your pardon?"

"I'll bet you dinner."

"I don't understand. What do you mean, dinner?"

"At the restaurant of your choice."

Richard blinked again. "You mean dinner with *you?*"

"Exactly."

Richard took a breath, exhaled slowly. "Sergeant," he said. "No offense meant, but I don't *want* to have dinner with you."

"Of course not," Sergeant Clark said. "That's the whole point."

"What?"

"The winner names the restaurant. Any restaurant in Manhattan. The loser takes him there, pays for everything, and sits there during however many courses dinner takes, and listens to the winner explain his theory of the case and how he happened to be right."

"Son of a bitch," Richard said.

"Oh?" Clark said. "I thought it was a very gentlemanly bet."

"It's fine except for one thing," Richard said. "I'm not involved, and I *have* no theory of the case."

"Your theory is merely that the murder of the John Doe isn't related. So I can understand your being hard pressed to pontificate about that for any length of time. So, more to the point, if I win you shall hear my theory of the case and how it proved to be right. If you win, I'll be forced to give you my theory of the case and explain how it happened to be wrong."

Richard blinked. A smile spread over his face. "Done," he said.

He extended his hand. Sergeant Clark extended his, and the two men shook hands.

"Now that's out of the way, Sergeant," I said, "you might want to tell us why you're here today."

"Good point, Stanley," Richard said. "I suppose I should have ascertained that first."

"Do you wish to retract your bet?" Clark said.

"Do you have anything to say that might make me want to?"

"I don't think so," Clark said. "I've come here following up routine inquiries in the death of the boom man, Charles Masterson."

"Any progress that you can tell us?" I asked.

"Just routine," Clark said. "Masterson had a wife and two children."

"Shit."

"That's not news," Clark said. "We knew that much from his W-4 form. But they have been confirmed and notified. He had a wife, Ellen, thirty-two, a daughter, Betty, six, and a son, Alan, age four."

Damn. How fast life hits you. I'd been standing there, getting off on the idea of Sergeant Clark and Richard Rosenberg making a bet, and there it was, a kick right in the face. The death of the boom man wasn't fun and games. A wife had been deprived of a husband. A little girl and boy had been deprived of a father.

Son of a bitch.

"There you have it," Sergeant Clark said. "A perfectly ordinary, simple family man. No apparent problems at home. No trouble with the union. Didn't work too much or too little. Didn't make waves. Just a sort of ordinary, nebbishy guy. Not particularly liked, but not particularly disliked either. Not the sort of guy anyone would be apt to have a grudge against. In short, hard to believe anyone killing him for any reason."

"From which you conclude?" I said.

Clark cocked his head at me. "I *conclude* nothing. I present the facts for what they're worth. I would say they tend to *indicate* that Charles Masterson was not the intended victim."

"Do they indicate who *was?*" Richard said.

"I'm not prepared to go into that at the present time," Clark said.

The door to one of the Winnebagos opened and Jason Clairemont came out. I could see him size up our little group and categorize it instantly as nonessential personnel—just cops and the screenwriter. With the barest obligatory nod in our direction, Jason Clairemont walked right by and out onto the dock.

"Now, why is that face familiar?" Richard said.

"That's the star," MacAullif said. "Jason Clairemont."

"Oh?" Richard said. *"To Shoot the Tiger?"*

Jesus Christ.

Even Richard.

"That's right," I said. "Our star, Jason Clairemont. Who happens to be the intended potential victim Sergeant Clark doesn't feel like discussing at the moment."

"Oh?" Richard said. "Now *that's* very interesting. Particularly when you tie it to the murder of a John Doe in a warehouse. I can't wait to hear how you made the connection."

"I repeat," Clark said. "There is not sufficient data to warrant discussing that at the present time."

"But why is it a possibility?" Richard wanted to know.

When Sergeant Clark didn't answer, I said, "If the original shooting schedule had been adhered to, the first shot would have involved Jason Clairemont leaning on that rail."

"Is that so?" Richard said. "That wasn't on the evening news."

"And I don't want it to be," Sergeant Clark said. "Which is why I didn't want to discuss it to begin with. I would appreciate your cooperation in this matter."

"Or all bets are off?" Richard said. "Have no fear. My lips are sealed."

Before Sergeant Clark could respond to that, the door to the other trailer opened and our newest cast member stepped out. It was the actress playing Cassie, or Hot Babe Number Two.

I had not seen her before. That I can swear to. I would have remembered. As hot babes go, she went. She made the actress playing Blaire look positively tame. This woman was amazing. She had curves in places most women didn't even have places.

And all were on display. She was wearing a string bikini. I'm not sure whether it's a fact or merely my perception, but it seems the older I get the skimpier bikinis get. Hers would have proved my theory. String wasn't the word for it. I'm talking dental floss.

Anyway, she came bouncing down the steps from her trailer, flashed a dazzling smile in our general direction, and sashayed right by, goodies flopping in all directions.

We gaped like morons. Two homicide sergeants, an attorney-at-law, and a private eye, all rendered speechless by a natural phenomenon.

Richard recovered first. There were a lot of things he could have said, such as, "Wow," "Get a load of that," "Check it out," or any number of typical sexist remarks. But no, he chose to say, "Where did *she* come from?"

It was to date my proudest moment on this draggy flick. I smiled, shrugged, said modestly, "I created her."

24.

"What's the story?"

"You already heard."

"No, no, that's bullshit," Richard said. "I mean the *real* story. How are you involved?"

Richard and I were sitting on a bench near the dock, waiting for the crew to get set up. Sergeant Clark had dragged MacAullif off to confer about something or other. I hoped it wasn't me.

"I'm not involved. Not really."

"There no reason to think you did it?"

"Well . . ."

"What do you mean, *well?*"

"It appears I've been named by some of the crew members."

"Named?"

"As a possible suspect."

"What?"

"I know it's ridiculous, but—"

"They suspect you of killing the boom man?"

"No. No one had a motive for killing him. But if the intended victim was Jason Clairemont, they give me a motive there."

"Oh? And what is that?"

I told him about Jason Clairemont rewriting my scenes.

Richard shook his head. "As a motive, that's thin as hell."

"Oh yeah? Just wait till you see some of the dialogue this kid comes up with."

"I know you feel that way, but it's nothing you'd kill for, and no one seriously thinks you did. Clark's an asshole, but he's not stupid. There's nothing else tends to indicate you, is there?"

"Well, I scouted the location."

"Oh?"

"And I was the last one down because I wanted to work out a sequence I was writing."

"Oh? Didn't happen to have a saw in your pants, did you?"

"No."

"Was this before or after rehearsals started?"

"Before."

"And at the time you got no motive, right? You don't know the kid's rewriting your script."

"True. But I *had* scouted the location, and I could have gone back later."

"Is that right?"

"Yes. In fact, I would have *had* to. Because that's an active construction site, and the eighth-floor scaffolding—that's where the guy fell—hadn't even been built when we scouted it the first time."

"When *was* it built?"

"I don't know. But I imagine Sergeant Clark's found out."

"Yeah, I imagine he has. Anything else implicate you?"

"Not in that murder."

"Don't tell me."

"Yup. In the previous one, the bum in the warehouse—the one the schmuck won't let go of, and I can't *wait* till you win that bet, I wish I could go along and watch the guy eat crow—in that one, unfortunately, I got to the warehouse ahead of everybody else. The murder didn't happen that day, but still."

"And the day the murder *did* happen?"

"I was in the production office that day and would have had access to the keys."

Richard looked at me. "That's it?"

"Yeah. That's it."

"You don't have any obscure reason for wanting to kill a bum in a warehouse?"

"How could I? Nobody even knows who the bum in the warehouse is."

"You don't have to know who someone is to want to kill 'em."

"Richard—"

"I'm not saying you did. I'm just making a point."

"Well, the fact is, no. I didn't know him and, no, I didn't want to kill him."

"What about the warehouse?"

"What *about* it?"

"You have any stake in that? In whether the movie company used it or not?"

"Absolutely not."

"You sure?"

"I'd never seen it before and I couldn't have cared less."

"You don't have someone in real estate who owns a piece of the building? Your wife's uncle, or something?"

I stared at him. "Richard. Why the hell do you say that?"

"Do you?"

"Hell, no."

"You're not connected at all?"

"No. Not at all."

"It doesn't matter to you one way or the other where this movie's filmed?"

"I wouldn't go that far."

"All right. But you couldn't care one way or another whether it got filmed in that warehouse?"

"Well . . ."

"You hesitate?"

"Oh, for Christ's sake."

"You *did* hesitate, didn't you?"

I exhaled. "Richard. I hesitated, but it doesn't mean anything."

"Everything means something."

"Oh, shit."

"Hey, this is what cross-examination is. It's what I do."

"Yeah, I know, Richard. But it's not like you tripped me up or anything. You just brought up something totally irrelevant which I now have to explain. I hesitated because you said shooting in the warehouse didn't matter to me one way or another. As it happens, it does."

"Why?"

"Because when we got into the warehouse, Sidney Fuckface Producer-Director spotted a whole pile of packing cases upstairs and thought wouldn't they be nice for the warehouse fight scene. Well, there *was* no warehouse fight scene, and there wouldn't be one now if he hadn't seen those fucking cases. When you asked me if it mattered to me one way or the other if we filmed in that building, it sure as hell did. But it had nothing to do with the guy in the elevator. Who was already dead long before Sidney Garfellow got his bright idea from lookin' at the stack of boxes."

"Tell me about it."

"Huh?"

"Tell me about Sidney looking at the boxes."

"Why?"

"Humor me."

I took a breath. "What do you want to know?"

"When did it happen? Was it before or after you found the body?"

"Before, of course."

"There's no *of course* about it. It's *of course* to you because you were there when it happened. But to me, from what you told me, he could have rented this building and then got the idea for the scene two days later."

"Well, that's not what happened. He saw them on the location scout. Before we found the body. He had already asked me to write the scene. I was already preoccupied with that when the elevator came down."

"With the body in it?"

"Right."

"Where were these packing cases?"

"On the second floor of the warehouse."

"That's the same floor where you found the body in the elevator?"

"Right."

"So you went to the warehouse, checked out the ground floor. Went up to the second floor. Sidney spotted the boxes. Then the elevator came down with the body in it. Is that right?"

"Yeah. So?"

"How long was it from the time you got to the second floor to the time you found the body?"

"I don't know. First we had to fumble around, find the lights. Then looked around some. Sidney had his great idea. Everyone was discussing whether the place would do for a sound stage. Then how we'd get the equipment in. Jake mentioned the elevator. He found it, pressed the button, and the corpse appeared."

"Which took how long?"

"I don't know. Five, ten minutes."

"No more than that?"

"I wouldn't think so."

"When did Sidney ask you to write the scene? Was that closer to the beginning of that time or the end?"

"I would say the beginning."

"Why?"

"Because it wasn't just before the elevator came down. Because that's when they were discussing getting power and equipment upstairs."

"So it must have been fairly soon after the lights were turned on?"

"I suppose it was. So?"

"So that's interesting."

"Why? What are you getting at?"

"I like a challenge. You tell me about the murder of this bum, tell me there's absolutely nothing to go on. Well, I don't know anything about it. I haven't seen the crime scene. I haven't questioned any of the witnesses except you, and already I know something."

"What's that?"

"The producer-director who was kind enough to let me on his set walks into a warehouse and within minutes of the lights being turned on is pointing to a stack of packing crates and asking you to write a scene. It certainly could have happened that way, and if the guy is one of those flighty genius types, maybe it did. But with some of these, quote, genius types, unquote, it's all an act. They plan and rehearse these flashes of inspiration."

I frowned. "What are you saying?"

"I'm saying it's possible Sidney Garfellow had seen those crates before. That when he walked into the warehouse he knew they were there, that he'd already planned on a warehouse fight scene, and knew he was going to ask you to write it." Richard smiled. "Which would mean he'd been in the warehouse before. When? The day before when he killed the bum."

"Good god."

Richard put up his hands. "Hey. I'm not saying he did. I'm just making a point. When you tell me there's nothing to go on. Well, maybe *Sergeant Clark* has nothing to go on. But that doesn't mean there is.

"But to get back to my original point. There's nothing to connect you to the death of the bum in the warehouse?"

"No."

"And the death of this boom man—even if we concede you had a reason to hate Jason Clairemont—Sergeant Clark, for all his failings, is relatively rational. I can't believe he really thinks you did it."

"I'm sure he doesn't."

"Good," Richard said. "Then as your attorney I'd like to give you some advice."

"Advice?"

"Yes. My advice to you is forget it. You're not involved. It's got nothing to do with you. Now, Sergeant Clark and I may have a bet, but that's got nothing to do with you either. Don't get some crazy idea you gotta win my bet for me. If it happens it happens, but it's got nothing to do with you.

"Now, then, this movie you wrote—the one you took four weeks off from my work to watch 'em film."

"What about it?"

"You say this kid's fuckin' it up. Well, maybe so. That's your area of expertise, not mine. Even so, you got your movie being filmed. It's a once-in-a-lifetime thing. Never happened before, may never happen again. It's a big deal. Which is why as your attorney I advise you to leave this murder to Sergeant Clark. It's got nothing to do with you. But as to the movie . . ."

"Yeah?"

Richard smiled, shrugged.

"Enjoy it."

25.

Easy for him to say. Richard Rosenberg never wrote a word in his life outside of a legal brief. And he couldn't have given a damn whether anyone rewrote him unless it directly cost him money. The way I saw it, what Jason Clairemont was doing to the script was *indirectly* costing me money, but that was the least of it. He was also tearing my heart out and stomping on it with soccer cleats.

Aside from that, what Richard said made sense. I wasn't involved in this murder, and I was under no obligation to solve it. Sergeant Clark, though not to my taste, was a perfectly competent investigator. No, that's not fair. To give him his due, the man was damn good. If he wasn't, I wouldn't have this nagging desire to wipe that smug smile off his face by solving the crime first.

No. Bad thoughts. Stick to Richard's advice. Enjoy the movie.

Hell, that was the problem. With the movie a hopeless mess, the impulse was to run from it and embrace the crime. It was almost as if Jason Clairemont had beaten me and I had conceded defeat, and now I needed to reassert myself by beating Sergeant Clark.

I was sitting alone on the bench thinking that. Richard had

strolled off and was on the dock watching them rehearse the scene they were about to shoot. And so was every other male within a hundred yards, thanks to the extraordinary attributes of Hot Babe Number Two.

Actually, if the truth be known, the young lady was Hot Babe Number Four. Because you don't shoot a movie in sequence. As I said, you shoot all the exteriors first. And since Hot Babes Two and Three appeared only in interior scenes, we had skipped directly to Hot Babe Number Four.

I was actually rather proud of her. As I said, I'd created her, and I'd created her out of whole cloth. Sidney had asked for four hot babes. There was only room for three in the script. Try as I would, I couldn't crowd the fourth one in. Unless I made one of the girls twins, which didn't really fit with the plot.

Sidney, naturally, was totally unsympathetic—he wanted four hot babes, and there were gonna *be* four hot babes. It was up to me to fit 'em in, and if I couldn't, it was my damn fault.

Which is how Cassie was born. Since there was no room for her in the plot, I added her to the movie without affecting the plot. During the chase scene at the end of the movie where the bad guys are all after Rick, I have him come screeching into the boat basin, run to the end of the dock, and steal a yacht. Just as he pulls away, who should wake up but Hot Babe Number Four, who had fallen asleep while sunbathing on deck. She's there for the entire chase, adding visual delight and chipping in an occasional one-liner. Actually several one-liners, in the hopes two or three of them would be funny enough to survive the final cut.

Anyway, after seeing her bikini, I had to admit it probably would be worth it even if *none* of them survived the final cut.

Perhaps it was that thought that drew me to the dock. At any rate, I found myself walking toward it. I went out, joined the crowd at the far end. It was standing room only. I had to stand on tiptoes, crane my neck to see.

It was worth it. Hot Babe Number Four was in position,

lying on her stomach on the deck of the yacht. The back of her bikini bottom consisted of an invisible string running up the crack of her ass. It might as well have not existed. The string of her bikini top *didn't* exist—it had been untied. Her oversized breasts were bulging out from under the sides of her body.

While I watched, they did the final rehearsal of Jason Clairemont jumping off the dock and stealing the boat.

Ever do something, you want to shoot yourself in the head? I did just then. Because I had written the sequence of Jason stealing the boat. And here's what I'd written: Jason hops in the boat, starts the engine, he pulls away from the dock, and the bimbo wakes up.

What a schmuck. Why couldn't I have written: Jason hops in the boat, starts the engine, the bimbo wakes up, and he pulls away from the dock? I mean, here is this hot babe, with more pounds of breast than you would see on most entire cheerleading squads, lying there with her top off, and I don't have her hop up until the boat's out in the middle of the fucking river. Why did I write it that way? Was I out of my mind? Was I in a coma?

Yes, I'm a sexist pig. I wanted to see them. But give me a break. We're talking natural phenomenon here. Even the *women* on the dock wanted to see them.

No such luck. After we shot the scene they'd rehearsed, cutting before the boat pulled out and the bimbo woke up, they moved the camera onto the boat and took off for the middle of the river. The two principals, Jason and the bimbo, and a skeleton crew of essential personnel. These included the producer-director, the director of photography, the first assistant cameraman, the sound mixer, and the script supervisor.

No, they did not include the screenwriter.

They didn't include the first AD either. As the boat pulled out from the dock, she came walking up to me.

"Say, what's with him?" she said.

"Who?"

She jerked her thumb. "The cop."

"Sergeant Clark?"

"Yeah. What's his story?"

"Why? Is he bothering you?"

"I'll say."

I looked at the end of the dock. Clark, MacAullif, and Richard were in the crush of people watching the yacht sail away. Well, hell, no one's *letting* me enjoy the movie, and if she's gonna come dump it in my lap . . .

"It looks like we're not needed here," I said. I jerked my thumb at the catering truck. "How about grabbing a cup of coffee?"

We went ashore, got coffee, strolled over by the Little League field.

"Okay," I said. "What's the problem?"

"The problem is, what right has he got to intrude on my personal life?"

"What do you mean?"

"The guy wants to know where I was the night before the boom man fell."

"It's no big deal. He's asking that of everybody."

"No. He just asked me."

"Huh?"

"He came here this morning just to ask me. He spoke to Clarity too, but he didn't ask her that at all."

"It doesn't mean anything."

"The hell it doesn't. What business is it of his if I went out with Jason Clairmont?"

I'm afraid my eyes widened slightly.

And she caught it. "See? See? You too. And there was nothing to it."

I put up my hands. I wanted to placate her, but I was sure nothing I could say was gonna work. "I'm sure there wasn't," I said. "What you're saying is, you're the one he took out to dinner?"

"What's wrong with that?"

"Absolutely nothing. But Sergeant Clark came here this

morning, asked you a lot of questions about it, and got you upset. Right?"

"Yes. Yes, he did."

"If you hang on a moment, I think I can explain." I took a breath. She was obviously upset, and I had to be careful not to offend her. "Well, look," I said. "The problem is, Jason Clairemont is young."

I offended her. "So I shouldn't go out with him?"

"No, no. Not at all. This is nothing to do with you, it has to do with him. The thing is, when he was questioned by Sergeant Clark he said he'd been out to dinner with someone but he wouldn't say who."

"That's ridiculous."

"Exactly. That's why I say he was young. It was a young thing to do—protecting your good name."

"But this policeman noses around, finds out about it, and asks me all these questions."

"Of course. You can see why. Jason Clairemont gave a rather dubious alibi. Of course he's gonna check it."

"Oh, yeah? So why's he care about my personal life?"

"I just explained."

"No, not that. No, he wants to know about me and Sidney."

"Oh."

"Yeah, and what business is that of his? He wants to know, were Sidney and I dating? Did we break up? *When* did we break up? Why did we break up? Who broke us up? Who broke up, me or him? And did Sidney know I was going out with Jason Clairemont?"

Well. Easy enough to follow that line of reasoning. Sidney Garfellow, the jealous, jilted lover, attempts to bump off rival Jason Clairemont. There were a few flaws in it, like why give him an eleven-o'clock call so the boom man dies instead, but as a working theory it had possibilities. It was certainly interesting that the attractive AD had gone out with the nerdy twerp superstar.

And that he hadn't wanted anyone to know about it.

26.

You know the expression, Don't rub it in? Happens to me a lot. Getting it rubbed in, I mean. On this occasion it was the sexist-pig bit. Because I'd just admitted to being one with regard to Hot Babe Number Four, when who should come driving up but Jake Decker with our new boom man.

Who was a woman. Which shouldn't have been that much of a surprise. It was just that with no one knowing Charles Masterson's name, everyone referred to him as the boom man. And with him getting killed, everyone was referring to him. So the words *boom man* had been on everyone's lips.

Bad words. Sexist.

Because now we had a boom woman. Only you didn't say boom woman. *That* was sexist. So what did you say, boom person? No, that was sexist too. You wouldn't call a boom *man* a boom person. So what the hell did you call her?

Jake Decker solved the problem for me. "Stanley," he said as they came walking up. "I'd like you to meet Judy Bloom. Judy's our new boom operator."

Yes, of course. Boom operator. Totally nonsexist.

Except.

It immediately reminded me of *telephone* operator, a traditionally female job.

I know. Don't rub it in.

Anyway, as Jake led the distaff boom man out to the dock, it occurred to me she was now the one person on the whole movie crew who wasn't a suspect in Charles Masterson's murder.

Until I realized, as the new boom operator she was the one who profited most from his death.

Just kidding.

I watched as she and Jake Decker walked out on the dock. Richard and MacAullif were still standing there looking out over the river where the action was taking place. I wondered how much they could actually see. Probably not much. Still, I considered joining them.

I realized I didn't see Sergeant Clark. I looked around, trying to spot him, but he was nowhere in sight. I looked some more, saw what might have been the back of his brown suit jacket disappear behind Jason Clairemont's Winnebago.

I wasn't about to go see. But surely there was no harm in walking a little ways along the riverbank. Which is what I did. And now when I glanced back over where the production vehicles were parked, I could see the other side of the Winnebago just fine.

Sure enough, there was Sergeant Clark. He was talking to Dan the gofer, who had just driven up.

That computed in my mind. Of course. Dan was the one who'd originally picked up the keys to the warehouse. Sergeant Clark, having bet that crime would tie in with this one, now had to prove a link. Hence he'd start with Dan.

I looked back over at the dock, where Richard and MacAullif still stood watching. I wondered if I should warn Richard. I immediately stopped myself.

Schmuck. It's none of your business. It was Richard himself who told you that.

To hell with it. I wandered over to the catering truck for another cup of coffee. The girl from the truck was arranging a tray of blondies, those delicious, scrumptious, incredibly high-calorie vanilla brownies that only a saint could refuse. I am not a saint. I would have succumbed, but the girl informed me they were for lunch.

I contented myself with a coffee. As I wandered off sipping it, I realized it was my third this morning. I also realized I hadn't been to the bathroom since my first.

Anytime you start thinking how glamorous the movies are, try hanging out on a location set and drinking lots of coffee. Jason Clairemont and the bimbo had bathroom facilities in the Winnebagos. The rest of us had to use the john on the crew bus.

It was small, cramped, and stunk. Really stunk. The thing reeked to high heaven. I took one whiff and almost gagged. And, wouldn't you know it, when I finished peeing I got an attack of diarrhea and had to stay in there.

I have to tell you, I thought I was going to die. I sat there on the toilet thinking, what else can go wrong? I wondered if the diarrhea was the result of too much coffee or if it had been brought on by nerves. Anyway, I took my infirmity as a final sign, a message from the gods, stay out, schmuck, you're not involved.

With that firm resolve I washed my hands, pushed open the bathroom door.

And heard, "He's onto you!"

A female voice. Fearful. Hushed. Urgent.

Then, in counterpoint, a male voice, cocky, assured. "Relax. It's all right."

I froze in the doorway. Listened.

"You're gonna get caught."

"No, I'm not."

"And you'll get *me* in trouble."

"I won't."

I pushed the door open slightly, peered out.

There were two people in the front of the bus, but I couldn't see either clearly. The woman was leaning against the arm of one of the seats with her back to me. The man was behind her, out of view.

There was something vaguely familiar about the woman's

long brown hair, but I just couldn't place it. Then her head turned slightly and I caught a glimpse of her features. The ski jump of her nose.

Of course. The girl from the catering truck.

Her head moved again and I saw the man behind her.

It was Dan.

My stomach felt hollow. Jesus Christ. Talk about signs from the gods. Here it is, laid out for you. Sergeant Clark questions Dan. Minutes later the girl warns him. *He's onto you!* Sorry, Richard. I'll butt out on the crime if I can. But if they're gonna go drop it in my lap.

"Dan—"

"Oh, Christ," Dan said. He looked around. As his eyes darted my way, I instinctively pulled the door shut. But not so much that I couldn't see what he was doing.

He took a deep breath, blew it out, ran his hand over his head. "Oh, all right," he said. "I give up. You win."

The girl looked up at him. "Huh?"

Dan put his arm on her shoulder. "All right. When you're right, you're right. Come on. I'll put it back."

"Dan."

His left hand was on her shoulder, escorting her off the bus. Now his right hand came up into view.

In it was something small and rectangular. Something I thought I recognized.

A vanilla brownie.

"Come on," Dan said. "I'll put the blondie back."

And with that they were gone.

Do I have to tell you how stupid I felt? Suffice it to say, that was the last kick I needed to drive the point home.

Hey, I already said I wasn't investigating the crime.

They didn't have to rub it in.

27.

The phone rang in the middle of "L.A. Law."

I hate that. Even if Alice and I gripe about the plot lines and say the show's not what it used to be. Still, come ten o'clock Thursday night I like to relax and wind down from the day. I do not like to answer the phone.

But I did. Because that late at night I'm always afraid it's an emergency. And I can't bear the thought of someone making an emergency phone call and having my answering machine pick it up—not when I'm really there. I rolled over on the bed and grabbed the phone on the second ring.

It was Richard.

With something on his mind.

"Do you think he's gay?"

"What?"

"Sergeant Clark. Do you think he's gay?"

"Good god, why do you say that?"

"He wants to have dinner with me. I was just thinking. Isn't that strange? Wanting to go to dinner?"

"Richard, I think it's just what it appears to be. You pissed him off and goaded him into making a bet. He's a cop, so he doesn't want to bet money. So he bets you dinner. He's also a smug son of a bitch, who'd like nothing better than to lecture you on how he happened to be right."

"Yeah, I suppose," Richard said. "It just occurred to me. The guy's so cold, aloof, and snobbish, maybe he's gay."

"I don't think those are necessarily gay attributes."

"You know what I mean. The man's a cipher. He strikes me as asexual, so how can you tell? It just occurred to me, maybe he thought *I* was gay. Which I'm not. I'm a bachelor, but I'm not gay."

"Richard," I said. "I think you're off on the wrong track. You remember when the bimbo with the boobs walked by? Clark was staring goggly-eyed like everybody else."

"So what?" Richard said. "Every man, woman, and child was staring at her."

I glanced over at the TV. Alice had hit the record button on the VCR, since I was missing half the show. It occurred to me, Richard was a lawyer and *he* wasn't watching "L.A. Law." I wondered if that was a comment on the show or on him.

"Richard," I said. "Is this what you called for?"

"No. I wanted to thank you for getting me on the set."

"No problem."

"That Sidney Garfellow is all right."

"Uh-huh."

"You don't sound too enthusiastic."

"Richard, I told you what they're doing to my script."

"It can't be that bad. He was damn nice to me."

He was indeed. When Sidney Garfellow had gotten back from photographing the bimbo in the boat, and I'd finally been able to introduce him to Richard, the man had been cordiality itself. I realized he always was with the public. It was only with insiders, with the cast and crew, that he let his hair down and slipped into the persona of ruthless bastard. Sergeant Clark, as the investigator of the murder, had been let into this inner circle. Richard Rosenberg, as a visitor to the set, had not. So Richard had seen only the genial facade.

"That's nice, Richard," I said. "I'm glad you had a good time."

"So that's why I'm calling. I forgot to ask him."

"Ask who?"

"Sidney Garfellow."

"Ask him what?"

"About dailies. I've never seen dailies on a motion picture. Could you ask him to let me in?"

"Tomorrow?"

"No. It's Friday, I go home early. Sometime next week."

"I'd have to know which day."

"I don't know which day. Just ask him in general. If he says yes, I'll see what my schedule is."

"Okay, I'll ask him. But I have to tell you something."

"What?"

"About dailies."

"What about them?"

"They're boring as hell."

"Sure, if you have to see 'em every day. I only want to see 'em once."

"Even so."

"I'll take my chances," Richard said and hung up.

"What was that all about?" Alice wanted to know.

"Richard wants to go to dailies and he was wondering if Sergeant Clark was gay."

"I got all that," Alice said. "What about the bimbo with the boobs?"

"I told you. Hot Babe Number Four in the string bikini. The biggest tits I never saw because I wrote the scene backwards."

"And even Sergeant Clark stared?"

"Turn the TV off."

"Huh?"

"We missed the whole middle of the show. Let's watch the tape when it's over."

"We didn't miss that much."

"We missed enough. Turn it off and come here."

"Oh?"

"Just turn it off."

Alice turned the TV off, came over to the bed. I put my arms around her waist.

"Do we owe this to Hot Babe Number Four?" she asked.

"If so, it's the first thing this movie's done for me."

I have to tell you, when the phone rang again it was an even bigger imposition than the first time. I would have let it ring, but it was after eleven. Which was prime time. No one called after eleven unless it was an emergency.

I groped wildly for the receiver, put it to my ear. "Hello."

It was MacAullif. "Turn on the TV," he said.

"What?"

"Turn on the TV. Channel four."

"MacAullif—"

"Now, schmuck!"

And the line clicked dead.

I slammed the phone down. "Where's the remote control."

From somewhere beneath me, Alice mumbled into my shoulder, "You gotta be kidding."

"MacAullif says it's important. Channel four."

"It's recording," Alice said.

She was right. Serendipity. We were able to concentrate on more important things. Still, the TV was back on a damn site quicker than it would have been if MacAullif hadn't called.

I rewound the tape. Without getting up and switching the VCR over from clock to digital counter, I was doing it by guesswork. I rewound a few seconds, then hit *play*. Alice and I watched the screen. There came that interminable two-second lag before the tapes kicked in.

"Look!" Alice said.

She needn't have bothered. I was looking, all right.

And there on the TV screen was Sidney Garfellow, large as life. Just in case there was any doubt as to the issue, the graphic, SIDNEY GARFELLOW, appeared across his chest. Just below that was the slightly smaller graphic, PRODUCER-DIRECTOR.

The shot was a medium close-up. It was an exterior, night. The location was in front of Sidney Garfellow's apartment building. Sidney's face was lit with floodlights. A number of microphones were thrust in front of him.

"That's right," Sidney said. "I said *murder.* The tragic death of our boom man, Charles Masterson, was not an accident, as you have been led to believe. It was cold-blooded, premeditated murder. The rail was sawed in two, and that is why he fell.

"But that's the least of it. There is every indication—and this has also been withheld from you—but there is every indication that the intended victim was *not* Mr. Masterson, but was actually our young star, Jason Clairemont."

That statement was greeted by a number of shouted questions, but Sidney put up his hands, fending them off. "Hold on, hold on," he said. "There's more. I would like to make a brief statement at this time."

Sidney reached into his jacket pocket, pulled out a paper, unfolded it. He pushed his glasses up on his nose and began reading. "As a result of the murder attempt on the life of my star, Jason Clairemont, which resulted in the death of my boom operator, Charles Masterson, I am convinced that someone is attempting to halt production of my movie, *Hands of Havoc, Flesh of Fire.* I hereby serve notice on that person or persons. This is *my* movie. I raised the money for it personally, and I am producing and directing it myself. And I am here to assure my investors that I will not be stopped. This production will go on. I am not intimidated."

Sidney extended his right arm. As he did, the camera pulled back to include Jason Clairemont, who stepped into frame.

Sidney put his arm around him. "And Jason Clairemont is not intimidated." Sidney smiled at him, then turned back to the camera. "But I *am* concerned for his safety. And toward that end, I have acquired the services of a personal bodyguard . . ." Here Sidney extended his left arm, and the camera pulled back farther to include a small mountain of a man who strode into frame. ". . . to insure Jason's safety on and off the set."

The camera held on the three of them for a moment, then slowly zoomed in on Sidney's face. I don't know how, but I swear Sidney must have directed it.

Because it was just perfect. Just as the camera moved in on him he raised one finger and said solemnly, "Because I assure you, ladies and gentlemen—just as I assure each and every one of my investors—that no matter what . . ."

Here Sidney paused, waited until the camera had come to a complete stop.

"The show must go on."

28.

It was a media circus.

When I got to the location at seven o'clock the next morning there were already four or five TV crews there ahead of me. I wasn't bothered though—immediately recognizing me as a nobody, the reporters let me push by.

Not so Jason Clairemont. When the nerdy twerp superstar's limo arrived they surrounded it, cameras up, microphones at the ready.

Not that they got anywhere near Jason, however. When the door to the limo opened, it was the burly bodyguard who emerged. He closed the limo door behind him and stood there glowering. The effect was awesome. Cameramen actually moved back a pace at his glance.

The bodyguard spotted the two cops from the mayor's office assigned to traffic control and motioned them over. At his direction, they cleared a path through the TV crews. Then and only then did he open the back door of the limo. Cameras were rolling, but the man who emerged was not Jason Clairemont but production manager Jake Decker. He and the bodyguard stood, two giants flanking the door.

Next, producer-director Sidney Garfellow stepped out. He stood there a moment or two in the TV light. Then, I swear

182

to god, he gave stage by stepping sideways and gesturing to the door of the limo.

From which emerged Jason Clairemont.

It was a star's entrance.

Jason neither cowered nor shrunk. He stepped out and stood, haughty, proud, disdainful.

Sidney, Jake, and the bodyguard quickly surrounded him and whisked him onto the set. But not before Jason had a chance to smile, nod, and wave to the cameras, not to mention the crowd of more than two hundred people that the TV crews had already attracted to the location.

But I didn't tell you what it was. The location, I mean. I'm doing it again. Telling the story out of sequence. Just like they filmed my script. Or at least Jason's version of my script.

Anyway, the location just happened to be the *USS Intrepid*. That's a ship that's permanently docked in Midtown Manhattan on the Hudson as an air and sea museum. It's an aircraft carrier with all types of old war planes on the deck. Which made it a neat place for a chase scene. In the script I had Jason dive off the yacht with Hot Babe Number Four and swim to the pier where the *Intrepid* was docked—no, not today, they shot that yesterday; if Hot Babe Number Four were here I can't *imagine* what the TV crews would have made of *her*.

Today we were shooting the stuff on the *Intrepid* deck. Jason running up the gangplank, hiding in a cockpit, jumping on a bad guy from the wing of a plane, bluffing guys out with a prop gun from the museum, and what have you.

The location was nice in that it was functional for the script, and it was nice in that it was confined to the deck of a ship that had access only by the gangplank, which made it easy to keep the media out.

Not that that was apt to appease Sergeant Clark much. I had a feeling the gentleman was going to be most prodigiously pissed.

Sidney Garfellow, the DP, the AD, Clarity, the gaffer, the

art director, and sound man Murky Doyle were on deck inspecting a World War II fighter plane when Clark arrived.

I was standing with MacAullif, who had just arrived himself, and the two of us were watching the scene and speculating on what would happen when Sergeant Clark showed up.

Not much. At least, no fireworks. And it occurred to me, Sergeant Clark was probably the only officer on the whole force who wouldn't have blown up under the circumstances. But he was remarkably calm.

"Mr. Garfellow," he said. "If I might have a word with you."

While apparently cooperative, Sidney managed to give the impression of being terribly put upon. It occurred to me the man was an excellent actor. As well as a colossal prick.

"Yes, Sergeant?"

"It has come to my attention that you have hired a bodyguard for Jason Clairemont."

"Yes. So?"

Clark nodded. "Probably a good idea. Where is he?"

"I don't know. Where is Jason now, in makeup?"

"Yes," the AD said. "They're set up belowdecks." She pointed. "Through that door there and down the stairs."

Sergeant Clark nodded his thanks and went off the way she'd indicated.

"Jesus Christ," I said to MacAullif.

"What?"

"He didn't ream him out."

"I told you he wouldn't."

"How did you know?"

"It's not his way."

"Nine cops out of ten would have chewed his ass."

"Not Sergeant Clark."

"That's one of the reasons he pisses me off. He's not a man, he's a machine."

"It's just his style."

"Yeah," I said. After a pause I added, "Do you think he's gay?"

"What?"

"Sergeant Clark. Do you think he's gay?"

"Christ, no. He's got a wife and three kids."

"Sergeant Clark?"

"Yeah."

"He's got a wife and kids?"

"You find that hard to believe?"

"Yeah, I do."

"Why?"

"Partly me. I've always had trouble thinkin' of cops as having families. Until they get shot. Then they always do."

"You're a cynical fuck, aren't you?"

"And then him. Like I said, he's like a machine. I just can't see him with a wife and kids."

"Well, he's got 'em. What made you think he's gay?"

I told MacAullif about Richard Rosenberg. That struck him funny.

"No shit," he said. "So, the ambulance chaser's homophobic. I'll have to kid him about it the next time he gives me a hard time."

"Aw, shit, MacAullif," I said. "You can't tell him I told you."

"You're kidding."

"No, you can't do that."

"Spoilsport."

"Hey, I gotta work for the guy."

"Yeah, I suppose you do," MacAullif said. After a pause he said, "You gonna tell him he's got a wife and kids?"

"Sure."

"How you gonna tell him you found out?"

"I'll tell him I asked you."

"And why did you tell me you wanted to know?"

"Why do I have to give you a reason?"

"What, are you kidding? Rosenberg's an attorney. He's gonna ask you a couple of questions, if you don't have the right answers, he'll tie you up in knots. You really think he won't find out you told me?"

I exhaled. It occurred to me, Jesus Christ, life was hard. "Hey, MacAullif," I said. "If he *does* find out, I'll let you know, and then you're free to kid him about it. Otherwise, keep your fucking mouth shut."

"Nice talk."

I heard footsteps on the deck and looked around to find Sidney Garfellow bearing down on us. If the safety of the young movie star was troubling him, you wouldn't have known it.

"Ah, what a location, what a location," Sidney said. "Do I know how to pick 'em, or what?"

I didn't point out that Sidney had had absolutely nothing to do with choosing the location, since I had actually written this particular one into the script. I merely smiled and nodded.

"And you, Sergeant," Sidney said. "I wanna use you in the shot."

MacAullif frowned. "I beg your pardon."

Sidney put up his hand. "No, not today. Next week. In the street scene. Check the schedule. I wanna use you then."

"Oh," MacAullif said. He didn't seem particularly happy.

"By the way, Sidney," I said. "Thanks from Richard Rosenberg."

"Who?"

"My boss."

"Oh yeah," Sidney said. "He wants to visit the set?"

I took a breath. "He was there. Yesterday. At the dock. I introduced you."

"Oh," Sidney said, without the slightest trace of embarrassment. "Is that who that was? So how'd he like it?"

"Just fine, thanks. But he wanted me to ask you if he could come to dailies."

"Tonight?"

"No. Sometime next week. If it would be all right."

He made a face. "I don't like the public seeing dailies. Just raw takes. Unedited. No effects. People don't understand. They look at it, they think it's shit. You could screen the rushes for *Citizen Kane,* you'd think what a boring flick, you know?"

"So, I should tell him no?"

Sidney shrugged, "Hey, if he can stand it, what the fuck do I care? Just tell Clarity when he's coming." Sidney clapped us on the arms, just one of the guys. "Now, if you gentlemen will excuse me, I gotta check out a plane."

And off he went.

"Does your technical expertise extend to aircraft?" I asked MacAullif.

"No, but what does it matter? No one's asked me for my technical advice yet. Frankly, I don't know why the guy hired me."

"He wants you as an actor."

"Yeah. Right."

"What's the matter? Stage fright?"

"Fuck you. I never acted before. You're the one used to be an actor. Why don't he pick on you?"

I hadn't thought of it. I guess I'd been too obsessed with the script. But it occurred to me, a cameo would sure be nice.

While I was thinking that, Sergeant Clark came out on deck. He looked around, spotted me and MacAullif, came up to us.

"Well," he said. "The bodyguard's name is Norman Pollack. Works for Randell Investigations. Small Manhattan agency. He's about as bright as you'd expect, but he seems tough enough. I just hope he knows his job."

"Uh-huh," MacAullif said. He turned to me. "You wanna ask him?"

"Ask me what?" Clark said.

"Why you didn't take Sidney Garfellow to task. For talking to the media."

"What would be the point?" Clark said. "What's done is done."

"That's not the way you felt about Richard Rosenberg," I said. "I remember when you weren't happy with him, you had a lot to say on the subject."

"There's a vast difference," Clark said. "He's an attorney-at-law."

"And therefore beneath contempt?"

"No. And therefore in the game. Sidney Garfellow's a civilian. Richard Rosenberg's a player."

"You really think of it as a game?"

Sergeant Clark grimaced. "I was speaking metaphorically. Surely you know what I mean. The public will only cooperate so far, and there's no use getting angry when they stop. An attorney-at-law is an officer of the court. I expect him to play by the rules."

"I recall you having opinions about me as well."

"You're a private detective," Clark said. "Isn't that obvious? Another kind of player. But tell me. Why does this bother you so much?"

"Bother me? It doesn't bother me." I frowned. "Well, yes, I guess it does. You know what, it's like you letting Jason Clairemont go home the other day. Now Sidney Garfellow blabs to the media and you don't say boo. It's like you're kowtowing to the movie folk."

"I assure you that's not the case," Clark said. "I take a pragmatic approach. I mean, what's really happened here? Sidney Garfellow's hired a bodyguard for Jason Clairemont. Which isn't that bad an idea. In fact, I might have even suggested it. So why should I be upset?"

"Because it isn't true," I said. "That's the whole thing. Sidney Garfellow isn't concerned with Jason Clairemont's safety. You think he seriously believes anyone's trying to kill the kid? He just *says* he does for the publicity it generates. He says, my god, here's a chance to get on TV and publicize my movie before it's even shot. He didn't hire his bodyguard for protection. He hired him as a publicity stunt."

"Of course he did," Clark said. "But what's the difference why he hired him? It's still a good idea."

I opened my mouth to retort. Couldn't think of one. Closed it again.

"Not that we need him much today," Clark said. "We're kind of isolated up here."

"Oh?" I said. "You don't think it's one of the crew?"

"I didn't say that."

"Then what difference does being isolated make, since they're all on board?"

"So are we," Clark said. "I don't expect anything to happen right under our noses."

"It did at the construction site," I said. "You weren't there, but we were."

Then I saw the look MacAullif was giving me. He didn't need me reminding Sergeant Clark that had happened right under his nose.

"That was a slightly different situation," Clark said. "At the time, you suspected nothing. You weren't looking for it. Now we're forewarned. And that was a booby trap. A wooden rail was sawed in half. We're on a ship. The rail's made of steel. How are you going to booby-trap that?"

"Obviously you can't," I said. "But why does it have to be the rail? Maybe the killer booby-trapped something else."

"Such as what?"

"I don't know," I said. I was standing next to some sort of single-engined fighter plane. I put my hand on the gun turret. "How about this? The ship's got all these weapons on display. What if someone figured out how to load one?"

I'd said it as a joke. But when I saw the look on Sergeant Clark's face, and then the one on MacAullif's, I suddenly felt sick.

"Oh, my god," I said.

There came the sound of a gunshot.

29.

No, it wasn't the nerdy twerp superstar falling dead at the hand of a cowardly assassin firing a museum piece affixed to the wing of a biplane aboard the deck of the *USS Intrepid*.

No, the gunshot turned out to be our prop man firing a blank gun for the purpose of a level check for the benefit of sound man Murky Doyle.

Which I probably could have figured out if I'd had my wits about me. After all, I'd written the damn scene. I knew there were gunshots in it. It just didn't occur to me at the time.

It hadn't occurred to Sergeant Clark or Sergeant MacAullif either, but once they got the idea they were none too pleased.

The scene had *lots* of gunshots in it. The scene called for lots of bad guys firing lots of blank cartridges from lots of guns. Those guns and cartridges now all had to be checked out, which was time-consuming and a pain in the ass. Moreover, the prop man, whom I hadn't really paid any attention to before but who turned out to be a sour individual who could put Murky Doyle to shame, was less than thrilled by the investigation, which he appeared to take personally.

Which was too bad for Sergeant Clark and Sergeant

MacAullif. As for me, I kept out of it. It was none of my business. Not that I'd want you to think me hardhearted. I was merely following the advice of my attorney—I wasn't involved, and I was enjoying my movie.

Which wasn't that hard to do this morning. We were filming an action sequence and there weren't any lines for Jason Clairemont to rewrite. And the action sequence wasn't half bad, particularly since anytime it called for Jason to do anything the least bit strenuous, he'd step aside and let the stunt double do it. The double, who was just a bigger, stronger, handsomer, more talented and athletic version of Jason Clairemont, was absolutely fine. He was a pro, and executed each bit of business with the same precision with which he had executed the spin kick.

At the construction site.

Just before the boom man fell.

Shit.

As I stood there on the deck of the *USS Intrepid,* watching the stunt double crouch on the wing of a fighter plane preparing to leap on the back of a bad guy as he passed by, it occurred to me to wonder, if Jason Clairemont *had* fallen from the construction site, would the stunt double have been elevated to his part?

Maybe not.

But he might have *thought* he would.

I saw Sergeant Clark standing on the other side of the deck, watching the action. I considered going over and suggesting the idea to him. I immediately talked myself out of it. Butt out, schmuck. You're an amateur. Clark and MacAullif are pros. Let them handle it.

Which they did. All morning long. Through a hail of gunshots.

Because when we got down to it, it turned out this was my Rambo scene. Or my reverse Rambo scene. The hero never fires a shot. He's unarmed, does it all with his bare hands. But the bad guys sure do. Through take after take after take, the bad guys fired shot after shot after shot. And each time the guns were reloaded, they had to be checked out by MacAullif and Clark.

I can't tell you what that did for the demeanor of the prop man. Not to mention slowing filming down to a dead crawl.

On the bright side, with the action confined to the ship, if someone *should* shoot Jason Clairemont—not that I was rooting for that to happen, you understand, but if it did—at least we could narrow our search down to the people actually aboard.

By lunchtime we had shot enough takes for MacAullif and Clark to have come to the conclusion it probably *wasn't* going to happen, and to realize their inspection of the prop guns and blank cartridges was probably a waste of time. In fact, I had that opinion from Sergeant MacAullif himself. He sidled up to me at one point after checking the guns and muttered out of the side of his mouth that the whole thing was a major pain in the ass, and an easier way to tell if the guns were loaded with blanks would be to shoot Jason Clairemont's bodyguard and see if he died.

Anyway, we got through the morning shooting without incident and broke for lunch.

Which was a brand-new ball game.

Naturally, there was no way to drive a catering truck up on the ship. The caterers had set out the hot trays and tables on the shore next to the gangplank. Which was a rude surprise for Sergeant Clark, who'd been up on deck and hadn't seen them setting up. But when the AD called lunch break, there were the caterers at the top of the gangplank, ready to usher everyone off the ship.

Which created a small jurisdictional dispute. Clark, for security's sake, wanted the caterers to bring the food and tables up on deck. Sidney wouldn't hear of it. If he didn't feed the crew now he risked going into meal penalty, which would cost him a fortune, and how would Sergeant Clark like to be responsible for the resultant tab?

A compromise was quickly reached—the crew would eat on shore, Jason Clairemont would eat on deck.

That pleased the TV crews that had stuck around about as much as one would expect.

It wasn't the way Sidney Garfellow would have liked it either, but he made the most of the situation.

"Ladies and gentlemen of the media," he declared, striking a pose at the foot of the gangplank and making sure to wait until the cameras were rolling. "I know you're waiting to see Jason Clairemont. I regret to inform you he will not be coming down. Because of the threat to his life, Jason Clairemont is lunching on deck."

The announcement was met by a chorus of boos.

Sidney held up his hands. "I know you're disappointed, but this is not my decision. I am following the orders of the New York Police Department."

With that, Sidney turned and strode back up the gangplank.

I was standing next to MacAullif. "Clever son of a bitch," he murmured.

"Yeah."

Sergeant Clark came over. "That man turns everything to his own use, doesn't he?"

"You're not eating on deck?" I said.

"No."

"Who is?"

"Jason, Sidney, the bodyguard, and the assistant director."

"Oh, that's interesting," I said. I shouldn't have.

"Why?" Clark said.

"The dynamics. She was messing around with Sidney, then she went out with Jason Clairemont."

Clark gave me a look. "Are you conducting your own investigation?"

"Not at all," I said. "She volunteered the information. Yesterday, she came up to me, wanted to know why you were hassling her about going out with Jason Clairemont."

"You say *she* brought this up?"

"Yes. But not like she had anything to hide. More like, why did people care about her personal life?"

"Thank you for that insightful assessment," Clark said. "For the moment, if I could ask a small favor."

That surprised me. "What?"

"If you gentlemen could keep your eyes open. I'm not at all happy about the crew eating down here."

"Why?" I said. "Jason Clairemont's eating up there."

"Yes, of course," Sergeant Clark said. "But we've only Sidney Garfellow's word for it that Jason Clairemont's the one the murderer is after. Just because you're working on a movie is no reason to get taken in by the hype."

With that. Clark moved off to inspect the perimeter.

There was indeed a perimeter. We were eating within a circle formed by police sawhorses and a rope. The rope extended from one side of the back to the catering truck and ran around a huge circle encompassing all the tables, ending at the other side of the back of the catering truck. The sanctity of the circle was being maintained by the two policemen from the mayor's office who, all things considered, weren't doing a bad job.

I took Sergeant Clark's hint, looked around for potential saboteurs. Saw none.

"I don't see anybody looks like they want to kill anybody," I said to MacAullif. "Whaddya say we eat?"

"Yeah. Right."

We grabbed trays and hopped on the buffet line. Which was slower than usual. Mamma and the girl were waiting on the party on deck, which left Papa serving alone. It occurred to me to wonder whether a slow lunch line could trigger meal penalty.

Finally, MacAullif and I got our food. We took our trays and sat down at a table with Clarity Gray.

"How you doing?" I said as we sat down. "You recover yet?"

"Recover?"

"From the questioning. I remember you weren't too happy about it."

"Oh," she said. "No, that was all right. I just get flustered. Can't remember things."

"I can't imagine that," MacAullif said.

"Oh, yes," Clarity said. "I'm a regular scatterbrain."

"You're kidding," MacAullif said. "With a job like that?"

"Well, not on the job," Clarity said. "That's something else. If it's job-related, I know." She frowned, shook her head. "In fact, that's part of the problem. If it's not job-related, I don't have to remember it, so I don't. See what I mean?"

"Was there anything Sergeant Clark wanted you to remember that you couldn't?"

"Remember? No. There were things he wished I'd seen that I hadn't. But nothing I couldn't remember." She smiled, shrugged. "Unless I'd forgotten it completely."

MacAullif and I both laughed, and I was relieved. It had bothered me that she'd been nervous about being questioned. It was nice to think that was just a normal apprehension about cops and didn't mean anything.

I smiled, felt good for the first time in some time.

And who should come walking up to our table but Murky Doyle.

Damn. I hated him for breaking the mood. Whatever the pain in the ass had to say, I didn't want to hear it.

"We're collecting for Charlie's wife and kids," Murky said. "Anything you'd care to donate would be appreciated."

Damn. The ultimate bring-down. Just when I want to resent the guy, he's doing something good. That's for starters. But what he's doing is killing the mood with widowed wives and orphaned children. Thanks, Murky. Thanks a lot.

I put in twenty dollars, not rich enough to afford more but feeling like it wasn't enough. I felt somewhat vindicated when MacAullif and Clarity kicked in twenties too.

When Murky moved off, none of us felt like talking. I attacked my food and looked around the dining area. Murky had moved on to another table and was making his spiel. I didn't have to watch that again. I looked some more.

Another table seemed to be composed of the department heads. Along with Jake Decker were the art director, the gaffer, the DP, and the cranky prop man.

At another table were the second assistant director with a bunch of actors, including Jason Clairemont's stunt double.

At a far table was a young man I recognized but for a moment couldn't place. A tall, gawky young man. Of course. Jason Clairemont's personal gofer. Now that Jason had a bodyguard, he was odd man out.

As I watched, he was joined at the table by the original gofer, Dan. My one triumph in this investigation. The kid I'd caught red-handed in the petty theft of a blondie.

I was aware of someone setting a tray down next to me and turned to look. It was Sergeant Clark.

"Well," he said. "Everything seems secure for the moment. I guess I can eat."

There came the sound of an explosion, like a loud gunshot.

It wasn't.

It was thunder.

And it began to pour.

30.

As Robin Williams would say, it was déjà vu all over again.

There we were, back at the warehouse, dripping wet, about to shoot a cover set. Just like day one.

Only we didn't have Hot Babe Number One, she was wrapped. And we didn't have Hot Babe Number Four, she was just exteriors on the boat. But we did have Hot Babe Number Two, called in expressly for the purpose of shooting some cover-set scenes that were to include—ta da da da!—partial nudity. So despite the change in the weather, I was actually feeling pretty good.

Sergeant Clark, probably unaware of that wrinkle in the shooting schedule, was not.

"Check your equipment," Clark said.

Sound mixer Murky Doyle gave him a look. Murky, like everyone else on the crew, was crowded around the catering truck, trying to get a cup of coffee to warm up from the rain.

"What was that?" Murky said. It was almost a sneer.

"I want you to check your equipment. Make sure it didn't get wet."

"It didn't get wet," Murky said.

"I want you to check it."

197

"Hey," Murky said. "It's *my* equipment. You think I'm not going to check it out?"

"I'm sure you are. I just want you to check it particularly."

"Why?"

"Isn't this how your first boom man got hurt? Isn't this how Charles Masterson got a shock?"

"No. Someone messed with the wires."

"So you say. But weren't the circumstances the same? They're filming outdoors, it rained, they came indoors, and on the first take this happened?"

"Yeah, because someone crossed the wires."

Murky was now one spot away from the coffee urn, and not to be deflected, no matter how persuasive Sergeant Clark's arguments were. Perhaps sensing this, Clark waited until he got his coffee before trying again.

"Fine, Murky," he said. "I accept the idea someone crossed the wires. Aside from that, isn't this exactly the situation you had before? The equipment was outside, got wet when it rained."

"Absolutely not," Murky said. "How many times do I have to tell you? The equipment *wasn't* outside. Sound wasn't called for the street scenes. I was home in bed. I rushed over here, set up the equipment, and it happened."

"You may not have been there, but the equipment was. On the camera truck. If they unloaded it to get at something else, wouldn't the equipment have gotten wet?"

"Sure. But nothing would have happened if someone hadn't crossed the wires."

"There's no chance of the same thing happening today?"

"Not at all. I've been using the equipment all morning and it's fine."

"And it wouldn't make any difference if it got wet?"

"If it got wet, I'll dry it off. Big deal. It's not gonna hurt anyone. Not unless someone was screwing with the machine. And they didn't. I was using it all morning. It's fine."

"What about lunch?"

"Huh?"

"What about lunchtime? You were down on the dock. Eating lunch. Taking up a collection, as I recall. Where was your equipment then?"

"On board the ship."

"Who was watching it?"

"Huh?"

"During lunch. Who was watching your equipment then?"

"I dunno."

"So. Anyone could have tampered with the equipment then."

Murky gave Sergeant Clark a look, then stomped off toward the set.

"You really think that's true?" I asked Sergeant Clark.

"I have no idea."

"Well, who could have gotten on board the ship to tamper with the equipment? I mean, they'd have had to have come up the gangplank. Someone would have seen them."

"The caterers came up."

"What?"

"And some people were there already. Jason Clairemont. Sidney Garfellow. The bodyguard and the AD. And who'd have given it a moment's thought if, while they were waiting for lunch, one of them had wandered over to the set."

My eyes widened. "You really think they did?"

"Not at all," Clark said. "I don't really suspect anything of the kind. I just want the man to check his equipment. Now he will."

MacAullif and I got coffee and strolled over to the set. Sure enough, there was Murky Doyle puttering with his Nagra. He didn't look pleased. Of course, that was his normal expression. But after his conversation with Sergeant Clark, I had a feeling he was pissed off to find his equipment *hadn't* been tampered with.

While MacAullif and I stood watching, someone switched on the power, lighting up the set. It was Vivian's apartment. Vivian, of course, was Hot Babe Number Two. Though, actually, it occurred to me, she would be Hot Babe Number

One. Because, chronologically, she is the first hot babe in the script. But as I said, you don't shoot a movie in sequence. So Blaire, whom I'd come to think of as Hot Babe Number One, was really the second hot babe in the script. And Vivian, whom I'd referred to as Hot Babe Number Two, was really Hot Babe Number One.

Don't worry, there won't be a quiz on this later. I'm just trying to keep it straight in my own head.

Anyway, Vivian is the first hot babe Rick calls on when he breaks out of prison. That's because she used to be his girlfriend. You see, they had a *prior relationship.* That's why it was so stupid from a dramatic point of view for Rick and *Blaire* to have had a prior relationship. Because then it's the *same* fucking relationship, and you wind up shooting the *same* fucking scene.

I'm sorry. I'm just not rational on the subject.

Anyway, while we watched, the crew began readying the set, which had been designed by the art director, Mr. This-will-do-nicely, and constructed in the middle of the second floor of the warehouse. It was a modern apartment, consisting of Vivian's bedroom and bath. The latter was complete with fixtures, including toilet, sink, and shower. The toilet and sink were not functional, but the shower had been equipped with hot and cold running water.

That's where the partial nudity came in.

In the scene I had written, Vivian is taking a shower when Rick, who has broken into her apartment, suddenly joins her. This allows for a *Psycho* parody, but the real humor in the scene comes from the fact that when Rick steps into the shower he is fully clothed.

Vivian isn't.

And, condemn me or not, but in my humble opinion, that was probably why in this particular instance the crew was attacking the set with more vigor than they were usually wont to display.

"Are they gonna keep us out?" MacAullif said.

I didn't have to ask what he meant—when the babe got in

the shower, was Sidney going to declare a closed set and boot the crew?

"I don't know."

"You seen her yet?" MacAullif asked.

Actually, I hadn't. I'd never met the actress Sidney had cast and, due to the efficiency of the second AD, who'd called her from the ship when it had started to rain, she'd actually beaten us to the warehouse and was now in makeup.

"No, I haven't."

"If she's anything like yesterday . ." MacAullif shook his head. "Unbelievable."

Actually, she wasn't. And when I saw her, my estimation of Sidney went up a notch.

She was a real person.

The actress playing Vivian was a young woman of medium height and weight with medium-length brown hair, straight and cut in bangs, framing a bright, intelligent, schoolgirl face. She was full-figured, but not disproportionately so. As opposed to Hot Babe Number Four, the actress playing Vivian was an actual human being.

"So, what do you think?" Sidney said, appearing between me and MacAullif and clapping us on the shoulder.

"Huh?" MacAullif said. "What do you mean?"

"Her," Sidney said. He jerked his thumb out at the set, where the actress, dressed in sweater and skirt, was checking the props in her bedroom.

"Oh," MacAullif said. "Well . . ."

"Isn't she gorgeous?" Sidney said.

"Yes, but . . ."

"But what?"

"Well, the one you had yesterday—too bad *she's* not going in the shower."

"Well, there's where you're wrong," Sidney said. "The girl yesterday, I got her on the boat, she jumps up, flashes her boobs, that's fine and we're done with her." He pointed. "Now, this girl here. She's gonna strip and get in the shower. And let me tell you, the audience is gonna dig this more than that. Why? You see a stripper take her clothes off, no big deal, it's what she does. But you see an ordinary person. Like her. It's something else. It's the girl next door, taking her clothes off. The mind boggles."

Sidney paused, nodded in agreement with himself. "I did a documentary, *Down and Dirty*. You saw it, Stanley. You know. I've studied this shit. What turns people on. And here we have it both ways. We have the fantasy woman on the boat, and the reality woman in the shower. Hell, you wouldn't wanna shoot the same scene twice."

The thought *unless Jason Clairemont rewrote it* sprang to mind, but I did not voice it.

Sidney looked up at MacAullif and must have seen doubt on his face, 'cause he chucked him on the shoulder, said, "Hey, trust me," and went to check out the camera.

MacAullif may have had doubts, but mine sure vanished fast. Because I'd seen Sidney's documentaries back when we'd first started working on the script, and I knew the man wasn't kidding. Arousing prurient interest happened to be his strong suit. And when the unnamed actress playing Vivian, or Hot Babe Number One, or Two, as you prefer, who wasn't a hot babe at all but an actual woman, a living, breathing human being, began taking her clothes off, it was exciting as hell.

As for the partial-nudity bit, well, that's what it said in the script. Because that's what we'd see on the screen. That's the way Sidney was shooting the shot.

But the actress herself was totally nude. She took off her sweater and she took off her skirt. And then she took off her bra and she took off her panties. And then she turned on the shower and she stepped in.

And Sidney didn't close the set. We gathered around and we saw it all. Believe me, it was standing room only. Even Papa from the catering truck. Even the teamsters, who'd driven their trucks up in the elevator. The whole world watched that scene shot.

If that bothered the actress any, she sure didn't show it.

Boy, she was good. She took off her clothes without the slightest hint of embarrassment, just as if she were alone in her apartment. Then she went in the bathroom, turned on the water, adjusted the temperature, got in the shower, and then and only then pulled the curtain closed.

Setting up the entrance of nerdy twerp superstar.

And here he came, giving his Tony Perkins impression. He reached the shower curtain and, as the camera panned up his back, grabbed the top of the curtain and gave a yank.

The curtain flies open and Vivian gives a startled cry and wheels around to discover:

Rick, fully dressed and standing in the stream of water that hit him as soon as she spun around and moved out of it.

"You!" she cried. "What are you doing here?"

Which wouldn't have been that bad if Blaire didn't say *exactly* the same thing in Jason Clairemont's rewrite.

And if what he was doing there didn't happen to be standing on a box. Because, as I said, the actress was of average height, and, Jason being short, the relationship wasn't going to play. So the set crew had built a three-inch-high platform to cover approximately a third of the bottom of the shower where Jason had to stand. Otherwise, when the babe wheeled around she might slap him in the face with her tits.

All right, it wasn't really that bad. With the platform he was actually an inch or two taller than her. No, I'm just a middle-aged married man resenting the fact he's a young movie star and that *he's* in there now with this gorgeous naked woman who's about to throw her arms around his neck and kiss him.

Which she did.

Jason said, "Just dropped in for a shower."

Which *I* had actually written. I guess he hadn't had time to change it yet. But this being a cover set that they hadn't rehearsed, it occurred to me he'd probably rewrite it before they shot.

It also occurred to me it wasn't that great a line. Out of all the lines of dialogue he could choose to leave alone, the kid has to pick that one?

Anyway, Vivian said, "Oh, Rick," and threw her arms around his neck.

Hugging him to her. Pressing her body against his. Pressing her firm, young, full breasts to die for up against his chest. Till not just me, but I'd bet you every man in the place secretly wished he were him.

It had just occurred to me, to my chagrin, that I'd been so caught up in what I'd been watching that I hadn't even noticed that Murky Doyle had rolled sound ages ago and nothing bad had happened, when a sandbag whizzed from the ceiling and sent Jason Clairemont, nerdy twerp superstar, crashing to the shower floor.

31.

No, he wasn't hurt. It didn't hit him on the head. It smashed the platform he was standing on, and he fell.

It *could* have killed him. It nearly did. Just a few inches was all.

Actually, the actress saved his life. Pulled him toward her slightly in the embrace. Had she leaned in to him, they might both be dead. As it was, he was shaken but unharmed.

Not that that cheered Sergeant Clark any. I don't think I've ever seen him so upset. He actually raised his voice.

Clark strode out in the middle of the set and said, "All right, nobody move!" He turned, pointed to Jason. "Are you all right?"

Rather shakily Jason said, "I think so."

"Fine. *You* can move. Get up and get out of there. You too, miss. Get your robe on and get out of here. Everyone else, stay where you are."

Clark wheeled on MacAullif. "Sergeant, take the door. See that no one goes in or out. Is that the only exit?"

"There's a back door, but it's usually locked."

"*Is* it locked?" Clark demanded.

"It's locked," Jake Decker said. I hadn't even realized he was there.

"Good," Clark said. "Are there any other exits?"

"Just the freight elevator."

"Which will not be used," Clark said. "Is that clear? No one's leaving here till I have a list of everyone on the floor. Where's the script supervisor?"

"Huh? Right here," Clarity said.

"Yes. Miss Gray, is it? If you'd do me the favor. You have pencil and paper, you're good at taking notes. If you would assist Sergeant MacAullif, please. I want to clear this area, send everyone downstairs. If you would please check them off as they go. That's right, over there with Sergeant MacAullif. Go on now, thank you very much."

"See here," Sidney said. "You can't stop me from shooting."

"I just did," Sergeant Clark said. "And if you thought about it, you wouldn't object. This was no accident. This was an attempt on Jason Clairemont's life. One that very nearly succeeded. You can hire all the bodyguards you like and give speeches on TV, that's fine in terms of publicity, but you must see it hasn't done a particle of good in terms of protecting your star. I don't want to tell you your business, but I should think that would be your first priority. As for right now, I expect your entire cooperation. Help me out here and you might be shooting before the afternoon's over, though frankly I doubt it. But stand around and argue and I guarantee you there'll be no time for anything at all."

For a moment the two men stood there glaring at each other. It was almost funny. Sidney towered over Clark, but it was clear which man had the upper hand. I wondered how Sidney would save face.

He did so by agreeing wholeheartedly, probably even as newspaper headlines danced in his head. "All right, you heard the man," Sidney said, addressing us all. "There's been an attack on our star. It's rally-round time. We gotta close ranks, pull together. Get beyond this. Above all, we gotta show Jason we're in his corner. Anyone who doesn't cooperate with the sergeant here will answer to me personally."

Sergeant Clark, ever pragmatic, was quite content to let that self-serving statement stand. "Thank you, Mr. Garfellow. To begin with, I want everyone downstairs. Please, everyone form a line at the door. Sign out with Sergeant MacAullif and wait downstairs."

Sergeant Clark turned. "Except you, Mr. Clairemont. Please stay here." He turned to the bodyguard, who was hovering solicitously if somewhat sheepishly and who gave the impression that while not quite bright enough to figure out if this was actually his fault, still he had managed to grasp the idea some people might not be entirely satisfied with the performance of his job. "You too, Mr. Pollack," Clark added with just a trace of irony. "If you would be so kind."

Clark turned to the actress. "You too, ma'am. And you, Mr. Garfellow. The rest of you, line up and check out."

I wasn't sure if he meant me. I didn't want to go, but I didn't want to ask either. As a compromise I got on the end of the line, so I could talk to MacAullif after everyone else left.

Fortunately, that didn't take very long. Clarity was efficient. She also had a crew list. She didn't have to write the names, just check 'em off. Within minutes they were all downstairs and I had reached the door.

"Is that everybody?" I said.

"Seems to be," MacAullif said.

"You want me downstairs?"

"Good lord, no," MacAullif said. "I want you up here to solve the crime."

If Clarity hadn't been standing there I would have had a choice comment. As it was I just smiled. At least I wasn't headed downstairs.

"Here's the list," Clarity said. "Do you want it, or should I hang onto it?"

"No, I'll take it," MacAullif said. "Thanks."

"Should I wait downstairs?"

"Yes, if you wouldn't mind."

Clarity smiled. "Then I'll check me off."

She did so, handed the list to MacAullif, went downstairs.

"I think she likes you," I said when she was out of earshot.

"Don't start with me," MacAullif said. "We are in deep shit."

"Clark's really pissed, isn't he?"

"Yes, he is. Do you know why?"

" 'Cause Sidney's bodyguard didn't do any good."

"Fuck the bodyguard. Who gives a damn about him. *We* didn't do any good. Me, you, Clark. But particularly him. Look what happens here. The boom man does a brodie right in front of our noses, we don't see nothing. Well, we weren't lookin' for it. But now we're all on the set, we're all lookin' out for everything. You, me, Clark, we're all there, ever vigilant. And what happens? The kid almost gets taken out, and we don't see a thing."

"It happens."

"Yeah, it happens. But it couldn't have happened worse. You know why?" MacAullif jerked his thumb. "Her. The babe. There's a naked broad running around. A nudie cutie on the set. Now, it don't make two shits worth of difference, 'cause no one would have seen the thing comin' anyway. But as far as the brass are concerned, we're all standin' around with our dicks hangin' out, oglin' a pair of tits while a murder attempt is taking place. And what's the implication? If we hadn't been droolin' over the naked broad, we would have seen who did it."

"That's ridiculous."

"Did you see who did it?"

"No."

"There you are."

"If you gentlemen wouldn't mind."

MacAullif and I turned to see Sergeant Clark standing there.

"I hate to interrupt," he said. "But we do have this murder attempt. If you wouldn't mind."

I can't think of anyone else in the world Sergeant MacAullif would have let talk to him like that. It occurred to me, it wasn't as though Clark was his superior officer—they were both homicide sergeants. But in Sergeant Clark's case, MacAullif never seemed to answer in kind.

"Right," MacAullif said. "We were just discussing our present publicity problem."

"It's not a problem," Clark said. "It's just an unfortunate situation. When Sidney Garfellow gives his next press interview, we are going to look like the Three Stooges. But there's nothing we can do about it. Trying to suppress it would make us look even worse."

During this, Sergeant Clark had led us back over to the set, which was now bare.

"Where is everyone?" MacAullif said.

Clark pointed. "In wardrobe. The woman's getting dressed. Jason Clairemont is hanging out with his bodyguard. Sidney Garfellow is with them. I left him nominally in charge."

"To keep him away from the press?"

"Partly. I want him up here out of harm's way."

"Him?" I said. "This was clearly an attack on Jason."

"Perhaps," Sergeant Clark said. "But even so. He strikes me as a secondary target somehow. Anyway, his job is keeping them entertained and away from us. Which will also keep *him* away from us."

"So what have we got?" MacAullif said.

"Your simple, basic booby trap. I'd like to leave it there for the time being, but do take a look." He stepped aside, indicating the bathroom. "I've turned the water off," he said, "but aside from that, it's just the way it was."

MacAullif and I squeezed past the camera and took a look.

The sandbag was lying in the middle of the shower floor. There was a good-sized pool of water around it, as it happened to be blocking the drain. Pieces of wood from the splintered platform floated in the water.

The sandbag was the type used on movie sets, usually to anchor the base of light stands, a canvas bag which if laid out flat would be a long rectangle. That in turn had been sewn into four rounded rectangular pouches of sand. Sewn into the strip between the middle two pouches was a steel ring, in case you wanted to hang the sandbag from something.

Which is what had been done in this case. A rope was tied to the steel ring. It ran up to the ceiling and over a pipe there. The other end of the rope hung down behind the back wall of the shower.

"About ten feet," Clark said, reading my mind. "On the floor, I mean. Back there. The ceiling's about twenty feet high. So you've got twenty feet up, twenty feet down. About ten feet of slack on this side and ten feet back there. We can measure it later, but say sixty feet in all. Now, when your sandbag is hoisted to the ceiling"—Sergeant Clark pointed up to where the rope went over the pole—"the perpetrator is about sixty feet from there."

Clark looked back at us. "Not to labor the obvious," he said, "but this is not a booby trap in the conventional sense. That is, something that is rigged that the victim trips, springing the trap. Obviously, in this case the perpetrator held onto the end of the rope and released it at the proper moment."

"So," MacAullif said. "If we measure the rope, we can figure out where he must have stood."

"Without even measuring, we could simply hoist it up again," Clark said. "But we'd be guessing, because it must have gone over another pipe too."

"How do you know?" I said.

"Take a look," Clark said.

We went out of the bathroom and around to the back of the set where the rope hung down.

"See," Clark said. "You could stand here, pull the rope, hoist the sandbag up to the ceiling. It would be out of sight. But see the rope? It would come straight down behind the back of the shower wall. Not in the shot, but right in plain sight. Surely someone would see it. Any distractions on the set not withstanding. And the killer's not going to want to stand there, right next to the set, holding a rope. Too good a chance he'd be seen."

"I wouldn't count it out," I said. "The guy doesn't have to be bright."

He waved it away. "It's a moot point. Look at the floor. Where would you tie it off? There's no place to tie the rope. And it must have been tied off, because it had to be rigged in advance. No one climbed up there and threw that rope over the pipe this afternoon while everyone was working on the set. It was rigged in advance and tied off. Then this afternoon it was untied, held till the proper moment, then released. If it couldn't have been tied, it wasn't here."

"It's a long rope," I said. "After it's pulled up, I mean. It could have been tied off anywhere."

"Right," Clark said. "But you take the rope, you walk to the back wall. Pull it tight and tie it off. Then you have a big diagonal of rope from ceiling to floor going across the whole warehouse. And if it's there for a while, someone's going to see it. No, the rope has to go over another pipe. Like over there," he said, pointing to the ceiling near the back wall. "There's a bunch of pipes up there, it's got to be one of them. It went over there, around the pipe, and down the side wall. You could tie it off anywhere—to a pipe, to a valve, to a two-by-four. It doesn't matter. That's where the rope was, and that's where the killer was. And that's a big break-through for us."

"Because someone might have seen him there?" I said.

Clark shook his head. "No one saw him there. Everyone was watching the set. That's what the killer counted on and he was right. Very clever. But maybe a little too clever."

"What do you mean?"

"We now know who the killer *wasn't*. Anyone who was on that set. Jason Clairemont. Sidney Garfellow. Just to name the obvious. That's not to say they couldn't be involved, they couldn't be an accomplice. But they were not the perpetrator of that particular act.

"And who was? Someone who wasn't there.

"Which we can determine. We have a list here of everyone who was on the floor. One person on that list wasn't watching the shower scene being filmed. If we can eliminate everyone who was, we'll be left with who wasn't."

"Jesus Christ."

Sergeant Clark said, "It's not that bad. You're a witness. I'm a witness. Everyone on this list is a witness. And everyone will have seen someone. And every little bit will help."

"Hold on a minute," I said.

"What?" Clark said.

"I have a problem with the whole premise."

"Oh. What's that?"

"I'm just trying to picture it in my head. The rope goes over the two pipes, the sandbag's hoisted up, the killer stands there."

"Yes. So?"

"So how does he know when to drop the rope? He's behind the set, he can't see a thing."

"Yes, but he can hear. He listens for the cue. That's the beauty of the little platform they built. He knows where Jason's going to stand, so he doesn't have to see him at all."

"Yeah, but how does he know the cue? How does he know he's there?"

"He watches the rehearsal," Clark said. "And that's our real clue. It was someone who was there when they rehearsed the scene, but wasn't there when they shot it. Because that's the way it had to be. The guy stood there and watched them rehearse. The dry run, as it were, with the shower off and the actress clothed. Then Sidney said, Let's go for picture. And your killer slipped out of the crowd, around to the back of the set to the back wall, untied the rope, and waited for the cue."

"Fine," I said. "That makes sense. But tell me something. Do you have any idea who this killer was?"

"That's a difficult question," Clark said. "I have *ideas*, but I don't think they're founded on the type of evidence you're talking about. Like personal observation. So I'd have to say no, I don't."

"Me neither," MacAullif said. "If I had to name someone

who was there for rehearsal who wasn't there for the shoot, I couldn't do it. Could you?"

"No way," I said.

"Fine," Clark said. "How about the other way around?"

"I beg your pardon?"

"Who can you name who definitely *was* there when we shot?"

"Oh," I said. "That's easy. Jason Clairemont. The actress."

"Yes, I thought you'd get them," Clark said dryly.

"Ah, Sidney Garfellow. The DP."

"Just a minute. Did you actually see them, or are you just assuming they were there?"

"I saw them," I said. "The DP was sitting at the camera. Sidney was standing next to him. I both saw and heard him, because he said 'action.' The AD said 'roll it'—the first AD, the woman. Murky Doyle said 'speed.' I heard that. I didn't see him, but I know I heard it. Because it didn't register on me until later that he'd rolled sound but nothing had happened. It hadn't shorted out, I mean. Because that's what we were worried about. And it occurred to me the man had called 'speed' and everything was all right. But it wasn't."

"Thank you for that succinct assessment," Clark said. "If the other witnesses' thought processes are as convoluted, we'll be here all day. Go on. Anyone else?"

I frowned. Thought. "MacAullif," I said.

"Excellent," Clark said. "That narrows it down. I can see the case is almost solved."

"Thanks a lot," I said. "Tell me, do you intend to be as sarcastic with the general public?"

"Not at all," Clark said. "I'm trying to get it out of my system now."

I took a breath. Exhaled. "Papa," I said.

Clark frowned. "I beg your pardon?"

"The guy from the catering truck. We call him Papa. I remember he was there."

"For the actual filming?"

"Had to be. He was looking at naked flesh. Also, some of the teamsters."

"*Some* of the teamsters?"

"I don't know them by name. But I recognized some of them there."

"Would you know their names if you heard them?"

"I'm not sure."

"Well, they're on the list. If you don't know their names, you may have to ID them."

"Great," I said. Identifying teamsters didn't exactly strike me as the healthiest of occupations, even if it was merely to exonerate 'em.

"Anyone else," Clark said.

"Well . . ."

"Great," he said. He turned to MacAullif. "Sergeant?"

MacAullif took a breath. "I would like to point out, he has already named the people who were obviously there."

"Thanks a lot," I said.

"Which is why my list is so short," MacAullif went on, irritably.

"And just who is on it?" Clark said.

MacAullif took another breath. Exhaled. "You are."

Sergeant Clark shook his head. "Thank you, Sergeant," he said. He clapped his hands together. "Gentlemen. We would appear to have our work cut out for us."

32.

Our work may have been cut out for us, but it was Sergeant Clark who did it. The questioning, I mean. He handled it all by himself. First he told Sidney tough luck but filming anymore today wasn't going to fly, and sent Jason Clairemont and the bodyguard home. He sent the actress home too, and commandeered the makeup room for questioning. He sent MacAullif to ride herd over the mob downstairs, and consigned Sidney and me to the herd. I can attest to the fact that neither of us was particularly thrilled.

The questioning took all afternoon and then some. The crew hung out in the rehearsal hall next to the catering truck, which Clark had wisely allowed to be driven onto the freight elevator and brought downstairs. We all stood around drinking coffee in dwindling numbers, as crew member after crew member was summoned and led away, never to return.

Sergeant Clark didn't get to Sidney Garfellow till around six o'clock. He must have had a good deal to say to him, or vice versa, because MacAullif didn't come back for the next one till six-fifteen.

It was eight-thirty when he came to get me. And when he did, I was the only one there. Dead last. That figured.

Only it turned out Sergeant Clark didn't want to question me at all.

"Sit down, gentlemen," Clark said when MacAullif ushered me into the room.

The makeup room, which was an impromptu affair thrown together with two-by-fours and Sheetrock, consisted of a makeup counter, some clothes racks, and half-a-dozen canvas folding director's chairs. MacAullif and I sat down facing Clark, who was seated beside the makeup counter. On the counter in front of him was a stack of papers. He picked them up, put them in his lap.

"All right, gentlemen," he said. "Let me give you what I've got."

"Anything promising?" MacAullif said.

"Could be worse."

"What's all that?" I said, indicating the papers.

"Crew lists," Clark said. "Well, not the entire crew. But lists of everyone who was on the set when the incident took place. I had the secretary type it up from Clarity's list. So it's not just the crew—it's a complete list of everyone who was on the set."

"What about the rest of them?"

"I beg your pardon?"

"The rest of the papers."

"Oh. They're all crew lists. I had her xerox them. They're all the same list. A hundred and some-odd copies."

I frowned. "What's the point?"

"One for each witness," Clark said. "Hang on and let me tell you what I've got. Each person I questioned, I asked them who they saw on the set. At the time of the incident. Like I did with you. Whoever they saw, I checked off on the sheet." He picked up the top paper. "And on the master sheet. So from these," he said, pointing to the pile, "I know who saw who. And from this," he said, holding up the top sheet, "I know everyone who was seen."

"Is it helpful?" I said.

"Absolutely. Taken at face value, these eliminate over half the crew. Maybe three-quarters."

"Can you take 'em at face value?" I asked.

"For the most part." Clark shrugged. "People may be inaccurate, and they may lie. But in many instances there's corroboration."

Clark put down the top sheet, picked up another paper from the makeup counter. He held it up and turned it around. It was another list with several check marks after the names. "See. Here's a cumulative summary. A bit messy, but still a help. Tells how *many* people saw each person. In almost every case, if someone was seen by one person, he was seen by at least two. There are only four names with only one check mark next to them. Two are teamsters who saw each other. Another is the caterer. The one you call Papa. No one saw him but you."

"He was there."

"I don't doubt it," Clark said. "It just so happens no one else saw him."

"What about the other caterers?"

"No one saw them at all."

"No, I mean, why didn't they see him?"

"They weren't there. At least, the woman wasn't. She was working on the truck. The girl *should* have been working on the truck, but I gather she was trying to take a peek at the set. Anyway, she names half-a-dozen people she saw there, but not him."

"Too bad."

"She does name the gofer, Dan. That's the other one with one vote. She's it."

"But he didn't name her?"

"No, like I said, no one did. As I recall, he named a whole bunch of people, but not her."

"Then they weren't together?"

"Why should they be?"

"I don't know. It just occurred to me there might be some attraction there."

"That's possible," Clark said. "Which would explain why

she would notice him. While he would be too preoccupied with the shower scene to notice her."

"What about the people no one saw at all?" MacAullif said. "How many are there of them?"

"Entirely too many," Clark said. "I haven't actually counted, but let's run them down." Clark switched papers, picked up the master list. "Some of these fall into groups. Like the two caterers. We also have four teamsters."

"That no one saw?"

"That's right."

"Well, you didn't do a sheet on me. I may be able to help you there."

"Maybe, maybe not," Clark said. "You wouldn't know the names."

"Right."

"Then you couldn't do it tonight. Because they're gone. And your information may or may not be valuable."

"Why?"

"How many did you see?"

"Two or three."

Clark grimaced. "See? That's where your information becomes somewhat less than useful. There's no such thing as two and a half teamsters. A teamster was either there or he wasn't. If you're not sure, it doesn't count."

"I'm sure."

"Oh, really? And how many faces were you sure you saw?" Before I could frame an answer, Clark went on. "Another reason it doesn't matter is that there weren't four teamsters, there were eight. Four were seen, four weren't. So the ones you saw may just duplicate the ones I've already checked off."

"I find that strange," I said.

"What's that?"

"That you haven't got them all. I would think they would be in a group. Would alibi each other. But four of them don't."

"That's not all that surprising," Clark said. "Just between

us, these are not the swiftest gentlemen in the world. I wouldn't trust their powers of observation on the one hand, or their veracity on the other."

"That's a rather elitist attitude," I said.

"Please," Clark said. "I'm not trying to win an election, I'm trying to solve a crime. The fact is, I would expect some of the gentlemen in question to misunderstand why I'm asking who they saw at the scene, and to deliberately refrain from naming their buddies as a matter of course. If this is an unfair assessment, I'm sorry. But the fact is, I don't seriously consider the teamsters as suspects."

Clark referred to his paper. "If we could move on. The next group are gofers. Two of them. Harold and Phil."

"The names don't help," I said. "Who are they?"

"Phil is Jason Clairemont's driver. Harold's the other one. Let me see. Oh, at the construction site, he was the one who gave us the hard hats."

"Right. And they didn't see each other?"

"No. Or Dan either. Though, from what I gather, they didn't tend to hang out as a group."

"It's odd they'd all be on the set though," I said. "You'd think some of them would have work elsewhere, like in the office or running errands."

"You're forgetting what we were filming," Clark said. "No matter what their jobs, somehow everyone on the crew managed to find time to take a look."

"Right," I said. "Who else?"

Clark went down the list. "Two grips. Three electricians. Two carpenters." He took a breath, turned the page. "Three stunt men."

"Stunt men? Wait a minute," I said. "What stunt men?"

"From the ship. This morning. They were eating lunch when it started to rain, so they were brought back here with everybody else. They went to wardrobe, changed out of costume, and were wrapped." I smiled to see that Clark was beginning to pick up movie terminology. Fortunately, he didn't notice. "A couple of stunt men went home," he said, "but most of them stuck around to see the shoot. Of those, three of them weren't seen on the set."

"Wait a minute," I said. "Of those, was one of them . . ."

"What?"

"Jason Clairemont's stunt double."

"Let me see," Clark said. He consulted his notes. "What's his name?"

"I don't know."

"No matter, I marked it. *SD* for stunt double. Nelson Kilmer is the one, and, no, he wasn't seen."

"Son of a bitch."

"What?"

"Well, that's significant."

"Why?"

"He's Jason Clairemont's double. If Jason were to die, he could do the part."

Sergeant Clark didn't seem impressed. "How could that be? Hasn't Jason already been filmed? I mean up close? Haven't we seen his face?"

"Well, yes."

"So there you are. How could this actor step in? Unless you filmed those scenes over. And on a picture with this budget, how could that be done?

"Besides, Jason Clairemont is a star. This fellow isn't. How could you do a picture with him? I imagine some of the funding is even tied up with Jason Clairemont's name."

"Maybe so," I said. "But this guy could *think* he'd get Jason Clairemont's part."

"Just because you think so?" Clark said. "From talking to the fellow, it seems the furthest thing from his mind. Though you needn't point out that the killer would necessarily lie. I'm taking that into consideration. So your idea is noted. It's been a long day. If we could move on."

Clark referred to the paper. "Most of the department heads are present and accounted for. That includes the more obvious, like the DP, who was operating the camera, and Murky Doyle, who was running sound. As well as both their assistants, the boom operator and the first assistant cameraman, who was pulling focus on the shot. The second assistant cameraman, who was supposedly loading film magazines, was not seen, by the way.

"Anyway, the key grip and his best boy were operating the dolly. The gaffer had nothing to do at the time, but was spotted by several people watching the shot." Clark raised his head. "The art director wasn't."

"Why is that significant?" I said.

"Well, you would think someone would have noticed."

"Why? Because he's black?"

"Exactly," Clark said.

"Why?" I said. "The guy's been working on the crew all week. You think people still notice the guy's black?"

"Absolutely," Clark said. "And particularly then."

"What do you mean by that?"

"Because a white woman was nude."

I looked at Clark. "I can't believe you said that."

"Oh, for god's sake," Clark said. "You're entirely too sensitive, you know it?"

"Sensitive, hell. That's an incredibly racist statement."

"Yes, of course," Clark said. "And one we must consider."

"I beg your pardon?"

"I'm sorry to offend your sensibilities, but racism does exist. Ignoring it doesn't make it any better. Out of a hundred-odd people, there are going to be some who are offended by the idea of a black man watching a white woman undress. It may be racist, but it's a fact of life. I would expect someone to be offended and mention the fact. When no one does, it's worthy of notice. If observing that makes me a racist in your eyes, I'm sorry, but I'm trying to solve a murder here."

"Could we move on?" MacAullif said. "I'd like to get home before dawn."

"Fine," Clark said. "I have another serious omission."

"Who's that?"

"Jake Decker."

"Oh."

"Yes. No one saw him. Which is somewhat extraordinary when you consider his size." Clark turned to me. "I suppose you'd care to take offense on behalf of large people?"

I took a breath. "It's been a long day for me too," I said. "Are you seriously considering Jake Decker?"

"He's certainly a suspect," Clark said. "After all, he scouted the construction site. And originally arranged for the warehouse."

"Good lord," I said.

"What's the matter?"

"You still think that?" I said. "About the bum in the warehouse? Even after what happened today?"

"Of course," Clark said. "Why does this change anything?"

"Isn't it obvious? This trap was specifically for Jason Clairemont."

"So?"

"I think that would confirm the suspicion. The trap the boom man fell into was also intended for Jason Clairemont."

"There's a strong possibility," Clark said. "But I don't see why that makes any difference."

"You don't?"

"No," Clark said. "And I don't want to debate it now. I want to wrap this up and get home."

"Here, here," MacAullif said. "What else have you got?"

"Just a bit more," Clark said. "Now, she's not really a suspect, but the most important witness of all turns out to be the secretary, Grace."

"What?" I said in dismay.

Clark nodded. "Not one person saw her on the set. And for good reason. She wasn't there. She was downstairs typing in the office when the incident occurred. She heard the crash, jumped up, and ran upstairs. She was standing near the top of the stairs when I sent MacAullif to guard them. Is that right?"

"Absolutely," MacAullif said.

"Why is she important?" I said.

"Because the office is right next to the stairs. She heard the crash, got up, and went to the stairs. And no one came down them. A significant fact. That she is sure of. From the time the incident occurred, no one went down the stairs. By the time she got to the top of the stairs I had taken charge and was sending MacAullif over. He and she overlap. Between the two of them, we can prove no one went down those stairs. So whoever dropped the rope, they did not escape, they were there on the floor . . ." Clark pointed. "And they are here on this list."

"Unless they went up," I said.

"What?"

"Unless they went upstairs. The killer dropped the rope, went up to a higher floor, and he's hiding there now, laughing at us."

"It's a possibility," Clark said. "And I'm not going to reject it out of hand. But I'm not going to consider it, either. For the purpose of the present investigation, I am acting on the assumption I have the killer here. Should that prove not to be true, I'll be happy to admit that I'm wrong. But that's my present assumption. To move on."

"There's more?" I said.

"There's the murder weapon. Or attempted-murder weapon. The sandbag."

"Ah," I said. My interest picked up again. "What about it?"

"It was apparently from the grip truck. I say *apparently* because the key grip is somewhat less than helpful. His personal opinion is that a sandbag is a sandbag. It's just like the type they use—that he admits. And there's nothing about it to distinguish it from any of the other sandbags used on the set. On the other hand, he refuses to identify it or concede that it's his."

"Isn't that perfectly natural?"

"Absolutely. No one wants to claim a murder weapon. But in this case it's not like anyone's trying to blame the grips.

During shooting, the trucks are parked on the floor. They're open and unlocked, and the teamsters are somewhat less than vigilant. Anyone could hop in the back and take a sandbag at almost any time."

"He'd risk being seen."

"That goes without saying. But the point is, it could be done. Now, I understand that aside from today it also rained Monday and Tuesday. Both days you shot here on the set. So the sandbag could have been taken either day."

"Why not today?"

"We went over that. Because the trap had to be rigged in advance."

"Right."

"Now then, as to the earliest it could have been rigged. This particular set was built last week. It was finished on Friday, a week ago today. That's everything including the shower. All set, ready to go. Except for one thing."

"What's that."

"The platform. The one Jason Clairemont stood on. That wasn't built till Tuesday afternoon."

"Oh?"

"Yes. The way I understand it, when it rained Monday you came inside. There was the initial incident where the boom man got a shock. After that everything settled down, filming was smooth. At some point during the afternoon, in between takes, Sidney Garfellow and Jason Clairemont checked out the set. The shower set, I mean. It was at that time that they decided to build the platform."

"I didn't know that."

"No reason why you should. But that's what happened."

"How'd they come to that conclusion? I don't recall seeing the actress there."

"She wasn't."

"Then how'd they know they needed the platform?"

"Clarity Gray."

"Oh?"

"Yes. The woman's sharp. She had it in her script notes.

The fact the woman was tall. When they checked out the shower, she brought it up."

"In front of Jason?"

"No. Discreetly, to Sidney Garfellow. He in turn discussed it with the DP. Who confirms the conversation. At least I think he does—I never understand half of what that man says. Anyway, they worked it out that Jason should stand on a platform. Sidney ordered it built and it was finished the next day. That's Tuesday afternoon. I can't pinpoint the exact time, but sometime around three. That is when the platform was built. That is the time after which the killer could know that suspending the sandbag above that platform would be the way to target Jason."

"So the trap was rigged sometime after that?" MacAullif said.

"Exactly," Clark said.

"Unless . . ." I said.

"Unless what?"

"Unless it was rigged simply to hit the shower. And the construction of the platform was merely fortuitous."

"Possibly," Clark said. "But the sandbag *did* hit the platform. Hit it dead center, from what I can tell. Which would *not* be dead center of the shower. As things turned out, dead center of the shower would have been a direct hit on our young star. But the sandbag landed dead center on the *platform*. Which is what saved Jason's life. Because the actress pulled him to her." Sergeant Clark held up his finger. "Which the killer could not have known, since the scene was never rehearsed.

"So, there's our problem," Sergeant Clark went on. "Someone stole the sandbag, probably Monday or Tuesday while you were shooting on the set. Somebody rigged it, most likely sometime after Tuesday afternoon when the platform was in place. There's no way they could have rigged it then—Tuesday afternoon, I mean—everyone was here shooting, something like that would be seen. But Tuesday night there would be no problem."

"How would they get in?" I said.

"Easy. They'd simply stay."

"I beg your pardon?"

"Like you said before. How do I know the killer's not hiding on an upper floor? Frankly, I don't think he is—I think there was time to blend into the crowd, but not time to get away. But one day after work, what would be simpler than to slip upstairs, wait till everyone was gone, then come back down and rig the trap?"

"And how would they get out?" I asked. "Isn't the warehouse locked up tight?"

"In theory," Clark said. "But several people have the keys."

"Oh? And who is that?"

"Practically everybody. All the production people. That's the production manager, the gofers, and the AD's. Sidney, of course. And the secretary and the script supervisor. Then there's the department heads. Some of them have keys. The art director, for instance. And he's given it out to the carpenters, to get in and work on the set. And the gaffer has one. Not that he needs it. I gather he wanted one because the art director had one. He's the type of guy who's always afraid he won't be given his due."

I nodded. That was a damn good assessment.

"On the other hand," Clark went on, "the DP and the sound mixer don't have keys and don't want them. The attitude is, why should they have to get here ahead of everybody else and be responsible for keys? Places should be opened *for them.*"

Sergeant Clark smiled. "The key grip had a key. I suppose that figured. At any rate, the poor man was mighty reluctant to admit it. He seemed to feel I was accusing him of something. I can't say that I blamed him. Between that and the sandbag, he must have thought I was getting ready with the handcuffs.

"Let me see, who else? I think that's about it, but it's quite a collection." Clark turned to me. "You didn't have a key, did you?"

"No. Why? Were you getting ready with the handcuffs?"

"How about you?"

"Not me," MacAullif said. "I'm just the technical advisor."

"Yeah, that's us," I said. "Nonessential personnel."

"Anyway," Clark said, "with that many keys around, getting in is not a problem. Getting out is a little harder. That is, if the warehouse is all locked up and the padlock's in place. Then you can't open the door from inside. But there'd be ways around that. There's other ways out of the building."

"Without smashing a window?"

"Sure. You could open it from inside, then pull it shut behind you after you go out."

"How would you lock it?"

"You couldn't. Not then. You'd have to lock it the next day when you came to work."

"I see," I said. "But wait a minute."

"What?"

"You say this happened Tuesday night?"

"At the earliest. It could have been done as late as last night."

"Not by someone who didn't have a key. Taking your premise that someone stayed in the building after work. Monday and Tuesday were the only days we were here. Wednesday and Thursday we shot outside. So if someone hung around after shooting, it would have to be Tuesday night."

"Right. What's your point?"

"You say he couldn't lock the window till he came back to work. Well, again, we weren't here Wednesday and Thursday. We didn't get back here till today. So the earliest he could lock the window would have been this afternoon."

"Obviously."

"Did anyone see anyone locking a window?"

"No one said they did."

"Did you ask?"

"Yes, of course. But that doesn't mean it didn't happen. Just that no one saw it. And that's only one possibility. A person with a key wouldn't have to hide here after work. He could open the door and go in any time."

"Right," I said. I exhaled. "So, we're no further along than we were before."

"Not at all," Clark said. "We're making considerable progress. I would hope to wrap this up soon."

I looked at him. "You're kidding?"

"Not at all."

"Are you saying you know who the killer is?"

"Oh, no. Nothing like that. But I will. It's just a matter of time. I have no doubt I'll nail the killer. Right now I've really only one concern."

"What's that?"

"To catch him before he kills again."

33.

Sergeant Clark called Saturday afternoon to tell me there'd been a break in the case. He caught me just as I was preparing to take Tommie out to the movies. I left that pleasure to Alice, went out, and hopped a subway downtown.

I certainly had mixed feelings. It had been a hell of a first week's shooting, to say the least, and I'd been looking forward to the weekend off. On the other hand, Sergeant Clark had invited me to his office to discuss the case and, unless he considered me a suspect, which I sincerely doubted, that was rather gratifying.

He hadn't told me what his news was either, so I was curious as all hell. Clark had said he couldn't discuss it on the phone because he had other calls to make. I wondered if that was true, or a ploy on his part to get me to come in.

I took the subway down to Chambers Street, walked over to One Police Plaza.

The last time I'd been in Sergeant Clark's office it had been to apologize for thinking he was an asshole. I wondered if he recalled the incident. Somehow, I was sure he did. Anyhow, it was all I could think of when I walked in the door.

Sergeant Clark was seated at his desk, just as he had been then. But at that time he'd been reading a paper. This time he was watching a TV. That was a new addition to the office—a TV and VCR on a stand. The tape was playing, and on the screen I saw a boy's face contorted in pain.

Sergeant Clark picked up the remote control and froze the frame, cutting off the boy's anguished cry.

It seemed familiar, though I couldn't place it.

"What's that?" I asked.

"Sidney's film," Clark said. *"Straight Shooter.* I rented it." He motioned to a stack of VCR rental cases on his desk. "Along with *Down and Dirty* and *To Shoot the Tiger.* I've been screening them, hoping to get a clue."

I frowned. "I don't understand. Why?"

"Why?" Clark said. "Because of them. Sidney Garfellow and Jason Clairemont. I figure one or the other of them has to be the key to the whole thing."

"One or the other?" I said. "It seems to me all the attacks have been on Jason Clairemont."

"That's possible. Maybe even likely," Clark said. "But I'm not prepared to go that far. We also have the assault on the boom man."

"Which could have been directed toward Jason Clairemont."

"The fall, yes. But what about the incident with the tape recorder? If someone sabotaged the equipment, resulting in a shock, that was *not* directed toward Jason Clairemont. At least, I can't see any way it could have been."

"We only have Murky Doyle's word for that."

"Granted, granted," Clark said. "I don't really feel like debating the merits of the claim. All I'm saying is, aside from the theory that the killer is specifically targeting Jason Clairemont, I have to consider the possibility the violence is directed against the production in general. If so, who in the production is important enough to warrant consideration?" Clark gestured to me, inclined his head. "With all due apologies to the screenwriter, the most important people on this movie happen to be the producer-director and the star. It occurs to me I know very little about them, so I've been watching their films."

"And what did you learn?" I said. I was aware of a conscious effort on my part not to sound condescending.

"Frankly, not much. At least in terms of the investigation. But it certainly is interesting. For one thing, this Jason Clairemont is entirely different in person than he is on film."

"You noticed that?"

"How could you miss it? In person, Mr. Clairemont does not impress—one wonders how he could act at all. But on the screen he comes across very well."

"It's not him."

"I beg your pardon?"

"A lot of the scenes in *To Shoot the Tiger*—the action scenes—it's not Jason Clairemont you're seeing, it's a stunt double."

"Yes, I understand," Clark said.

A thought struck me. "I wonder . . ."

"What?"

"Is it the *same* stunt double? In *To Shoot the Tiger*—is it the same stunt man who's working this film?"

Clark frowned. "I have no idea."

"Couldn't you find out?"

"I certainly could," Clark said. "Though I don't really see what difference it would make."

Somehow I just knew he'd say that. It was in Clark's nature to belittle the idea just because it was mine.

"All right," Clark said. "That's about all I learned about Jason Clairemont. Sidney Garfellow is another story. Have you seen his documentaries?"

"Yes, I have."

"Pretty intense, aren't they?"

"Sure. Look at the subject matter. Child pornography and AIDS. And the guy got an Oscar nomination. He's bound to have some pretty hard-hitting stuff."

"Which one?" Clark said.

"Huh?"

"Which film got the nomination?"

I frowned. "You know, I don't remember. Does it matter?"

"No. I'd just like to know. Anyway, this gives me a good glimpse into Sidney's character. The way he goes after the people in these films. The interviews. The questions that he asks. The things he gets them to say. Hard-hitting, yes, but very exploitive, if you know what I mean. Kind of a ruthless disregard for the people themselves." Clark pointed to the TV screen where the picture was still frozen. "I mean, look at that. That's a boy with AIDS. Do you know what he's doing there? He's telling how he got it. About being brutalized by a superintendent in his building. A man with AIDS still walking the streets today. Now, that may be good theater, but think how the people in that boy's family feel, seeing this tape.

"Well, that tells me a great deal about our friend Sidney Garfellow. I mean, we've seen how far he'd go to make hay out of a tragedy, hiring this bodyguard to protect Jason Clairemont. But this goes beyond that. This shows a ruthless disregard for human feelings."

Clark leaned back in his desk chair, laced his fingers together behind his head. "I have to tell you something," he said. "I originally pooh-poohed the idea that Sidney Garfellow could be behind this himself, creating these crimes as a monstrous way to publicize his film. The idea seemed absurd."

Clark took his hands from his head, tipped the chair back down. "After seeing his documentaries, I'm not sure. I wouldn't put anything past him."

I took a breath. "Pardon me, Sergeant, but I thought you said there's been a break in the case. Or did you just bring me down here to discuss these video tapes?"

"Actually, I'm waiting for Sergeant MacAullif," Clark said. "No reason to go over the same ground twice."

"You called him too?"

"As a matter of fact, I called him first. But he had to come from Bay Ridge, so you beat him here. But I'd expect him any moment."

"Are we just gonna sit and wait?"

"Well, we can watch the tape."

Clark picked up the remote control, started it playing again.

I sat down to watch.

The boy on the screen started moving again, going over the horrors of his ordeal.

It was strange watching it. I'd screened it before, way back when, before I began writing the script. And I'd had such a different opinion of Sidney Garfellow then. He'd been my salvation, my savior, a lifeline, a way out of my dead-end detective job. An introduction into the magical world of film.

Oh, sure, I'd been somewhat cynical about his documentaries then. Particularly while writing a karate movie with four hot babes. But I'd taken them at face value. He was, after all, an Oscar-nominated director. I guess the difference was that my cynicism then was to regard Sidney as a *documentary* film maker, perfectly competent as such, but over his head trying to tackle a feature. Now, seeing his documentaries with the gift of hindsight, all I could see him as was a manipulative, exploitive son of a bitch.

MacAullif showed up fifteen minutes later. He did not look happy. Of course he'd been summoned to Sergeant Clark's office on a Saturday afternoon while on vacation, but even so. The man looked decidedly uncomfortable.

It didn't take long to find out why.

"I'm filmin' tomorrow," MacAullif said. "Not tomorrow, I mean Monday. I'm filming Monday. They called last night to let me know."

"Filming what?"

"Some street scene. I dunno. You wrote the damn movie. Scene one thirty-eight. Exterior. Street. Day. Rick cases crooks from across the street."

I frowned. "What are you playing?"

"What do you think? A cop."

"There's no cop in that scene."

"There is now. The cute-lookin' AD calls me up, tells me

I'm workin' Monday, to report to makeup at six o'clock. Hell, I been comin' in seven o'clock no problem, but six? Gimme a break. I ask her what I'm filmin', she says scene one thirty-eight. I get off the phone, look it up, doesn't tell me a thing. I call her back and she ain't there. I get her two hours later, she tells me not to worry, there's nothing in the script, Sidney will tell me what to do. Terrific. How the hell an I supposed to prepare, I don't know what to do till I get there?"

"There's nothing to prepare," I said. "It's not like there's any lines or anything. You just show up, they'll tell you where to go."

"I'll tell *them* where to go," MacAullif said.

"You're really going to be in the movie?" Sergeant Clark said.

"Whether I like it or not," MacAullif said. "This morning I get a call from the costume lady wanting to know my size. I say what for? She says the *uniform*. Jesus Christ, you know the last time I wore a uniform?"

"Why didn't you just tell her not to bother, you'd wear your own?" Clark said.

"It won't fit, that's why. It's too damn tight. I had to tell her I'd call her back and then my wife whips out the tape measure. Jesus Christ, you'd have thought I'd robbed the fuckin' bank. I mean, like an extra inch or two's the crime of the century, you know?"

I made a *T* with my hands. "Excuse me," I said. "Time out. I've been here for half an hour and I'm going nuts. What's the break in the case?"

"Yeah," MacAullif said. "What's up? It better be important to come all the way down here. Big-time actor like me."

"It's important," Clark said.

"Well, what the hell is it?"

"We ID'd the body."

34.

The photograph Sergeant Clark handed me was an eight-by-ten black-and-white head shot of the dead man in the elevator.

Sergeant Clark said, "This is the picture we circulated for identification purposes. And this," he said, handing me another photo, "is a picture of Peter Mertz of Minneapolis, Minnesota. Who is who our dead man turns out to be."

MacAullif, peering over my shoulder, said, "Not a great likeness."

MacAullif was right. The photograph showed a rather clean-cut young man in jacket and tie. Any resemblance to the bum in the elevator was entirely coincidental and not to be inferred.

"That may well be," Clark said. "But it's him, all right. They matched the fingerprints."

"And the man is who?" I said.

"Peter Mertz of Minneapolis, Minnesota."

"So you said. I mean, who is Peter Mertz of Minneapolis, Minnesota?"

"That is indeed the question," Clark said. "He's forty-four years of age, attended public high school in Minneapolis, went to Northwestern, dropped out after one year. He got a job as a used-car salesman, largely through strings pulled by Father, couldn't cut it, lasted less than two months. Left home later that year with avowed intention to make it in motion pictures."

"Son of a bitch!" I said. "Is that true?"

"It is, according to his mother, who still lives in Minneapolis."

"You're kidding," I said. I couldn't believe it. Sergeant Clark's prediction was coming true.

"Let's see," Clark said. "Left home with stated intention to make it in motion pictures. Headed for Hollywood. There's no record of when he actually arrived, but he certainly got there because he joined the Screen Actors Guild in 1972. He worked on half-a-dozen pictures over the next year and a half, nothing big, in fact mostly extra work. After that he dropped out of sight, his SAG card lapsed and was never renewed."

"Where did he go?" I asked.

"Immediately, I have no idea," Clark said. "But eventually he wound up in New York."

"And died on a movie set," I said. "Jesus Christ, is there any connection to Sidney Garfellow?"

"None that I can determine."

"Or to Jason Clairemont?"

"No. Though that's much less likely. There's a huge age difference. And Jason's first picture was last year."

"What about the rest of the cast and crew? Come on, don't make us pry it out of you. What's the connection?"

Clark spread his arms and shrugged. "So far, none."

"But it must exist," I said. "How'd you ID the guy?"

"As I said, through his picture. The picture was recognized."

"By whom?"

"Miss Virginia Finewald."

I frowned. "Who is she?"

"Miss Finewald is a concert violinist. Apparently very good. Has actually played Carnegie Hall."

"She recognized him? From where?"

"Miss Finewald also does volunteer work. On the weekends. At Saint Catherine's Church."

I frowned again. "Wait a minute. What kind of volunteer work?"

"Serving soup."

"Serving soup," I said. My eyes widened. "Wait a minute. You mean in a soup kitchen?"

"That's right."

"She knew this guy from working in a soup kitchen?"

"Exactly."

"He wasn't one of the people working there?"

"No. He came for soup."

"Son of a bitch," I said. "You mean he *was* a bum."

"I think Miss Finewald would take exception to that statement," Clark said. "She was very careful to refer to her clientele as the homeless."

A grin spread over my face. Son of a bitch. I didn't even resent the time spent coming downtown or the bullshit he put me through. Sergeant Clark had made my day.

"So," I said. "You lost your bet."

Sergeant Clark's eyes narrowed. "No such thing."

"Sure you did. You owe Richard Rosenberg a dinner."

"Don't be silly," Clark said. "The facts aren't all in yet."

"What facts? Rosenberg bet you the man was a bum, and he's a bum."

"That was not the bet."

"I beg to differ. MacAullif, you were there. Wasn't that the bet?"

MacAullif put up his hands. "Hey, don't ask me to take sides against a fellow officer. If he says that wasn't the bet, I suggest you let him explain."

"Explain what?" I said. "Look, with all due apologies, Richard Rosenberg's my boss. You think I'm not gonna tell him this?"

"By all means," Clark said. "You can tell him whatever you want. But don't tell him he won his bet."

"Why not? The dead man's a bum, exactly as he said."

"That was not the bet."

"Oh? And just what is your interpretation of the bet?"

"You'll recall the terms were somewhat vague," Clark said. "First was whether the crimes were related at all. Then it was whether this crime would shed any light on that crime. Or whether the identification of the dead man would shed any light on the other crime."

"And how was it left?" I said.

"As a gentleman's agreement. That we would know what we meant. That we would accept the outcome gracefully. That we wouldn't hide behind technicalities or attempt to argue a lost cause."

"Exactly what you're doing," I said.

"Not at all," Clark said. "The victim is a bum, but that is not the bet. The bet is whether there is a reasonable connection between his murder and the other crimes. While I concede the possibility that there is not, I am not ready to accept it as fact. We don't know who killed this man, or why. Until we do, there is no reason to assume the crime wasn't related."

"Wait a minute," I said. "That seems unfair. Are you saying that if the murder of this bum goes unsolved, you don't have to pay? That's a conflict of interest. It's like an incentive *not* to solve the case."

"No, no, no," Clark said. "In the first place, I expect the crime to be solved. But even if it weren't, once the other crime is solved, the murder of the boom man—and that I *do* expect to solve—well, after that, this crime will either have fit in or not. And if I can't fit it in, if I can find no link whatsoever between the two deaths, I will concede defeat and dinner's on me."

"Jesus Christ," I said. "I can't believe you're still pushing that. Look here, tell me something, will you?"

"What's that?" Clark said.

"There's a lot of euphemisms flying around here when you start defining the bet. *Shed light. Link between the crimes.* I don't know whether this is your bet or not, but tell me this. Is it your contention that we have a serial killer here? Do you still believe the same person killed both men?"

Sergeant Clark looked at me in surprise.

"Yes, of course."

35.

Alice and Tommie were home from the movies. She met me in the foyer when I came in the front door. I was carrying a red plastic bag.

"Video tapes?" Alice said.

"Yeah."

"What did you get?"

"*Down and Dirty, Straight Shooter,* and *To Shoot the Tiger.* Plus a tape for Tommie."

"Why?"

"It's a two-for-one rental. You have to get four."

"Don't be dumb. Why did you rent those tapes?"

"Because Sergeant Clark did."

"Uh-huh," Alice said. "So what's up? What's his big news?"

"Oh. The guy's a bum."

"Sergeant Clark?"

"Don't do that again, Alice. The bum in the warehouse. They ID'd him. And he *was* a bum."

"So. You were right."

"Yeah. But Sergeant Clark won't admit it."

"Why not?"

"Because he'd have to admit he was wrong."

240

"I don't understand."

"You and me both. The fact is, the murdered man was a bum, just like everyone thought. He's been ID'd as one of the homeless who used to get free meals at Saint Catherine's Church. There's no connection between him, Sidney Garfellow, Jason Clairemont, or anyone else on the picture."

"Well, that's good."

"Yes. Except . . ."

"What?"

"He used to be an actor. Worked in the movies."

"Oh? When?"

"Twenty years ago."

"Oh. So what's the connection?"

"That's just it. I don't see how there could be one."

"Uh-huh. So what's with the video tapes?"

"Sergeant Clark's been screening them. I don't know why, but he is. He says just to get a line on the parties involved. Maybe, maybe not. But if he's gonna screen 'em, I wanna screen 'em too."

"Why?"

"To see if there's something I missed."

"No. Why do you have to do it at all? I thought you'd decided it wasn't your job to solve this crime."

"Yeah, I know, Alice. But I'm right. About the bum in the warehouse. He's wrong and I'm right. It may be stupid, but it means something to me."

"It's not stupid. It may be a little obsessive, but it's not stupid." Alice pointed to the video tapes. "So what do you hope to find?"

"How about this?" I said. I reached into the red plastic bag, pulled out a photograph, handed it to her. It was a copy of the eight-by-ten ID photo I'd got from Sergeant Clark. "This is the dead man. The bum. This is how he looked now." I pulled out the other photo. "And this is how he looked then. As a young man. The truth is probably somewhere between the two."

"Yeah? So?"

"So, the best of all possible worlds would be to find this man in these films."

"That's what you plan to do?"

"That's right."

She shook her head pityingly. "Well, you haven't got a prayer. You can't even recognize Richard Dreyfus in a film, you're going to recognize some nondescript bum?"

"I'm going to try."

"Don't be dumb," Alice said. She picked up the bag. "Come on. I'll watch 'em with you."

It took all day.

We watched *Straight Shooter* first. Which was depressing as hell. I got to see the boy again, the one with AIDS, the one Sergeant Clark had talked about. As usual, Clark was right—Sidney's handling of the boy was brutal at best.

Down and Dirty was the same way. Sidney interviewed a teenaged prostitute, got her to cry on film. It was a telling moment. The girl started off tough and streetwise, talking about her job. Sidney turned the conversation onto her personal life, got her talking about her folks, asked her if they knew what she did, got her to break down.

Once again, brilliant theater, cruel as hell.

Sidney didn't appear in the documentaries, by the way. You heard his voice, conducting the interviews. But off camera. You never saw him on camera because he was *holding* the camera—that was his method, to shoot the interview himself while conducting it.

I had to admit it was an effective technique.

Aside from that, there was only one thing worthy of note—the credits for *Down and Dirty* listed the sound man as Murky Doyle. When I saw that, I recalled Sidney mentioning working with him before. And maybe it was just the power of suggestion, but I swear the sound in that documentary didn't seem as good, and it occurred to me it must have been the other one that got the Oscar nomination.

Anyway, we watched both documentaries and then we

sent out for Chinese food—Moo Shu Pork for us and chicken with broccoli for Tommie—and watched *To Shoot the Tiger*.

The dead man was not in any of those three films. I say that with absolute certainty. As bad as I am at spotting people, Alice is good at it. In movie theaters she's always jabbing me in the ribs and saying, "Do you know who that is?" I never do, but she does. Even if the actor is wearing a false beard, mustache, and two tons of makeup, she knows him. Hell, even if he's wearing a *mask*, she'll know him from his *voice*, for Christ's sake. So if Alice didn't spot the guy, he wasn't there.

Which was rather disappointing. I hadn't *really* expected the dead man would be in those pictures. On the other hand, I hadn't really expected he wouldn't.

"I'm sorry," Alice said.

I looked over at her. Smiled. "What? Like it's your fault he wasn't there?"

"Yeah, I know. But I feel like I failed."

"So whaddya think of the movies?"

"I've seen 'em before."

"Yeah. Me too. They just seem different now."

"How so?"

"Well, Sidney Garfellow's an asshole."

"You always thought that."

"Yeah, but more so. I look at these documentaries now, I don't see a guy getting an Academy Award nomination. I see a parasite feeding on people's pain."

"That's a little extreme."

"I know. I'm projecting. That's because two people are dead and Sidney's treating it like a publicity stunt. It colors my whole perception of him."

"No shit. What about the other movie?"

"What other movie?"

"To Shoot the Tiger."

I looked at her. "What do you mean?"

"Well, what do you think of that?"

"Do you have a point, Alice?"

"I don't know. You say your perception of Sidney Garfellow changed. What about Jason Clairemont?"

"What *about* him?"

"That's a little different situation. Sidney's movie you saw when? Six months ago. Jason's movie was when? Two or three weeks?"

"I saw it last year. When it first came out."

"Yeah, but you rented it again. When Sidney got him for the part. Now, I know what you said—it's Eastwood's movie, why is this kid so hot, he just happened to be in it—wasn't that how you felt?"

"Well . . ."

"I'm wondering if *that* opinion's changed."

I looked at her. "Christ, Alice. That was before the kid started rewriting the lines."

"Right. So what's your opinion of him now? You just saw the movie, so whaddya think?"

I took a breath. "He's a good actor. And I happen to know all the action stuff in there was a stunt double, but even so. He has a good screen presence, he projects sympathetically, and the kid can act. He comes across much better on the screen than he does in real life. In real life he's a fucking toad, and I'd like to strangle him."

"Un-huh. About what I figured," Alice said. "Tell me, are you capable of being civil in front of him?"

I frowned. "Of course I am, Alice. Why do you ask me that?"

"You've forgotten, haven't you," Alice said. "I suppose that's understandable, with everything that's going on."

"Huh? Forgotten what?"

"Tommie's off from school Monday. You invited us to visit the set."

36.

Monday was gorgeous. In terms of the weather, anyway. The sun was out, the sky was blue, the air was crisp and clear. All perfect for the filming of scene one thirty-eight, Exterior, Street, Day.

It's hard to describe how I felt that day. I was torn in so many directions. I mean, first of all, I was making a movie—through everything else I had not completely lost sight of that. I also had Alice and Tommie on the set. As well as that fresh new cinematic face, Sergeant William MacAullif. As well as Sergeant Clark of the NYPD with his ongoing homicide investigation. And not present but still voting, wager participant Richard Rosenberg of the law firm of Rosenberg and Stone. Not to mention Sidney Garfellow, Jason Clairemont, and the rest of the usual suspects.

But I'm doing it again—telling it out of sequence. My god, am I going to be cursed with this affliction until the damn picture finally wraps?

Okay, to begin with, today we were filming in the triangular block between Seventy-second and Seventy-third streets, bounded by Broadway on the west and Amsterdam on the east. Broadway and Amsterdam have just crossed each other at Seventy-second, Amsterdam running due north and

Broadway angling northwest, resulting in the small block known as Needle Park. Which is not its real name, of course, just the nickname given to it because junkies like to hang out in it and shoot up.

Today the junkies were out of luck. The movies had taken over the place—lock, stock, and barrel. When Alice, Tommie, and I drove up, there were production vehicles all over the place—trucks, campers, production cars.

Including mine. It was the first time I'd brought it to the set. For a number of reasons. One, it wasn't listed on our parking permit (Jake Decker, like everyone else, counting the writer as nonessential personnel), which meant finding a parking space at locations would have been a pain in the ass. And Alice needed it to drive Tommie to school. Today she didn't—there was no school, and he was with us. And I couldn't leave the car at home because it was on the bad side of the street and had to be moved for alternate-side parking. So the first thing on my mind as I drove up to the location was, what the hell was I going to do with it?

It didn't help to see the two cops from the mayor's office busily engaged shooing all other cars out of there. Or when the attractive AD stepped out in the middle of the street and flagged me down.

I rolled down the window. "I know," I said. "I've got no permit for it, but I had no choice."

"No, no," she said. "No problem. You gonna be here all day?"

"I don't know if *they* are. Why?"

"We need your car."

"What?"

"Picture car. In the shot. Once it's established, it's gotta stay. Can they go home by cab?"

They sure could. Which solved my problem. About parking, I mean. The AD and the cops directed me to make a U-turn and pull up on the east side of Broadway near Seventy-third.

I was happy just to have the parking problem solved, but Tommie was positively thrilled.

"Wow," he said. "Our car's gonna be in the movie."

So was Sergeant MacAullif. We found him drinking a cup of coffee and eating a doughnut on the other side of Broadway next to the catering truck which was set up outside of HMV. He was dressed in a policeman's uniform.

It was the most uncomfortable I had ever seen him.

Don't get me wrong, the uniform fit him fine. In terms of size, anyway. I mean it wasn't like he'd lied to the costume lady about his measurements over the phone.

But Jesus Christ.

Oddly enough, he didn't look like a cop. He looked like an actor hired to play a cop.

An amateur actor. Nervous, insecure, and terribly hassled.

That's what I saw, but that's not exactly how I phrased it to him.

"Hey, you look great," I said.

MacAullif and Alice had met briefly on one occasion, but I introduced them again.

I also introduced Tommie. His eyes were wide. "Gee," he said. "Are you an actor?"

"No," MacAullif said. "I'm a cop."

"Really? You look like an actor."

That was not exactly what MacAullif needed to hear, and I jumped right in. *"Today* he's an actor," I said. "He's playing a cop. He's got makeup on. That's why he looks like an actor. The makeup makes him seem not quite real. But that's just in person. On film he'll look exactly right."

I hope I didn't sound as dubious as I felt. As far as I was concerned, uniform or no uniform, MacAullif looked hopelessly out of character. In fact, the only thing that seemed normal about him at all was the doughnut and the cup of coffee.

At that moment Sidney swooped down upon us, doing the hail-fellow-well-met routine. "And who are these fine visitors to our location?" he inquired.

I introduced Alice to Sidney for what was only the third or fourth time since I had begun working for him, then introduced Tommie.

"And what a fine big boy," Sidney said. "Chip off the old block. And did you know how important your father is to this production? Did you know he wrote the very words the actors will be saying today?"

I closed my eyes and prayed that Tommie would not have heard, remembered, or be inclined to repeat any of the comments I had made to Alice on the subject of my participation in this particular movie. However, no such thoughts had crossed his mind.

"Is Jason here?" he said.

Sidney's broad smile indicated Tommie had asked just the right thing. "Yes, Jason's here," he said. He pointed up the street. "He's in his camper getting his costume and makeup on, but he should be out soon. You stick around and watch."

Although MacAullif had been there for the whole conversation, Sidney now seemed to see him for the first time. "Oh, and look at this," he said. He stepped back, spread his hands. "Fantastic. Can I pick 'em, or what? Is that a cop, or is that a cop?"

It was, from anyone's point of view, a very unhappy cop, but Sidney didn't seem to notice.

"Now, Sergeant, when we start filming, you're going to be over there in the park walking your beat. Don't worry about the specifics, when we get the shot set up, I'll tell you what to do." Sidney turned back to us. "So, nice meeting you. Stick around, I think you're going to like this."

And he trotted across the street to confer with the DP.

The door to Jason Clairemont's trailer opened, and out came the burly bodyguard.

"Wow," Tommie said. "Who's that?"

"Jason's bodyguard."

"Is someone really trying to kill him?"

Funny how some things don't compute.

I think of myself as a good family man. I love my wife and kid. But I have to tell you, it wasn't till Tommie said that that it occurred to me they might be in the least danger being on the set. Seeing the bodyguard drove it home.

I felt a cold chill.

Still, I tried to appear calm. "Tommie," I said. "We don't know for sure what's going on. That's why we're trying to be careful. That's why I want you and Mom to stay in the background. Not get too involved."

"Dad," Tommie said, giving it the full two-syllable treatment.

I'm sure Tommie would have had more to say on the subject, except at that moment Jason Clairemont came out of his trailer.

"Wow," Tommie said.

The bodyguard took Jason under his wing and the two of them crossed the street.

Tommie looked up at me. "Dad, he's so small."

"You have to remember. You're seeing him next to this huge bodyguard."

"Even so," Alice said. "He *is* small."

As Jason crossed the street with the bodyguard, I noticed something for the first time.

No TV crews.

No newspaper reporters.

The intervention of the weekend had robbed the Jason Clairemont story of its immediacy. Had pushed it off the front page. Not that it ever *was* on the front page, you understand—that's just a figure of speech. But in any event, the media had not yet arrived.

Sergeant Clark had, however. He came striding up to us. Took one look at MacAullif and said, with an absolutely straight face, "Good morning, Sergeant."

MacAullif muttered something unintelligible.

Clark turned inquiringly to me.

I made the introductions. Which was a bit of an event. Alice had not only never met Sergeant Clark, she had never even seen the man. But I'd certainly described him enough. And not exactly in glowing terms.

All I said now was, "Alice, this is Sergeant Clark. Sergeant, my wife, Alice, and my son, Tommie."

But, oh, the subtext.

Sergeant Clark and Alice both said the standard pleased-to-meet-you's, then we all stood there gaping at each other like idiots.

To save the situation, I jumped in with, "At least no TV crews."

"Yes," Clark said. "And do you know why?"

I frowned. "No. Why?"

"Mr. Garfellow and I came to an understanding. Last Friday, when I questioned him. We discussed shooting today. When it turned out he had the street scene scheduled, I suggested that if we were besieged by TV crews I couldn't guarantee enough policeman to keep the streets clear enough to shoot. You noticed there was nothing in the papers about Friday's incident?"

"Sidney's cooperating?" I said.

"Fully," Clark said. He shrugged. "Of course, when he finishes his exteriors and moves inside I lose my leverage. But for the time being, we are controlling publicity."

We were interrupted by the first AD calling, "Sergeant." But it was not Sergeant Clark she wanted. It was Sergeant MacAullif. "Ready on the set, Sergeant," she said.

The first AD must have been over her sulk, because she was smiling when she came to get MacAullif. She made the summons to the set an altogether pleasant invitation.

But you wouldn't have known it to look at him. MacAullif plodded off with all the enthusiasm of a man going to the gas chamber.

As I watched MacAullif cross the street, it occurred to me that this was what today was about—MacAullif's acting debut. That, as to the rest of it, it was of no importance. That, despite the presence of Sergeant Clark and Jason Clairemont's bodyguard and all that, as far as the murder investigation was concerned, today absolutely nothing was going to happen.

Wrong again.

37.

Scene one thirty-eight, Exterior, Street, Day, was a bit of a kick in the face. For me, I mean. Because I've been going on and on about Jason Clairemont and Sidney Garfellow and what they did to my script. And then here comes scene one thirty-eight and damned if they didn't do something that wasn't half bad.

Basically, scene one thirty-eight, Exterior, Street, Day, was a throwaway. All I'd written was that Jason Clairemont follows the bad guy from across the street. Which is just a setup for scene one thirty-nine, Exterior, Apartment Building, Day, Jason follows the bad guy home and learns where he lives. So there was nothing special about what we were going to shoot.

Or so I thought.

To begin with, I hadn't picked the location. I hadn't written, EXT: NEEDLE PARK—DAY, I'd just written, EXT: STREET. It was Sidney who'd decided on Needle Park. And when he began rehearsing, I saw why. It gave him a lot to play with. Instead of your street of storefronts, it had trees and park benches. Perfect for hiding behind or sitting on or what have you. He also had extras sitting on the benches.

251

Not to mention a cop. Which is where the bit of business comes in.

But I'm telling it poorly again. As usual. Let me just describe the scene. The one Sidney came up with. Or Jason. Or the two of them together. Anyway, whoever the hell was responsible, this was the bit.

To begin with, Jason is scouting the guy out from across the street. As I had written. To do this he's walking in the park, keeping in the shadows, behind the benches. All the time he's walking down the east side of Broadway, keeping his eye on the bad guy, who's walking down the west. Everything's going real nicely for Jason until there on the corner, right where he's heading, who should he spot but . . .

A cop.

Sergeant MacAullif making his acting debut.

Bad news for Jason. If he keeps creeping along behind the benches, the cop will get wise. If he steps out and walks along Broadway, he risks being seen.

The bench Jason is behind is empty except for a newspaper someone left lying there. Quick like a bunny, Jason sits down on the bench and buries his head in the paper.

The newspaper is the *New York Post.* And as Jason opens it and raises it over his face, there on the front page is the headline, "Escape." Underneath the headline is a mug shot of Jason Clairemont.

The cop, whose attention has been attracted to the man on the bench, comes walking over. He looks at the newspaper, taps his night stick a few times to build suspense, then keeps walking.

As the cop's footsteps retreat, Jason lowers the newspaper. And the photograph of his face gives way to his actual face, and that patented, endearing Jason Clairemont grin.

Damn it, it worked.

And one of the reasons it worked was Sergeant William MacAullif.

Which really blew my mind.

Because I had been feeling sorry for MacAullif. And perhaps a little smug. Because he had been so unhappy about being in the movie, which wouldn't have bothered me at all. And then when they started filming, MacAullif was actually good.

Which I should have expected. After all, I used to be an actor, I know what it's like to perform. You're always scared to death before you go onstage, and then when it happens you're fine. MacAullif was not unique in having stage fright. He was just an amateur, so he was no good at hiding it. Also, never having acted before, he didn't realize he'd get over it. Which accounted for his overwhelming depression.

But when they filmed the scene, MacAullif relaxed and was just fine.

And to give the devil his due, the man responsible for this was none other than Sidney Garfellow, who had no trouble extracting a performance out of him.

Which again shouldn't have been surprising. After all, Sidney was a documentary film maker, who was used to working with amateur actors. Hell, in a documentary, *everyone's* an amateur. So Sidney knew just what to do.

First off, he didn't start with the master. He started with MacAullif alone. He aimed a camera at him, slated it one thirty-eight double papa, or some such bullshit, and then proceeded to roll film while he told MacAullif what to do.

"All right, Sergeant, here you go, you're walking your beat, that's all you're gonna do, you're gonna walk down here and look these benches over. Only one thing—you can't look like that. You look like your jockstrap's on too tight. Is that the problem? You send wardrobe the wrong measurements? Don't worry, we can fix it. Hey, wardrobe, get in here. We need a new jockstrap for the sergeant.

"Hey, that's a good look, Sergeant. Now look at the bench over there. Take your time, you're an officer of the law, you don't have to do squat if you don't want to. But you wanna hassle someone, hey, that's why you took the job in the first place.

"Good look, Sergeant.

"Now, you're lookin' at this guy, he sits down, picks up the newspaper. And you're lookin' at the newspaper coverin' his face. The headline says, 'Escape.' Hey, that's good, but you didn't read the headline, Sergeant. I can tell 'cause your lips didn't move.

"That's it. Now, stand there. Tap the nightstick into your other hand. Nice and easy. And you're sayin' to yourself, this is Sidney Garfellow's head I'm tappin'.

"Good. I like that. The controlled rage. Smoldering power. Just the right sense of menace.

"And . . . You walk on. Slowly. Just walk away.

"And . . . Cut."

Absolutely brilliant. Not only had he loosened up MacAullif and coaxed a performance out of him, but some of that footage could actually be used. After all, this was a movie, You could cut in any bits you liked.

It occurred to me, this was how Sidney must have won his Oscar nomination. The people in his documentaries he must have talked to the same way. Well, not kidding them about their jockstrap being too tight, but just talking to them while they were on camera, getting responses from them that he could cut into his film.

It was a disturbing thought for me. This Sidney Garfellow, whom I'd come to think of as an opportunistic, egocentric schmuck, was actually a gifted and talented director.

Anyway, after he'd finished with MacAullif, Sidney rehearsed and shot the master. This was a long dolly shot, starting on Jason in the north end of the park, and dollying with him as he makes his way down the block hiding in the shadows behind the benches, until the camera stops moving and pans to include MacAullif standing and watching him. At which point Jason sits on the bench and picks up the paper. MacAullif walks over, looks at him, taps his stick a few times, and walks off.

It was a long continuous shot, and if Sidney hadn't worked with MacAullif first, there was no way they would have gotten through it. But by now MacAullif actually seemed to be having fun. And if his performance wasn't letter perfect, that didn't matter, as long as he kept going. Because there'd be enough takes, close-ups, and what have you to cut to, to get a shot where his performance *was* good.

Anyway, things went well. So well, in fact, that Tommie and Alice stuck around. Which was something in itself. Hanging out on a movie set was usually about as much fun as watching paint dry. So the fact Tommie and Alice lasted the morning was significant.

They also opted to stay for lunch. I think Alice had probably had enough, but not Tommie. The kid was in serious danger of becoming a movie groupie. They'd finished the street scenes before they broke, and Tommie wanted to know where they were going next.

The answer was, to shoot more street scenes. Lots more street scenes. None of them as interesting as what we'd just shot. The scenes scheduled for after lunch were simple shots of people walking down the street, walking into buildings, walking out of buildings, and what have you. And an occasional reaction shot of Jason Clairemont watching someone doing that. In short, exactly what I'd written for scene one thirty-eight, only without the embellishments. That scene was wrapped.

So was Sergeant William MacAullif. He emerged from the wardrobe camper in plain clothes and sporting a shit-eating grin, and was immediately engaged in fending off compliments from everyone from Sergeant Clark to Clarity Gray. Naturally, Alice, Tommie, and I chimed in.

"I think you've found a new career," I told him.

MacAullif gave me a look that told me if my wife and kid weren't there he'd tell me to go fuck myself. Instead, he joined us in the lunch line, and proceeded to blush splendidly each time someone else came up to compliment him on his performance.

Lunch was set up in Needle Park. In the later part of the morning, while Sidney had been shooting reverse-angle shots of the bad guys across the street, Papa had driven the catering truck around to Seventy-third Street and set up the hot trays in the north end of the park, which was where the cafeteria line was now wending its way.

There is an unwritten rule in the movies—production eats last. Producers, directors, production managers, writers, and scum of that type. Because production people are theoretically working *for* the production trying to *save* money. And the crew and actors are working *on* the production trying to *make* money. And the crew and actors have the unions protecting them and governing when and how they eat. And production people don't.

Within this class structure, there is no rule that says a crew member has to defer to an actor, and in many cases they don't. But another unwritten rule is most crew members will defer to a star. And in Jason Clairemont's case, when he wasn't being brought his lunch as on the *Intrepid,* the crew had been happy to bump him to the front of the line. And the nerdy twerp superstar had accepted this preferential treatment as a matter of course.

But not today. It turned out today's filming had inspired a sense of camaraderie. Which I must confess feeling somewhat jealous about, since I had nothing to do with it. But everyone had had a good time, spirits were high, and Jason Clairemont, in a rare display of graciousness, had not only seen fit to be one of those to compliment MacAullif on his performance, but had also opted to stand in line just like one of the gang.

Which is why he was there when it happened.

As I said, we were in the cafeteria line where the steam trays had been set out in a row, flanked by two long folding tables holding trays, plates, silverware, rolls, butter, and what have you. Papa, Mama, and the girl were all manning the steam trays, dishing out food to the cast and crew filing through. With the three of them serving, it was moving pretty quickly, but it was a long line and we had a ways to go.

While I was waiting I found myself standing next to Clarity Gray. Which is when it occurred to me, what with MacAullif making his acting debut and my wife and kid being on the set, it had totally slipped my mind to find out about getting Richard Rosenberg into a screening. So I asked her if he could come tonight.

To my surprise, the answer was no. And Clarity wasn't the type of person who liked saying no. Her nose wrinkled up, and she fidgeted a bit, and then she explained. What with the accident Friday with the sandbag falling and all, there'd been no dailies Friday night. So we were a whole day behind. We had two days worth to watch, and tonight was going to be a double session. It would be a real grind, people would be apt to get testy, and it would be a poor night for visitors to come.

However, tomorrow night would be fine.

I agreed to that readily enough, and shuffled along in the lunch line.

As I did, it occurred to me that by coming tomorrow night, Richard Rosenberg would get to see the footage of Sergeant MacAullif. I figured he'd like that.

Then it occurred to me that what they were screening tonight, which he *wouldn't* get to see, was Thursday and Friday's footage. Which just happened to include the topless bimbo on the boat and the nude shower scene.

I figured if he knew that, Richard would be somewhat less than thrilled with shots of Sergeant MacAullif.

Anyway, there I am in the lunch line thinking Richard won't be going to dailies tonight but I will, and I'm standing there next to my wife and kid with visions of naked breasts dancing in my head.

And I hear Alice say, "Look who that is."

I have to tell you, I was totally disconcerted. Bad enough to have my lecherous daydreams interrupted by my wife, but why did it have to be that? "Look who that is."

It's the type of thing Alice is always doing to me. Because I'm so poor at faces, and she's so good at it. Usually, like I said, she does it in the movies, nudges me and says, "Look

who that is." And there's some actor up there on the screen
and I haven't the faintest idea who he is because he has his
hair combed different. Or sometimes it will be on the
street—"Look who that is," and I haven't a clue. Whether
it's the father of one of Tommie's classmates, or someone I
went to school with, or some celebrity I don't recognize, or
what.

Anyway, I'm jolted back to reality by those dread words,
and find myself in a cafeteria line holding a tray with a plate,
knife and fork, and paper napkin, and my wife next to me
holding a tray and looking up into my face expectantly.
Good god. Look who that is? Who the hell could she mean?

There were a lot of people around us, a lot of possibilities,
but they *weren't* possibilities. They were all people I knew.
Aside from the caterers, the only people in the immediate
vicinity, the only people near enough to count, were:

Clarity Gray.

Jake Decker.

The attractive first AD.

Sound man Murky Doyle.

And Jason Clairemont.

38.

I spoke to Sergeant Clark during lunch.

He was skeptical.

Then Alice talked to him.

After that, he was a little less skeptical. Alice has that effect on people.

After talking to Alice, Sergeant Clark began dragging people away from lunch to talk to them.

First he talked to Jake Decker.

Then he talked to Sidney Garfellow.

Then he talked to Murky Doyle.

Sergeant Clark's face was grim when he finished. He had a few words with me and MacAullif, got in his car, and drove off.

He wasn't around for the filming that afternoon. Neither were Alice and Tommie. I sent them home. On the one hand, it was going to be dull. On the other, it might be dangerous to have them stay.

Tommie, who hadn't been told why, was mighty reluctant to leave. I felt bad about not telling him. He's a good kid, but still he's a kid. I left it to Alice to work her magic. I don't know what she said to him, but by the end of lunch I saw them out on Broadway hailing a cab.

Good.

One less thing on my mind.

Now I could enjoy filming my movie.

Sure, Richard.

Fat chance.

I stuck close to MacAullif while we filmed the afternoon street scenes. He stuck close to the catering truck, mainlining coffee as if it were going out of style.

What a day it had to be for him, making his acting debut in the morning and cracking a murder in the afternoon.

If that's what we were doing. The thing of it was, there was no word from Sergeant Clark. He didn't catch up with us at Columbus Circle, where we filmed Jason following a bad guy out of Central Park. He didn't join us on West Fourteenth Street, where Jason hails a cab. And he wasn't there in SoHo, where Jason follows a bad guy into a loft.

That left only the shot on Wall Street, where Jason follows a bad guy into an office building. When Sergeant Clark didn't show up there, we grabbed the shot and then wrapped.

I got in the car with MacAullif and we headed back uptown to watch dailies of the bimbo in the boat and the broad in the shower, Hot Babes Two and Four.

We never got to see 'em. When we got there, Sergeant Clark was waiting outside. He'd spent the afternoon tracking down the information, and he'd got it. So instead of watching the dailies, we sat in his car and went over what we had.

Which wasn't really much.

"It's all conjecture," Clark said. "There isn't a shred of evidence."

"Yeah," I said. "But it's true." When Clark said nothing, I said. "You *know* it's true."

"Of course I do," Clark said. "But I can't act on that. It's not enough for a warrant. It's not enough for anything."

"So what *can* you do?"

Clark shook his head. "Forewarned is forearmed. The only thing now is to watch, wait for another attempt."

"You can't mean that."

"The alternative is more questioning. Pointed questioning. But if I do that, I tip my hand. And with nothing to go on . . ."

"Yeah, I know."

"So we have to wait."

I shook my head. "No good."

"Oh? Do you have a better suggestion?"

I took a breath. "I have an *idea*. I doubt if you'll think it s *better*."

"Let's not get hung up on semantics," Clark said. "If you can think of a way to force the issue, please tell me now."

I did. I'd had all afternoon to think about it, and I'd come up with a plan. Which I must say I rather liked.

I didn't expect Sergeant Clark to go for it though. Not conservative, conventional, by-the-book Clark. I was surprised he was even willing to listen.

I was floored when he went along.

But it occurred to me, the first time I'd met Sergeant Clark he'd let me pull my harebrained scheme just to see what would happen. Only, that time I hadn't known he was on to it. Hadn't known he was even around. But he'd let me do it all the same.

Still, it was quite a shock when he agreed. I guess it was exactly as he said—he *had* no plan of his own, other than wait and see, or resume questioning, and toward that end my scheme couldn't really hurt. If anything, it would only accelerate the process.

We batted it around some, there in the police car outside the warehouse. Then we got out of the car and waited on the sidewalk until dailies were over.

Then we picked up Jason Clairemont.

39.

There were still two and a half weeks of shooting left, but for all practical purposes the picture was over Tuesday night. From my point of view, anyhow. Everything after that was just anticlimax. But that night I will never forget.

It was the night we screened the MacAullif scenes.

Richard Rosenberg was there.

So were Alice and Tommie.

So was Sergeant Clark.

And of course Sergeant MacAullif.

And all the usual suspects:

Sidney Garfellow.

Clarity Gray.

The attractive first AD.

The gaffer.

The art director.

The DP.

Sound man Murky Doyle.

And Jason Clairemont.

Complete with bodyguard.

Dailies were held as usual in the warehouse, threaded up on the interlock projector by the multitalented gofer, Dan. For tonight, extra folding chairs had been rounded up from the set to accommodate our visitors, and the girl from the catering truck was on hand with a coffee urn and a tray of blondies, so to a large extent the atmosphere was that of a premiere.

This was enhanced by the fact I'd been unable to reach Richard Rosenberg other than to leave a message about the screening. So he was totally unaware of the latest developments, and was in high spirits when he arrived. The sandbag falling was news to him, and he had a great deal to say on the subject, and probably would have said it had not Sidney signaled Dan to start the projector and turn off the lights.

And suddenly, there we were in the dark watching Sergeant MacAullif's performance. A round of good-natured catcalls and applause greeted his first appearance. Richard, seated next to me, was grinning from ear to ear. The first time MacAullif walked over to Jason Clairemont and stood there tapping his nightstick, the place went wild.

It calmed down after that. After all, dailies are a boring thing. We saw the same scene again, take after take, and every ten minutes the reel would run out and we'd have to turn the lights on and sit and wait while Dan threaded up another.

By the fourth reel Richard had had it. The reel we'd just watched wasn't MacAullif anymore, just pickup shots from the afternoon of Jason following people everywhere, which was *really* boring.

"I think I'm shoving off," Richard said.

I put my hand on his arm. "One more reel."

He looked at me in surprise. "Stanley?"

"Trust me," I told him.

Richard shrugged, sat back down, and proceeded to needle Sergeant Clark about their bet.

Clark said nothing. And neither did I. And Richard remained in the dark. If he'd known the body had been identified as an actual homeless man, I'm sure Sergeant Clark never would have heard the end of it. But Richard didn't know that.

Among other things.

And so he continued to banter.

And the projector began rolling and the lights went out.

There was a moment's pause while the leader ran through the projector. Then the film hit the lens.

You could tell at once this footage was different. First off, it wasn't a street shot, it was an interior. Shot right here in the warehouse. And it wasn't shot with a camera dolly—from the slight movement of the picture, you could tell it was handheld. And the lighting was different—in fact, it was bad. As if there was none. As if the film had been shot with existing light.

As to the shot itself, it was a medium close-up of Jason Clairemont. Only he wasn't dressed as Rick Dalton, karate master. He was wearing his regular street clothes.

One other difference—no camera slate. No scene one forty-two, take one, or what have you. Jason just started speaking. Without any slate at all, he began the following scene:

INT: WAREHOUSE—DAY

JASON looks around, smiles.

JASON

It's perfect.
> (spreads his arms wide)

It's just perfect.

CAMERA PULLS BACK AND PANS RIGHT TO INCLUDE:

HOT BABE #2, Vivian of shower-scene fame, made up to look young in cotton pullover and jeans.

HOT BABE #2
(worried)

I don't know.

JASON
Hey. Trust me.

HOT BABE #2
I do, I do, but—

JASON
I tell you the place is perfect.
(pointing up to ceiling)
Look there.

SNAP PAN TO:

Pipe on ceiling.

Back on JASON and HOT BABE #2.

JASON
You see that?

HOT BABE #2
See what?

JASON
That pipe.

HOT BABE #2
What about it?

JASON
You could run a rope over that
pipe. Hang a sandbag. Drop it on
the set.

HOT BABE #2
No!

JASON
Yes. It's what we talked about.

                    HOT BABE #2
I know that, but—

                    JASON
That sound man—did you get his
name?

                    HOT BABE #2
Yeah.

                    JASON
Is it the same one?

                    HOT BABE #2
I think so, but—

                    JASON
Fine. Then I'll fuck up his tape
recorder.

                    HOT BABE #2
If you have to.

                    JASON
                (looks at her)
Have to? What's with you? Why
are we doing this? Why did you
get the job?

                    HOT BABE #2
To make trouble.

                    JASON
Right. To make trouble. So?

                    HOT BABE #2
Well, that's fine with the tape
recorder. That's all right. But the
sandbag. I mean, you could kill
someone.

>   JASON
> I don't care.

>   HOT BABE #2
>   (looks at him in horror)
> You can't mean that.

>   JASON
>   (strong)
> Oh, come on. Whaddya think this
> is, a game?

>   HOT BABE #2
> No, but—

>   JASON
> Well, it's not. It's real. It's hap-
> pening. And you know what? I
> don't *care* if it kills someone.
> Hell, I hope it does.

SOUND from out of frame, camera left. Rustle of cardboard boxes.

JASON & HOT BABE #2 turn to see:

STANLEY HASTINGS; dressed as homeless man, clambering to his feet from where he had been sleeping behind a pile of cardboard boxes. He gets to his feet, stands there, blinking at them.

JASON & HOT BABE #2 react.

>   JASON
> He heard us!

>   HOT BABE #2
> It doesn't matter.

>   JASON
> What, are you nuts? He heard the
> whole thing.

                    STANLEY
                (puts up his hands)
        Hey, mister. I didn't hear nothing.

                  HOT BABE #2
                    (pleading)
        See?

                    JASON
        He heard!

                    STANLEY
                (shaking his head)
        No. I don't know about no killin'.

                    JASON
        Son of a bitch!

                  HOT BABE #2
            (in anguish, grabbing his arm)
        No. Please.

                    JASON
                (pushing her away)
        Let go!

JASON wheels around, looks, sees:

A two-by-four lying on the floor.

JASON rushes to it, picks it up.

JASON turns and swings the two-by-four, clubbing
STANLEY to the ground.

HOT BABE #2 rushes into frame.

                  HOT BABE #2
                (grabbing Jason)
        My god, you killed him!

JASON
I had to. He heard everything.

HOT BABE #2
No, no. You didn't have to do it.

JASON
(grabbing her by the arms and
looking her right in the eyes)
Yes, I did. I had to. He heard too
much. He had to die.
(then, turning from her and
looking directly into the camera lens and speaking directly
to the audience)
Didn't he, Dan?

The film ran out.

The reels revolved.

The only sight was the white light projected on the screen.

The only sound the flapping of the film ends on the reels.

Someone switched on the lights.

And there was Dan, standing next to the projector, trans-
fixed, helpless, too overcome to even switch it off.

Jake Decker stepped up, did it for him.

And in the silence that followed, there came another heart-
wrenching sound.

The anguished sobs of the girl from the catering truck.

40.

It was sad.

It occurred to me, the first case I'd been involved in with Sergeant Clark had that sort of ending too. Sort of unsatisfying, in that the wrong person was guilty. That you didn't *want* them to be guilty. That you wanted the solution to be something else.

I'm talking about the girl. The girl from the catering truck. Dan you could feel sorry for, I guess, but not really. Not like her. Is that sexist? Probably. Everything is. But in Dan's case, I'm sure he was the driver, the mover, the actor, the one who did the deed. And she was just the accomplice. Equally guilty in the eyes of the law. But not in mine.

Or in Alice's.

She was the one Alice recognized, of course. The girl from the catering truck. That had to be a shock—there's Alice going through the lunch line and suddenly she recognized the girl dishing out the food. Well, not her, really, but her sister.

Damn it, I'm doing it again. Telling it out of sequence. For what I hope is the last time. Surely when this movie is over it will cure me of the habit. Movies do that to you. You shoot 'em out of sequence, and it screws up your head. Time is out of joint. Nothing happens when it should.

Funny, but in a way that was the solution to this case. Events happening out of sequence. Specifically, the murder of the bum in the warehouse. Which was why it didn't seem to relate to anything. Didn't seem to make any sense. The sequence was wrong. Because it was a crime committed to cover up another crime. Perfectly natural. Only, the crime it was committed to cover up *hadn't happened yet.* The crime, the dropping of the sandbag, had merely been *planned.* It was that *plan* that had been overheard, necessitating the murder. The one that happened out of sequence.

Damn. I'm *still* telling this out of sequence. I can't seem to get out of it.

Okay, where was I?

Alice.

The girl from the catering truck.

Right.

Alice went through the lunch line and recognized her. Actually, Alice had never seen her, but she'd seen her sister, and there was a strong family resemblance, and that was what she saw.

The girl in the catering truck was the sister of the girl in Sidney Garfellow's documentary *Down and Dirty.* The teenaged prostitute. The one Sidney got to cry on film.

That girl was dead.

No, she hadn't committed suicide. That would have been too pat. If her parents had seen the documentary, disowned her, and as a result she'd killed herself, hell, there'd have been no need for such an underhanded attack. Her family could have sued Sidney, smeared him with adverse publicity, and practically ruined him if they played it right.

But that wasn't the case. What the girl had done was to sink deeper into prostitution and drugs and eventually die of an overdose. Not enough to hang on Sidney legally, but enough to crucify him in her sister's eyes.

And in Dan's.

You see, Dan was her boyfriend.

She had come to New York from the Midwest, a runaway,

got picked up in the Port Authority by a pimp and put on the game. It was while she was turning tricks that she'd been discovered and interviewed by up-and-coming documentary filmmaker Sidney Garfellow.

Shortly after that she'd kicked the life, thanks largely to a young Columbia film student who'd taken an interest in her.

Dan.

She moved in with him and the relationship lasted several months.

Long enough for her to decide to communicate with her parents.

Long enough for her sister to get to New York to visit.

Then the documentary came out.

By Academy Award–nominated filmmaker Sidney Garfellow.

The film received critical attention. It played art houses nationwide and was screened on several college campuses.

Including Columbia.

It was in fact used for one of Columbia's film courses.

One Dan took.

A month later, the girl had moved out, was back into prostitution and heavy into drugs.

Two months later she was dead.

Dan and her sister met at the funeral. They spoke of their anger and frustration. They directed it toward Sidney Garfellow. They resolved to do something.

The rest you know.

It was no problem for Dan, as a Columbia film student, to get a job as a gofer on the picture. Once hired, he began looking for a position for the girl. He got the name of the caterers, she applied to them, and damned if they didn't have a job.

It was as easy as that.

Then came the fatal afternoon. Dan was sent to pick up the keys to the warehouse. Which in Sergeant Clark's eyes made him the prime suspect—and Clark as usual was right. When Dan got the keys he called the girl, gave her the address, and told her to meet him there. She did and they went in and up to the second floor, which Jake had said would likely be the shooting stage because he'd been told the floor was wood.

They looked around for things to booby-trap. Laid some plans.

And found the bum.

The real kick in the head, of course, was I heard them discuss it. That day on the bus. Don't have to rub it in, hell. I was sitting there in the john and heard the whole thing.

And then Dan turns toward the back of the bus where I'm hiding and, cool as cucumber, holds up the vanilla brownie and says, "I'll put the blondie back."

What a performance.

I wonder if he actually saw me. Recognized me as Stanley Hastings, I mean. As not just the screenwriter, but the man who was working with Sergeant MacAullif and Sergeant Clark. If he made the connection that I was his nemesis, that I was the investigator he had to fool.

Or did he merely see the door move and know that *someone* was there, and cover his tracks just in case?

In any event, the ad lib was brilliant. In one simple line, tying up and explaining away everything that had come before. Without turning a hair, without revealing a thing, without a moment's hesitation he turns to the girl and says, "All right. I'll put the blondie back."

Poor girl.

If only it were that simple.

If only there were some way he could have put the blondie back.

But from the moment he swung the two-by-four it was too late. They had passed the point of no return.

Poor girl.

Yeah, like I said, it's sad.

But life isn't like fiction, all clear-cut, black and white, the good guys and the bad.

Take Sidney Garfellow, exploitive opportunist—was he the good guy in the piece? He was the one I wound up having to protect. And he was with us at the end. Hell, he held the camera when we shot our little scene. Cooperated fully, and did everything I asked.

Yeah, I directed that scene. Wrote it, directed it, and acted in it too. I can take some pride in that. Even if the dialogue wasn't that hot.

Which wasn't Jason Clairemont's fault, by the way. He didn't rewrite me there. No, the dialogue wasn't that good because I wrote it there on the spot and there was nothing subtle about it—it had to be heavy-handed and right on the head. But for the record, Jason cooperated fully, said the words I wrote, and did his damnedest to make them play. And as I've said, the kid could act. I have to tell you, when he turned to the camera and talked to Dan, I felt a chill.

I'm sure Dan did too. Not that he confessed because of it. No, he held firm till the girl broke. Which didn't take long. After that he went noble, tried to take it all on himself.

And how it will all turn out I have no idea. They got separate lawyers, filed motions, fought for delays, and the whole nine yards. The first trial he was found guilty on all counts and she on two, but that's being appealed.

In the meantime, they're both out on bail.

Is there justice there? I think of the girl and I feel glad. But every time I start feeling sorry for those kids, I have to remind myself about boom man Charles Masterson.

And his wife and kids.

And it occurs to me, the story of Dan and the girl wouldn't make a movie. Totally unsatisfying. No happy ending. No winner.

Except Sergeant Clark.

He won his bet.

And Richard Rosenberg, to his credit, conceded as much. He didn't try to argue, as one might expect, that the bum in the warehouse had absolutely nothing to do with any of it, that he was just a poor soul who happened to be in the wrong place at the wrong time. No, Richard was as good as his word. He accepted the solution for what it was, and didn't try to get off on any technicalities. He called Sergeant Clark, offered his congratulations, and asked him where he'd like to dine.

The answer, Lutece, must have set Richard back a bit, but he didn't complain. As a matter of fact, I gather Richard actually got a kick out of hearing the solution to the case.

As to that solution, most of it you know. However, in Sergeant Clark's version, I gather, it was his brilliance rather than Alice's recognition of the girl from the catering truck that cracked the case. Well, that's not quite fair. I think the way he put it was the identification was merely confirmation of theories he had had for some time.

To begin with, he'd always suspected Dan. Because Dan was the one who had picked up the keys and could have gotten into the warehouse. Jake Decker wound up with the keys, but not until six o'clock, which according to the medical examiner was the outside limit when the man could have been killed. As to the rest of the suspects: Sidney Garfellow, the art director, the gaffer, the AD, the DP, Murky Doyle and, yes, yours truly—all of whom had been in the office that afternoon and would have had access to the keys on Jake Decker's desk—the big stumbling block was that they had only been in the office *once.* So they could have *taken* the keys perfectly well, but they couldn't have *put them back.* And they had to have been put back, because they were there on Jake Decker's desk when he went to look for them at six o'clock. (In response to the suggestion that in one visit to the office *wax impressions* of the keys could have been made, Sergeant Clark was reported to have said, "Yes, in a detective novel. The type I read and throw across the room.")

At any rate, it was Sergeant Clark's contention that, from the very first, the gofer Dan Mayfield was strongly indicated.

With regard to the murder of the boom man, Dan was also a prime suspect there. He went along on the preliminary location scout and was the one taught to run the construction elevator. As to who he was trying to kill, best guess was Jason Clairemont. Why? Because it would create the most havoc with the production. Why not Sidney himself? Because Dan didn't want to kill Sidney—he wanted him to live and suffer. On the other hand, if Sidney were to fall . . . what the hey.

As Sergeant Clark said way back then, this was sort of a hopeful crime. Weaken the board and see if someone falls. Dan could have suspected it would be Jason Clairemont after reading the action sequence I wrote, even if he couldn't be sure. But I don't think there was any way he could have known it was the boom man. That was just coincidence.

Don't tell MacAullif. He doesn't believe in coincidence. But some happen. You can buy one. A small one.

The coincidence is, it was the boom man, Charles Masterson, who happened to stumble into two traps. Neither of which was set for him.

The short in the Nagra was intended for Murky Doyle. That bit of mischief was deliberate and specific. Because Murky Doyle was the sound man Sidney Garfellow used on *Down and Dirty*. And a documentary's a lot different than a feature. There's no huge crew. Just Sidney Garfellow with a handheld camera and Murky Doyle with a handheld mike. They were the pair who filmed the girl. That's what I was referring to in my little movie—"That sound man—did you get his name?" "Is it the same one?" They got the sound man's name from the credits of the documentary. Just as I did. Murky was one of the original perpetrators, making him a specific target. They shorted out his Nagra. Only, it was the boom man who got the shock.

And the boom man who took the dive.

That's the coincidence.

Too much?

So sue me. Read a murder mystery sometime. As a coincidence, it's pretty tame.

But where was I? I keep getting lost in this case. Oh yeah, the various crimes.

Well, there's the sandbag falling. That's the one I think of as the real crime. Because it's the one the first murder was committed to cover up. Sergeant Clark's opinion there was just the way I laid it out in my movie. Initially it was just an idea—you could hang a rope there, drop a sandbag on the set. No particular target in mind.

Once the shower is built it gets specific. Jason Clairemont. Then when the little platform is built for him in the shower, it's better still. You know exactly where he'll stand.

Did anything implicate Dan? According to Sergeant Clark, yes. His interviews of all the witnesses. Only one witness named Dan as watching the filming.

The girl from the catering truck.

And no one saw her.

Why was that? Because she was lying. Lying to protect Dan. Neither one of them was there. She lied to give him an alibi.

He didn't bother to give her one because he figured if they alibied each other it would be too pat. Or he figured she didn't need one. Or he just didn't think of it. Or give a damn. Take your pick.

Anyway, Sergeant Clark *claims* that's how he knew they were conspirators. Frankly, I think that's bullshit. I grant Clark a lot, but not that. Tell you why.

Sergeant Clark also takes credit for the theory that the key to the vendetta against the movie could be found in Sidney Garfellow's documentaries, and points to the fact that he was screening them days before the denouement. Yeah, but he was also screening *To Shoot the Tiger*. The way I see it, he was exploring possibilities, but he didn't have them narrowed down.

But he *was* exploring them. And he *did* watch those documentaries over the weekend. After the sandbag fell. And it is my contention that if he *really* thought the girl was Dan's accomplice, was giving him an alibi back *then*, he would have recognized her sister in the film.

Is that a stretch? I don't think so. True, neither Sidney Garfellow nor Murky Doyle had noticed the family resemblance, and they'd actually *met* the girl. But it was years ago they'd shot the documentary, and why should they remember one particular prostitute?

But Sergeant Clark is a trained cop. I think he would have seen the resemblance if he'd been looking for it. And he *didn't* see it. Had no idea till Alice pointed it out.

Of course, after she did, everything fell into place. Sergeant Clark was able to investigate, identify the girl, find out who she was, where she came from, and the fact she was dead.

In my opinion, it was only *then*, knowing she had a sister on the picture who turned out to be the only one who had alibied Dan, that Clark linked those two together and sewed the thing up.

But that's a quibble. I have to admit Sergeant Clark was on the right track with the documentaries. And on the right track with Dan, and the whole bit.

In hindsight, a lot of things pointed to Dan. I mean, hell, that first day in the warehouse when we were all groping around in the dark, he was the one who switched on the lights. Easy enough—he'd done it the day before. The day he'd killed the bum. Killed him and stuck the body in the freight elevator and sent it upstairs, a nice little surprise to pop out at Sidney Garfellow and crew when they came to inspect the building the next day.

Yeah, it all fit pretty well. Even Richard had to agree. He called me after the dinner at Lutece to tell me Sergeant Clark was an insufferable man, but brilliant. Which coming from Richard was high praise. So, hell, maybe they'll wind up golf buddies after all—stranger things have happened.

As to the movie, yeah, we finished it. On schedule and under budget. Which was a bit of a miracle, considering the problems we had. A miracle of the Jake Decker kind. You wouldn't believe how that man rode the crew.

I'd like to tell you things went a lot smoother from that point on. After me directing my little film with Sidney Garfellow and Jason Clairemont.

I'd like to tell you that, but I can't.

If there's one thing history teaches us, it's that we learn nothing from it.

Sidney Garfellow and Jason Clairemont did not mend their ways. You think they shot my script? Guess again. Jason Clairemont rewrote the whole fucking thing.

The result was exactly what you'd expect—a low-budget B movie. No better or worse than the rest of the mindless garbage being churned out. The picture was lucky to get a theatrical release. It opened to disastrous reviews and disappeared inside of three weeks. It had a brief run on cable TV, then came out on video cassette.

You can rent it.

People still do, or so I gather from the residual check I get every six months from the Writers Guild.

No, it isn't much.

As to the usual suspects:

Sidney Garfellow went back to documentaries, which are his strength, if one can call it that. If he does well enough, someday perhaps he'll get another feature.

As to Jason Clairemont, he went on to bigger and better things. Being in the movie hurt him not one whit. As I said, even with bad material, he always came off well. Many of the negative reviews even said as much. No, no need to cry for Jason Clairemont. His star is definitely on the rise.

And, as for me, I'm back chasing ambulances again. I'd hoped my screen credit would be my passport into the world of motion pictures, but believe it or not, producers are not lining up to hire the writer of *Hands of Havoc, Flesh of Fire.*

No kidding.

I knew that the first day of rehearsal.

But that's the way it is with the movies. Even knowing it's doomed, you hang in there. You carry on. You chase the dream.

And what the hell—I got a movie produced. I know screenwriters much more successful than I, who've never had a movie produced.

Well, I have, and I can prove it too.

I own the video cassette.

I can watch it on my TV.

And I do.

Anytime I want.

Turn it on and watch the scenes and recall the whole thing.

The construction site.

The shower scene.

Sergeant MacAullif's acting debut.

With fast forward and reverse I can skip around, pick and choose the scenes I want to see.

And sometimes . . .

I must confess.

Sometimes I'll rewind it all the way.

To the top.

To the credits.

To *my* credit.

SCREENPLAY BY STANLEY HASTINGS.

Yeah.

In a way.

But what the hell.

And I chuckle to myself. Softly. Ironically. With just a tinge of regret.

So what if I'm a private detective again?

I had my fifteen minutes of fame.

I wrote a Jason Clairemont movie.